"Marry me, Charlie,"

Luke pleaded. "Let me take care of you."

Furiously, she pushed away from him. "Is that your idea of a solution? I'm not some helpless little twit who has to depend on a man at any cost—I'm not!"

Dismayed, Luke battled against a sense of hurt dejection. "I'm not suggesting you are. But it's all right to need someone."

"Not for me. I'm going to prove to everyone I can make it on my own."

"But you don't have to." Luke felt himself sinking deeper and deeper into a morass of emotional quicksand. "Didn't you understand what I said? I love you! I want you to be my wife!"

"And don't you understand I can't?" Charlie's mouth clamped down tight, and she threw up her chin. "I can't!"

ABOUT THE AUTHOR

"This book is very close to my heart," says
Suzannah Davis of *Evening Star*. Suzannah
has set her second Superromance novel in
the town of Natchitoches (pronounced
Nak-a-tush), Louisiana, only thirty miles
from her hometown of Coushatta. "The book
was a pleasure to write because the
characters are so familiar to me," she says.
"I hope that readers in other parts of the
country will enjoy the local color." The
popular author still lives in Coushatta with her
husband and three children.

Books by Suzannah Davis

HARLEQUIN SUPERROMANCE
359–AIRWAVES

Evening Star

SUZANNAH DAVIS

Harlequin Books

TORONTO • NEW YORK • LONDON
AMSTERDAM • PARIS • SYDNEY • HAMBURG
STOCKHOLM • ATHENS • TOKYO • MILAN

Published June 1991

ISBN 0-373-70455-0

EVENING STAR

In memory of
Gus, a Catahoula Cur who sang harmony
and
Lucifer, a Lab who hated snakes and green olives
and
for their masters, who miss them.

Special thanks to:

Dr. Bob Zinnikas, D.V.S.
Jay Adcock, Red River Farms
Johnny and Elvie Stuart, Stuart's Dusting Service
"The Boys" at the Red River Parish Farmer's Co-op

Home is the place where, when you have to go there,
They have to take you in.

—Robert Frost

CHAPTER ONE

"CHARLIE'S BACK in town."

Bertell Dickson, eighty if he was a day, casually tossed this tidbit of news into the ever-present circle of coffee drinkers passing the time at the Natchitoches Parish Farmer's Co-op. The crusty chrome-plated percolator on the rickety card table cluttered with crumpled napkins, plastic spoons and pink packs of artificial sweetener burbled alarmingly when Bertell depressed the lever and released the hot, aromatic stream into his white disposable cup. The potent brew was as black as sin and as thick as the gumbo mud clotting the tires of the pickup trucks lined up outside the co-op in the brilliant Louisiana sunshine. He took a cautious sip and waited for the inevitable questions.

At the cash register the broad-shouldered, loose-hipped man in faded denims and scuffed boots froze in the middle of passing Bob Tilley a couple of twenties.

"Uh, is that all, Doc?" Bob asked uncertainly.

Lucas Duval forced his attention back to the transaction at hand. "Yeah, that'll do it."

Nodding, Bob scribbled on the invoice, listing a length of rope, half a dozen metal hitches and two hundred pounds of dog chow, muttering to himself as he double-checked his addition. Luke watched Bob's labored efforts with a look of bland patience on his lean, sun-bronzed face, but his attention was riveted, albeit unwillingly, on the group gossiping around the coffeepot.

"Been a while since Charlie's been home, ain't it?" Melton Snipers asked, leaning back in his wooden chair.

"Who the hell is this Charlie fellow, anyway?" Bill Dozier demanded through a cobweb of white mustache.

"Ah, hell, Bill! She ain't no fellow!" Bertell said with some disgust for his crony's inferior memory. "You recollect little Charlotte Kincaid. That ne'er-do-well barnstormer's kid. Margaret Montgomery's granddaughter."

"Oh, yeah." Bill nodded. "Married that fancy-pants fellow from over Charleston way about ten years ago, didn't she?"

Nine years, seven months, and twelve days ago, Luke amended silently, then bit out a single explicit swearword under his breath at the damning self-revelation.

Bob looked up from his figuring. "What'd you say, Doc?"

"Nothing. Could you hurry it up?" Luke shifted restlessly. He threaded a hand through his sun-streaked brown hair, then pulled on a green baseball cap bearing a yellow John Deere logo. "Preacher Lamar's got a cow down, and if I don't get out there fast, he'll have my hide."

"Sure thing, Doc," Bob said, returning to his math, the edge of his tongue peeking out of the corner of his mouth to indicate his concentration.

"Well, anyway," Bertell said importantly, hitching up the legs of his khaki pants and perching on the edge of the wobbly table, "she's home. Gave her a lift from the bus station out to the Montgomery place myself not half an hour ago. And she weren't wearing no wedding ring, neither."

Hoary eyebrows lifted and heads nodded sagely.

So the prodigal returns. Luke's thoughts were bleak, and a cold knot tightened his stomach muscles. The amber brown of his eyes darkened until they were almost as black as the coffee in Bertell Dickson's cup. The knowledge that Charlie Kincaid's high-society marriage had failed should have given him pleasure, but there was only a strange twisting in his gut instead of the satisfaction he'd expected.

Charlie.

The name evoked long-buried memories of whiskey-colored hair and soft, vulnerable gray-green eyes. Who'd have believed that for a time the prettiest girl with the bluest blood in the parish had been *his* girl, a boy who'd grown up in a shack on Black Lake, the product of a family that society at its most charitable could only call "white trash."

She was the sweetest forbidden fruit, the product of impeccable breeding. A lady from her head to her toes and the epitome of everything he'd secretly desired and openly sneered at. Who'd have guessed one of the Black Lake boys would fall head over heels in love with Miss High Society herself, Charlie Kincaid? He should have known girls like her didn't play for keeps.

Luke made a soft sound of annoyance. What was the matter with him, anyway? he asked himself in sudden disgust. Why was he feeling sorry for Charlie Kincaid? If anyone was wounded, it wouldn't be Charlie. Hell, no doubt her return to Natchitoches was really a triumphal procession, a victory march after having stripped that sucker of a rich husband of hers for everything she could get. After all, Tyler Frazier could afford it, being part of the old money set in South Carolina.

Luke had seen the occasional news item in the *Natchitoches Times* about Mr. and Mrs. Tyler Frazier attending

this symphony benefit or that museum opening in
Charleston. And there had been notices of the St. Thomas
vacations and the European tours, and he'd seen the
spread in *Southern Interiors* on their meticulously re-
stored "single house" in the Charleston Historic District
with its Spode chandeliers and Aubusson carpets. In the
glossy photographs they'd been the ideal of a genteel
couple, Tyler with his blond prep school good looks, and
Charlie with her dark cloud of hair and luminous eyes.
Yes, Luke could almost find it in himself to feel sorry for
Tyler, losing a woman like that. No doubt all Charlie had
left in her wake was a bloodied stump of a man, sucked
dry of all life, emasculated and left penniless by a beautiful, heartless woman.

Well, Luke had learned the hard way, too. So what if
Charlie Kincaid was back in town? She wouldn't hang
around Natchitoches for long, not a jet-setting social
butterfly like her. So let her traipse around in her
Charleston finery. She didn't mean a damn to him anymore, and he was going to keep it that way. If she expected
to find *his* welcome mat out, she'd be disappointed. In
fact, he just might make a donation in her name toward
a ticket on the next bus out.

Luke reached for his paper bag of purchases.

"I'll get Alan to put that dog chow in your truck," Bob
said, and ducked through the swinging door behind him
leading to the co-op warehouse.

"Hey, Luke," Melton Snipers hailed, "you coming out
to see about my sow or not? I swear you vets are the
hardest fellows in town to track down!"

Although in no real mood to talk, Luke smiled easily,
a lopsided grin that never failed to charm. Many a business deal and lots of referrals came to him through "the

boys" at the co-op. "Sure, Mel. Hematoma in the ear, isn't it? I'll be out tomorrow."

"And you'll charge me an arm and a leg for a house call," Melton ragged, the expression on his craggy face showing that he was just joshing.

Luke scratched his chin thoughtfully. "Well, I've no objection if you want to load her up and bring her to the clinic."

Melton's chair legs hit the concrete floor with a snap. "Hell, no! That sow's meaner than a junkyard dog!" Instantly Melton realized he'd made a tactical error. "I mean...that is..."

His companions snickered into their coffee cups, and Luke's grin got wider. "That so? Guess I'll have to charge you for hazardous duty."

"Hell, Luke!"

Luke clapped the old man on the back. "Don't worry about it, Mel. I'll be out to lance that ear tomorrow. No extra charge if you can promise me a piece of Bessie's peach pie."

"Done!" Melton said.

"Should have paid him cash," Bertell cackled, the rooster's waddle of loose skin jiggling under his neck as he laughed. "Don't you know this boy's got a hollow leg? Better get Bessie to bake six or eight of them pies, Mel, and then don't expect to fill him up!"

"Now, Bert, I'm just a growing boy," Luke protested, patting his flat stomach. "And I've only had two candy bars and five honey buns so far today."

"And it ain't even lunchtime!" Bill Dozier hooted.

Bertell eyed Luke carefully. "'Spect you heard the news, huh? Saw Charlie Kincaid today. You two used to go 'round together, didn't you?"

"That was a long time ago." Luke kept his voice even and began to edge out of the circle. "Lot of water—and women—under that bridge."

The group grinned its masculine approval. It was well-known that Dr. Luke Duval could have his choice of the town's loveliest ladies, squiring debutantes and divorcées with equal aplomb. There had been a glamorous widow with the red Porsche, a model with legs up to *there,* and of course, there was Rachel, Luke's buxom receptionist. Everybody knew they'd been carrying on hot and heavy for some time now.

Luke repressed a grim smile at the success of his distracting ploy. It wouldn't do to give these old gossips anything to speculate about. At seventeen thousand inhabitants Natchitoches wasn't exactly a big town, even counting the university campus, and it was certainly still small enough and Southern enough for nearly everyone to know and take an interest in most everyone else's business. And Luke knew from experience that the coffee klatch at the co-op could outgossip their wives at Winona's Beauty Shoppe ten to one.

"'Peared to me like she was intending on stayin' a spell," Bertell offered.

"That's nice for her grandmother, I guess." Luke shifted his sack to the other hand.

"Yeah, those Montgomerys have always been a close family. Tighter'n a new cotton boll. Funny how she ain't been home since the wedding, though."

"Guess it's past time," Luke remarked, his manner offhand. Then his voice went husky with a question he damned himself for asking but couldn't contain. "How...how is she?"

"Still pretty as a picture. Yes, sir," Bertell said, his old rheumy eyes alight with appreciation, "that there's one pretty woman."

From deep in Luke's memory came the strains of Roy Orbison's song "Pretty Woman." Once those lyrics had symbolized all the hope a boy from the wrong side of the tracks could feel when the girl of his dreams noticed him. But the dream had turned into a nightmare.

Damn it! I'm too old to quiver like a moonstruck kid over a female! Luke thought furiously. Bitterness spilled into his soul like gall, and he clamped down hard on a pang of regret. "I'll see you fellows later," he said, and stalked out the door, head down.

"Hey, Doc!" Bob Tilley burst through the swinging door again, then drew up short at the sound of a pickup being gunned and the squeal of tires on gravel. Bob looked helplessly at the group huddled around the coffeepot. "The doc forgot his change."

Gray heads nodded and thumbs stroked lower lips thoughtfully. The old men looked at one another, but for once no one had anything to say.

CHARLOTTE AMELIA Kincaid Frazier stopped in the middle of the long, dusty driveway, set down her two suitcases, then sat on the largest one and proceeded to dump the white silt out of her flimsy Italian sandals.

She'd been a fool not to take Mr. Dickson up on his offer to see her to the front door of Evening Star, but somehow she'd needed to make this homecoming on her own. So she'd thanked him courteously for the lift, but had gotten out of his rickety pickup at the highway, a mile and a half from the stately white edifice that had been home to the Montgomerys since before the Civil War.

It had been hard enough deflecting the old man's well-meaning curiosity on the ride from town, anyway. She could see the questions in his avid eyes. Why had she been at the bus station in the first place, when her wealthy husband had provided her with her own Beechcraft to fly herself anywhere she wanted? Why was she visiting Natchitoches unannounced with just two battered suitcases? And most importantly, why was she coming home alone, without even the mark of a ring on her left hand?

But Bertell Dickson was a Southern gentleman of the old school, too well trained when gentle probing evoked no response to ask her these things point-blank, even though he'd been a friend of Milady's ever since Charlie could remember. So he'd gone off unsatisfied, but Charlie had no doubt he'd soon be drawing his own conclusions about her arrival and sharing them with his friends over a cup of bad coffee down at the co-op.

A wry smile curled her full lips at that thought as she slipped her sandals back on. Thank goodness some things never changed.

Like Evening Star plantation.

Charlie rested for a moment longer, letting her gaze travel over the expanse of flat farmland, the acres upon acres of cultivated parallel rows spreading out on either side of her as far as the eye could see. Cotton and soybeans, foot-high plants springing from the fertile soil of the Cane River Country as they had for generations. There was serenity here. At least she hoped, prayed there was. Oh, God, she certainly needed it.

Deliberately Charlie looked down the long driveway, shaded on each side by oak trees planted by her grandfather only three decades ago, but almost large enough now to touch spreading branch to spreading branch across the wide driveway. At the end of the driveway, gleaming in the midday sun, stood Evening Star itself, a raised cottage with a graceful arch of front staircase and tall white cypress columns supporting the roof. Massive azalea bushes skirted the green-painted lattice surround of the raised porch, and Charlie felt a stab of disappointment that she hadn't been here earlier to see them in full bloom, covered with so many fuchsia blossoms you couldn't even see the spring green of leaves beneath them.

So sharp was that pang that tears prickled behind her lids, but she determinedly blinked them away. There had already been enough tears. She was stronger than that now; even the doctors agreed. Strong enough to fly to a tiny Caribbean island she'd never heard of and obtain a quickie divorce from her husband of nine years. Strong enough to make some decisions about what she would do with the rest of her life.

Strong enough to come home.

She hoped.

Charlie tossed her tumble of shoulder-length, whiskey-colored curls out of her faintly damp face and swallowed despite a throat gone suddenly dry with apprehension. Failure wasn't allowed at Evening Star, and Charlie had failed at everything—miserably.

"Well," she said out loud to bolster her faltering determination, "I might as well get this over with."

She stood and dusted off the pure daffodil silk of her jacket and tailored pants, a remnant of that other life she'd left behind in Charleston, and wished she were wearing something practical for marching down a dusty Southern road in the heat of a May noontime. Something like jeans or—heaven forbid!—even shorts. But Tyler expected his wife to be dressed at all times as befitted her station in Charleston society, or at least as if the Junior League were expected for tea. So there hadn't been much for her to take in the way of practical apparel—just some designer sportswear and her aerobic shoes. But then she hadn't needed much where she'd spent the past six months. At any rate, her glass supplies, cutting tools, soldering irons and such filled up one suitcase, so there hadn't been room for any of Tyler's more extravagant purchases—those guilt offerings she hated—and that in itself was a blessing.

Charlie picked up her cases and trudged toward the beckoning house. The closer she got, the more she realized her initial assessment had been somewhat off the mark. There had been some changes at Evening Star. There was a new tin-topped shed to the rear of the compound, filled with monolithic equipment. Farther back, several pastures boasted new board fences, and horses dotted the green fields in little clumps. There had never been horses at Evening Star before, but Charlie smiled at the pretty scene. They fit right in, down to the new line of stalls adjacent to the old barn that housed her daddy's ancient crop duster. Improvements like these suggested prosperity, and that was a comforting thought, considering that she was coming home, at least figuratively, with her hat in her hand.

She was breathing hard by the time she reached the base of the front stairs. Mounting the steps, she crossed the shady expanse of porch to the front door, with its leaded glass sidelights and arched fanlight above, and set down her burden. As always, she admired the design in the beveled-glass panes. As a child, she'd imagined that was what diamonds looked like—warm and sparkly, breaking the sunlight into prisms of rainbow color. Only as an adult, wearing one on her hand, had she found diamonds cold and chilling.

Charlie hesitated at the door. Did one knock on the door of one's own home? What would Emily Post advise? she wondered wildly. Before she lost her nerve altogether, Charlie lifted the heavy brass knocker and let it fall.

A shadow moved through the foyer, and Charlie could hear the *click-click-click* of heels tapping on the varnished heart pine floors. She stepped back as the door flew open.

The tiny lady dressed in unrelieved navy blue and a single strand of pearls had an imperious bearing to match her crown of wispy silver hair. She stared at Charlie for a long moment. Charlie didn't say anything, nor make any sort of move, but merely waited with indrawn breath.

"You don't look as bad as I expected," Margaret Montgomery announced, inspecting her granddaughter from head to toe. "You kept your looks. There's that at least. Well, don't just stand there. Come in!"

Charlie picked up her cases and obeyed, entering the cool air-conditioned hall with a sigh of relief. She set the suitcases beside the Hitchcock bench, smiled at the matriarch who'd raised her after her mother had died giving her life, and bent to brush a kiss over her soft, lined cheek. "It's good to see you, Milady."

Before her lips touched Milady's face, a flurry of growls and barks erupted, and Milady drew back, agile enough, despite her seventy-three years, to bend and scoop up an armful of fat white dog.

"You hush that up, Miss Scarlett!" she admonished firmly. With a final sibilant growl the ugly, miniature poodle-size mongrel subsided, but her bulging black eyes were suspicious, and she watched Charlie carefully from the haven of Milady's arms.

"I see Miss Scarlett is as willful as ever," Charlie commented, wisely refraining from attempting anything so foolish as scratching the dog's tufted ears or the unusual circlet of fur that surrounded her neck like a clown's ruffled collar.

"She's old," Milady snapped. "It makes her irritable. Like the rest of us. So you've come home?"

"Yes, Milady," Charlie said, feeling like a runaway child, two years old at most, and not twenty-eight going on a hundred.

"That fancy hospital wasn't good enough for you?"

Charlie looked away. "It wasn't a hospital."

"Rest home. Sanatorium. Booby hatch. What *do* polite people call a place like that these days?" Milady demanded in an acerbic voice. Milady prided herself on calling a spade a spade, no matter how painful other people found it.

"Long Pines is what they called it. You can call it whatever you want. They were kind to me there, but it isn't home."

"Your home is in Charleston with Tyler," the older woman said harshly.

"Not any longer, Milady." Charlie's voice was quiet. There were things even Milady couldn't know about the breakup of her so-called marriage. But Charlie had been taught to please, ever the dutiful, obedient daughter, and she knew the things she could reveal wouldn't please Milady, so she said nothing.

"You could give the man another chance to sire a son off you," Milady said. "One pregnancy in nine years, and a miscarriage at that, isn't much of a contribution—"

"I'd prefer not to talk about it," Charlie said stiffly. "May I stay or not?"

"What kind of settlement did he make?"

"Nothing."

"What!" Milady's gray eyes went almost colorless. "You mean to tell me you're broke?"

"Not exactly," Charlie hedged. Although she knew the two hundred and fourteen dollars left in her private checking account wouldn't impress Milady, it was money she had earned herself from the sale of her own artwork. The important thing was that it was hers. "I didn't want anything from Tyler," she muttered.

"And that's what you got. You were always a fool, Charlotte," Milady said in disgust. "Well, don't think you'll get anything from me! You had that big wedding, the college expenses—everything else is tied up in Evening Star. You can ask Howard if you don't believe me."

"I won't have to ask Howard."

Howard Montgomery was a distant cousin who'd come to live at Evening Star and oversee the plantation now that Milady was getting on in years. His help had been invaluable, Charlie knew, and the plantation seemed to be thriving under his hand, as evidenced by all the improvements she had seen. And he and his wife, Gina, were companions to Milady, who'd had only the black couple, Sudie Mae and Hector Parrish, to care for her after Charlie's marriage.

Charlie felt suddenly tired and drained. It was a legacy of the depression in which she'd foundered after her miscarriage and the final blowup with Tyler. It had taken months in Long Pines to work herself back up out of that dark valley to where she could again see the first glimmers of light. Sometimes, like now, she had the feeling that her perch was very precarious, and if she wasn't careful, she'd slide back down into that yawning crevice.

"I don't expect you to take care of me," Charlie said, fatigue making her voice crack. "I'll find a way to support myself as soon as I can. I just want a place to stay for a while.''

"I'm hardly likely to turn away my own kin, am I?'' Milady demanded irritably. "What would people think?''

"What indeed?''

Charlie turned away to hide her stiff features, smoothing her wayward curls in the gilded mirror over the foyer bench. She was faintly surprised at how cool and calm she appeared. But then she'd always been adept at hiding her feelings, because nobody loved a whiny, demanding little girl and it was important to keep the peace. Even after all this time Milady still had the power to hurt her with just a word. What Charlie had always wanted was her grandmother's acceptance and approval. Somehow she'd always fallen short of the mark, no matter how hard she tried, no matter to what lengths she'd gone, even to the point of marrying the wrong man.

But it did no good to think about that. There were many reasons she'd stayed away so long, not the least of which was the chance of coming face-to-face again with the man who'd broken her heart at the tender age of nineteen. But she couldn't blame Milady for Luke Duval's lack of faith any more than she could blame herself for the hell Tyler Frazier put her through for nine years. She'd come a long way since the day she'd become almost catatonic with grief over the loss of her unborn child, and she'd learned a lot about herself, and more about how good it felt to stand alone. She'd begun to heal, and she'd come home to face her demons, to exorcise them if necessary. No one—not Milady, not Luke Duval—was going to stop her.

"Milady, have you seen my lace gloves?'' called a high voice from the paneled dining room. Heels tapped stridently over the floor again, and a tall, model-slim redhead appeared. "I said—oh! Why, Charlotte, dear! Wherever did you come from?"

"Gina. It's nice to see you again," Charlie replied.

"Well, how good you look!" Gina pranced forward, showing off considerable natural grace and an expensive luncheon suit. She bent, kissing the air beside each side of Charlie's face in a parody of the Southern ritual of greeting. Her sharp, copper-colored glance noted the suitcases by the bench. "Come for a visit, have you?"

"She's come to stay." Milady's razor-sharp edict wasn't to be denied.

Gina looked faintly surprised, then quickly smoothed away the expression. "How delightful for us all. And I'm sure poor Charlie could use the peace and quiet after her... ah, illness. I must run or I'll be late for the country club. We'll have a cozy visit later, all right, sugar?" She briefly kissed the air again next to Milady's cheek in farewell. "Here's Howard just coming in. I'm sure he'll want to hear all of Charlie's news."

Gina glided toward the French doors at the rear of the foyer, pausing briefly to whisper a remark into the ear of her thickset husband before exiting toward the garage. Howard Montgomery cast an assessing glance at the slender woman waiting in the foyer, and for an instant there was a flash of something in his expression that unsettled Charlie. She had no intention of threatening Howard and Gina's place within the household, nor even competing with them for Milady's affection. She'd learned long ago that the old lady bestowed it at will and not due to anything a person did or didn't do. But how could she assure the couple that she posed no threat and simply wanted a haven from adversity?

Charlie's lips quirked, and she hid a dry smile. She must really be getting well again if she could think it funny to find herself wishing Milady could be as affectionate with her as she was with Miss Scarlett.

Howard had thinning pitch-black hair, helped to that effect by some drugstore formula against graying. He wore a crisp checked shirt, creased tan slacks and about twenty extra pounds around his waist, but his round, swarthy face was determinedly jovial and welcoming as he hastened forward.

"Charlotte, how good to see you! You're just in time for lunch. I believe Sudie has made a pot of her famous shrimp jambalaya. Come tell us all about your trip."

He offered Milady one arm and Charlie the other, chatting in a friendly manner about the plantation, the price of fuel and soybean futures so that Charlie's apprehension evaporated. They reached the opening to the dining room, and there was a sudden crash of silverware against china.

"Lord have mercy! It's my Charlie-girl!" An energetic black woman in a bright Mother Hubbard apron surrounded Charlie in a warm hug.

"Sudie!"

"Land's sake, chile, if you ain't a sight for sore eyes! Let Mama Sudie look at her purty little girl!" Sudie's black eyes shone with tears, and her white teeth formed the biggest smile Charlie had seen since arriving at Evening Star.

Charlie felt a wave of emotion that made her light-headed. This was how a welcome home was supposed to feel. Sudie and Hector's acceptance had always been unequivocal. Warmth spread through Charlie that had nothing to do with the heat outside. She returned Sudie's hug with a kind of desperation, a taut-fingered grasping that touched the older woman's kind heart and told her more than mere words.

"There, there, chile," Sudie murmured. "It's gonna be all right now."

"Oh, Sudie!" Charlie whispered. "It *is* good to be home!"

"Now you set," Sudie ordered, pushing Charlie gently into her chair. "I'll get your dinner. Be right back!" she beamed. Pushing through the door to the kitchen, Sudie singsonged a message. "Hector! Hec-tor! You guess what? Our Charlie's back!"

"CHARLIE'S BACK."

The news hopscotched all over Natchitoches the rest of that day. When Luke Duval got back from Preacher Lamar's, he found the waitress at the Bonanza Restaurant discussing it with a booth of hungry businessmen, bankers and lawyers who did business with Milady Margaret Montgomery. At the barbershop Luke waited for his turn while Al Deaton clipped Sam Messick's hair and told him about the year Charlotte Kincaid had won the title of Lady of the Bracelet at Northwestern State University. And when Louise Bewley brought her daughter's new Siamese kitten into Luke's clinic that afternoon to be vaccinated, she confided to Rachel Aubert that Gina Montgomery had announced Charlie's return at the country club luncheon but, disappointingly, couldn't or wouldn't add any juicy details about her divorce from Tyler Frazier.

And later, when the day was finally over, Luke sat on his patio and watched the sun slip down into Sibley Lake, drinking bourbon, neat, no ice, and cursing himself for a fool.

Charlie Kincaid was poison, a spoiled and pampered doll, beautiful and useless, everything he despised. He'd pulled himself up out of the quagmire of his poverty-ridden childhood by his own bootstraps and made something of his life. He didn't need Charlie Kincaid coming around again all silky smooth and untouchable to remind him he'd earned his first paycheck gutting fish.

He knew all that, but it didn't help to alleviate the powerful urge to see her just one more time. Just for the satisfaction of having his evaluation of her substantiated, he told himself. To see for himself that she was just as selfish and self-centered as she'd always been and to count himself well rid of her.

And, his deepest dreams whispered, to see if she was still as fragile and lovely as a magnolia blossom. To discover if she still smelled of honey and flowers and looked like a Botticelli angel. To admire the grace of her slender hands as she spoke, hands that could touch a man in so many ways...

Luke cursed again, then defiantly drained the glass, letting the liquor burn raw down his throat. Then he poured another drink.

Poison was right. He hadn't achieved anything he had by being stupid. For as long as Charlie Kincaid hung around, he'd stay the hell out of her way. It was a damn sight smarter than any other alternative. It might even be a matter of survival.

He sat there until the dark settled around him and the pain in his heart was only a dull ache. And he could have sworn the wind overhead in the tall pines whispered the news that echoed in his whiskey-clouded brain.

Charlie's back... Charlie's back... Charlie's back...

CHAPTER TWO

CHARLIE PUSHED on the old barn door. The hinges creaked, and from high above in the rafters came the scuttle of mice and the rustle of pigeons' wings. She gave the other wide door a shove, and sunlight splashed into the dusty interior, forming golden bars of illumination on the gleaming black and yellow lines of her dad's crop duster.

She didn't quite know what had drawn her to the plane in the cool quiet of the early May morning, only that it was necessary. Wandering forward, she caught the scent of diesel fuel and oil. No matter that there was no one here to fly the Stearman; Hector still hadn't neglected it. He'd been an Air Force mechanic years ago in the "big war," and this baby was as much his as it had ever been Roy Kincaid's.

Charlie trailed her fingertips over a strut, then ducked under the wings and circled the craft as she made a visual inspection. It looked in as good a shape as when she'd first earned her pilot's license, that summer when she was seventeen and Roy had made one of his rare but eagerly anticipated appearances at Evening Star. Between them they'd cooked up the plan, Charlie's first outright defiance of Milady, but Charlie would have done anything to win her father's love, to somehow make him stay this time.

Of course, he couldn't, not that vagabond, Roy Kincaid. Milady's hostility for the man who'd stolen away her only child was too open, her contempt for his wanderlust life-style too evident. And instinctively Charlie knew, too, that there was too much at Evening Star that reminded Roy painfully of Emmie, Charlie's mother. So he'd taken off again to crisscross the country just like the old barnstormers.

Charlie sighed, her hand absently stroking the stripes decorating the Stearman's fuselage. That was really Roy's fatal flaw. He'd been born too late, and he'd spent all his life trying to find a place for himself. Crop dusting, private pilot, air shows—he'd done it all. Except raise his daughter. That he'd left to Milady.

He sent Charlie the occasional card from Tallahassee or Wicoma or Georgetown, called on her birthday and even came to see her once when he was passing through Charleston. Tyler hadn't been impressed with his long-lost father-in-law, and since the feeling was mutual, Roy hadn't come back. Charlie had accepted it because she loved her father, and it was the way he'd always been, dropping in and out of her life on a whim. The last she'd heard, Roy had been headed for Oregon, and she hadn't tried to contact him when she'd lost her baby. After all, what could he have done? But now, standing here, remembering the closeness of those lost summer days when he'd taught her the thing he loved best, Charlie wished he'd call. He, of all people, would understand how strange she felt, how isolated. There were times when even a big girl needed her daddy.

Shaking her head at that self-pitying fancy, Charlie turned her back on the Stearman and stalked out of the barn. Hadn't she learned anything? It had taken every ounce of her courage to shed her old life for the hope of something better. She'd lived up to everyone else's expectations for twenty-eight years, and this new determination to depend on no one but herself had been hard-won. It was time, by God, to do something about it.

Walking toward the big house, she was so busy with her thoughts that she didn't pay any attention to the brown pickup truck barreling up the lane from the horse paddocks. It passed her in a haze of white dust that settled over her silky peach blouse and knife-creased oyster slacks, then skidded to a halt fifty feet beyond. Grinding the gears, the driver reversed back up the lane, braking to a halt beside her. The passenger door swung open, and Charlie looked up into the tawny lion's eyes of the first man she'd ever loved.

"Heard you were back." Right arm draped over the seat, Luke Duval stared at her, his chiseled mouth compressed into a straight line. His gaze was coolly assessing, disguising an inner turmoil that threatened to eat him alive.

Damn all the luck! he thought.

Why did he have to run into her now after all the promises he'd made to himself? But he'd known, even before he'd passed her in the lane, who she was. It was as if some power outside himself had forced his booted foot onto the brake pedal. He hadn't planned this meeting, hadn't wanted it, but one glimpse of Charlie Kincaid and he couldn't help himself, any more than he could prevent himself from opening an old wound.

His glance raked her from her tousled mane of whiskey-brown curls to her dusty toes. There was grudging admiration in his golden-brown eyes. "You haven't changed."

Heart pounding, Charlie struggled with her composure and won. "Hello, Lucas. It's good to see you again."

Pleased with the polite friendliness she'd infused into her voice, Charlie told herself it was ridiculous to be so affected by a man she hadn't seen in nine years, no matter how they'd parted, no matter that he was just as lean and blatantly sexy in his jeans and western shirt as when he'd been the town rebel. A certain amount of awkwardness was to be expected, but they'd really been no more than kids when he'd broken her heart. People made mistakes, as she knew to her grief. There was no profit in holding a grudge, but she couldn't help a certain wariness, either. She cast around for an innocuous topic. "Are you here at Evening Star on business?"

One wheat-colored eyebrow lifted while his amber gaze followed the slim line of her legs in her narrow slacks. His drawl was lazy with subtle insinuation. "As opposed to pleasure?"

"I mean, are you visiting in a professional capacity this morning?" she asked stiffly.

"Yeah."

Exasperated, her voice grew tart. "I see veterinary school did a lot for your powers of communication."

He smiled at her comment, and her stomach performed a precision somersault. As if he guessed what that smile had done, he grinned even wider, lifting his broad shoulder in a negligent shrug. "Howard's colt has a swollen ligament, and he wanted me to take a look."

"Is it serious?"

"Anything can be serious when you're dealing with a hundred-thousand-dollar racehorse."

Charlie couldn't prevent the gasp that escaped her. "A hundred thousand! Howard has a horse worth *a hundred thousand dollars?*"

"More than one, I'd say. Thoroughbreds don't come cheap, especially if there's a chance they'll become runners."

"Oh." Charlie's brain reeled. Things must be going very well indeed at Evening Star, no matter what Milady said.

His white teeth flashed in a mocking grin. "You sound surprised. Is that why you left the Charleston high life and came home? To size up what's left of your inheritance?"

Her expression became closed and stony. "You haven't changed much, either, Lucas. You still have a talent for offending people. Good day."

She walked away, her elegant chin high with disdain. Luke let the pickup roll forward so that he could keep pace and watch her out of the open door.

"Touchy, touchy!" he taunted. He knew he was being deliberately nasty, but perversely, he couldn't stand to see her disappear so soon. "Get down off that high horse and I'll give you a ride to the house."

Pausing, her sandals sinking out of sight in the white silt of the lane, she glared at him. Her gaze dropped with contemptuous appraisal to the dusty, cluttered seat of the truck, littered with fast-food wrappers, veterinary instruments and assorted bottles and vials of medicine.

"No, thank you. Your filing system leaves a lot to be desired," she said in a chilly tone, dubiously eyeing the floorboards as if a tentacled alien might appear from beneath the morass.

"Some of us are too busy working to bother with appearances. What's the matter, princess, too good to ride with the po' folks?"

His poisoned arrow struck home. She was a quiet person, an interior personality. It was unfortunate and galling that time and again the cool serenity that was a part of her nature had been mistaken for snobbishness. She knew it was foolish to feel she had to prove anything to Luke Duval, but before she realized it she had taken a step forward.

"Very well. I'd appreciate a lift."

Luke's long arm reached out, scraping the assorted litter into a pile and spilling it with total unconcern onto the floorboards to join the inches-thick accumulation of several weeks. "Hop in."

Gingerly Charlie climbed into the high cab, settling onto the slippery tan vinyl seat. Luke reached across her to slam the passenger door shut with one hand.

He was suddenly close—too close. His muscular arm beneath the rolled-up cuff of his plaid shirt was barely an inch from Charlie's breasts. She could feel the heat of his lean body and smell the scent of his skin. Caught off guard, she pressed backward against the seat, amazed she could feel anything of a sexual nature toward any man. Why did it have to be Luke Duval who brought her back to an awareness of herself as a woman?

"That damn door can be a bit stubborn. Got to put your back into it to get it to shut," he explained.

"I see." Charlie knew her color was high.

Snap out of it! she ordered herself. There was no reason to become a bundle of nerves simply because she'd met up with an old boyfriend. Memory sneered at that appellation, and she conceded that Luke Duval had been much more than that to her. But she'd been little more than a kid then! Surely a full-grown woman had more sense than to fall prey to an unscrupulous man simply because he oozed virility. She'd made a fool of herself once over Luke Duval, but she wouldn't make the same mistake again.

Luke sat back, hit the gearshift and set the truck in motion. *Damn! He was making the same mistakes again!* He'd crowded her on purpose, but the little male sexual game had backfired on him. Her warmth, her floral feminine scent, the soft luminescence of her eyes sent his senses reeling backward into time. He'd *known* it would be a mistake to see her again! Clenching his jaw, he drove in silent determination, his fingers curled tightly around the steering wheel. He'd dump her at the house and get the hell away before she worked her feminine wiles on him again.

They bumped down the lane in awkward silence. After a few minutes, Charlie chanced a surreptitious glance at Luke's profile.

The only evidence of the passage of years in his sun-bronzed face was the tiny laugh lines that radiated from the corners of his eyes. His tawny, sun-streaked hair and the strong, tanned hands on the steering wheel were those belonging to a man accustomed to long hours and hard work out of doors. He'd always been more experienced, more worldly, but the years had ridden him easily, only emphasizing his masculinity and increasing his attraction. The truck cab held the musky nuances of male skin, shaving cream and piny after-shave, and Charlie shifted her feet uncomfortably, appalled that even after all this time, after all that had happened between them, she could still feel the tug of Luke's powerful magnetism. Their silence had become oppressive, and desperately she searched for a safe topic.

"How's your family?"

Luke cast her a quick look, then stared back at the narrow road. "Scattered. All except Dad. He's still drinkin' and fishin' and drinkin' down on Black Lake."

"Oh." Charlie bit her lip. Luke's father had been borderline alcoholic as long as she could remember. He'd run a little fishing camp and eked out a marginal living as a fishing guide, but the family had lived a hand-to-mouth existence, the kids growing up half-wild and hungry after Luke's mother died. Luke had been the only one to show any ambition, going off to the army, then coming back to go to college on the GI Bill. She was glad that ambition had paid off for him.

"Well, tell him I said hello, will you?" she said.

"Sure," he drawled, amusement lighting his eyes at her inevitable good manners, even toward an old drunk.

Battling a peculiar weightlessness that nestled in the core of her stomach, she looked out the window at the fields dotted with grazing horses. "It is beautiful here, isn't it?" she asked softly, then shook her head, slightly bemused. "I still can't believe Howard's invested so heavily in racehorses."

"I didn't think that kind of money was more than a drop in the bucket to a Frazier," Luke remarked.

"Then you think wrong." Charlie glanced down at her hands, found her fingers clenched tightly together and forced them to relax. Though pricked by his insinuations, she owed Luke Duval no explanations. She didn't have to tell him she'd been out of touch with life at Evening Star because she'd had her hands full with her own problems. "Anyway, I'm not a Frazier any longer."

"I heard about your divorce. That's too bad."

"The grapevine in this town is remarkable," Charlie muttered, her irritation plain. "Privacy doesn't mean a thing."

"Nope. Especially not down at the co-op."

"Mr. Dickson?"

"Who else?"

Charlie sighed. "I knew it."

"Taking your maiden name again, are you?"

"Yes."

"Typical," Luke said cryptically. "My, my. Who'd have thought Ms. Charlotte Kincaid was a feminist? I'll bet that's not all you took Tyler Frazier for."

Charlie's expression grew frigid, and her voice became quietly angry. "I'll thank you not to speculate about something that's none of your business, Lucas."

Luke pulled the pickup to a stop in front of the big white house. He gave her a considering look. "That got your dander up. I wondered what it would take to make the ice princess thaw."

Charlie sucked in a ragged breath at his deliberate effrontery. "You bastard."

He tsked between his teeth. "Such language from a lady! Is that any way to treat an old friend?"

"We haven't been friends for a long time, and you know it!"

He caught her arm when she made a move toward the door, and his voice was suddenly husky. "That's not the way I remember it."

"Then your memory's faulty!"

"Is it?"

"Yes!" Stung pride made her stretch for a bravado she didn't feel. "Just because I had the bad taste to be infatuated with you once, don't try to make more out of it than it was."

"If memory serves, nothing came of it." He dragged her closer, his angry lion's gaze hooded. "I figure that was our one mistake. But maybe it's not too late to fix it."

Charlie froze. Suddenly there was no air in the truck cab, and she couldn't catch her breath. Her lips tingled under Luke's heated appraisal. She could almost feel his gaze touching her skin, scorching it. Needs she'd thought long dead surged to vibrant, aching life. Her lashes began to drift downward.

This can't be happening, she thought.

This can't be happening, he thought.

But it was. She was as soft as he remembered, her lips ever so much more tempting now that they were really here and not the images of some fevered dream. He knew without doubt that her taste would be just as sweet, just as addictive...

"No!" The word ripped harsh and guttural from his throat, and he shoved her away roughly, muttering, "You're not worth it."

"W-what?" She could barely breathe, couldn't think, could only feel. Suddenly let loose from the invisible cords of throbbing tension, the haze lifted, leaving her weak and appalled.

"I was right," he said, his jaw flexing. "You haven't changed at all." There was no tenderness in the lion's eyes.

Cheeks burning, she shook her head in confusion. Had the charged moment been all on her part? How humiliating! How utterly galling! Only a lifetime of training gave her the composure to rise above her embarrassment. Trying to ignore what had almost happened made her voice stiff. "I don't know what you mean."

"Sure you do, honey," he drawled. His words dripped contempt. "You're a pretty woman, Charlie, but you're haughty and spoiled, sure that nothing in the world is quite good enough for you."

"You have no right to say that! You don't know me at all!" Incensed, she slid across the seat to climb out, but his hand again fastened on her upper arm.

"That's where you're wrong." His golden eyes blazed. "I know you up one side and down the other. Now that you've gotten what you wanted out of Frazier, you've come running home to grandma until another meal ticket comes along."

With an infuriated cry, she swung at him, but he caught her hand easily, his lazy smile half pitying, half contemptuous.

"You've never been more than a pretty parasite, princess, so don't waste your time hanging around Natchitoches. The pickings around this town are too slim for a woman like you. You might as well pack your bags tonight. Face it, you don't belong here anymore."

His scorn scalded her; his arrogance infuriated her. "You can't tell me what to do, you arrogant, conceited...ape!" She tugged at her captured hand. "Let me go!"

He released her. "Sure, princess, just as long as we understand each other."

Free, she fumbled with the door handle and bolted from the truck cab. Breathing heavily, she slammed the vehicle's door as hard as she could. "You haven't got the brains to understand a gnat's behind, Luke Duval! How dare you call me such a vile thing!"

He laughed at her outraged expression. "Come off it, Charlie. The truth hurts sometimes, but I'm sure you'll live to prosper. Your kind usually does."

"You...you..." She was so enraged that she spluttered incoherently.

"Relax, princess, or you'll have a stroke. I've enjoyed our little talk. It's always good to know where we stand." He shrugged, an infuriatingly cocky grin creasing his cheek.

Teeth clenched, she glared at him through the truck window. "You're *standing* on Evening Star, so get the hell off and don't come back!"

Luke scratched his chin. "Did Tyler teach you to cuss, honey? I didn't know a blue-blooded lady was allowed."

"Get out."

He shrugged and cranked the truck. "Before you throw me off Evening Star, you'd better check with the boss. Howard says who comes and goes."

"I'll do that!" Swinging on her heel, she stormed off. The truck pulled away, and the sound of Luke's mocking laughter followed her into the house.

Every molecule in her body pulsing with anger, Charlie charged up the steps and into the foyer. Gina's dulcet tones and Milady's starchy comments came from the direction of the breakfast area in the huge country kitchen, and Charlie veered away, heading for the solitude of her room to nurse her rage.

The bedroom was as she'd left it nine years ago, the four-poster cherry bed and dressing table a delicately carved heirloom set, the Irish lace curtains at the windows, the pale, cool yellow of the woven bedspread. It was airy and feminine, with framed pictures of the family lined up precisely on the nightstand and cut-crystal perfume bottles on a mirrored gallery tray on the dresser. Even during high school there had been few signs of a typical teenager's room—no pennants or banners or remnants of dried corsages pinned to a bulletin board. Milady wouldn't have thought such things "proper" decor for a young lady. Now Charlie, with an uncharacteristic, *un*ladylike flounce, threw herself down on the immaculate coverlet and fumed.

Damn Luke Duval! Who the hell did he think he was? Parasite.

The word left a bad taste in her mouth. Is that what he thought of her? Certainly, when she was younger, Milady had insisted on observing the proprieties, insisting on the "right" friends, the "right" schools. Did everyone think it was *her* idea to attend that snooty eastern finishing school Milady had chosen? She'd wanted nothing more than to attend Northwestern, the local state college, as an art major. She and Milady had compromised finally, Charlie going east to school during the regular semesters, and attending locally during the summers. Milady had wanted her to devote her time to attending the "right" social functions when she was home, but even that matriarch couldn't quibble about the value of a college education. And Charlie couldn't reveal that by that time one of the major attractions on campus was a dangerously exciting, flirtatious scoundrel by the name of Luke Duval.

Charlie rolled over and dragged her fingers through her curls, sighing loudly. It was clear he'd never thought of her as anything but a pleasant diversion, a casual flirtation with the poor little rich girl. The memory of his almost-kiss made her face burn again. He'd done it just to humiliate her, she decided, using his famous magnetism on her vulnerable feelings just so he could laugh at her. She couldn't think of a name vile enough to call him. Still, it puzzled her that he was so openly contemptuous and hostile. After all, he'd been the one to make it clear they were through, not the other way around. But if he'd been less brutal in breaking things off, maybe she wouldn't have jumped into her hasty marriage with Tyler.

She'd worked hard at that marriage, at least at first, before Tyler's jealousy and possessiveness destroyed the genuine affection she'd felt for him then. Maybe he'd known from the start that he had never truly possessed her heart, but other couples made it on less. It wasn't from lack of trying on her part. Tyler got everything he wanted in a wife—a hostess, a leader of Charleston society and

philanthropy, and a pretty, smiling helpmate to stand at
his side as he climbed the corporate ladder. And Charlie?
Well, she'd gotten a taste of living hell.

Charlie sat up abruptly, closing the door on the painful memories. Parasite! That scathing condemnation
made her burn with a cleansing anger. It occurred to her
suddenly that Luke's words had set off a charge within her
that was bringing her out of the self-imposed protective
stupor she'd developed in the hospital. No amount of
counseling or therapy had galvanized her the way Luke's
comments had.

All right, so she'd had to come home feeling like a
whipped dog. It was humiliating to admit failure, but she
didn't intend to sponge off Milady forever. She'd show
Luke Duval and Milady. She'd show them all. But mostly
she'd show herself.

Charlie rose and went to the closet, grabbing the suitcase she hadn't yet unpacked and swinging it into the
middle of the rumpled bed. She unsnapped the latches
and threw it open. Soldering irons, spools of lead solder,
nylon line, suction cups, and articles wrapped in tissue
paper filled the case. Feverishly she began unwrapping the
packages, revealing squares of jewel-toned glass in every
color of the rainbow—cobalt, emerald, crimson, ame-
thyst. She unwrapped the largest bundle carefully, laying
the half-finished panel on the bed.

She'd intended it as a gift for Bunny Morrison, a friend
whose wealthy husband had just built his wife a new
house. The unicorn in the design matched a scrap of
wallpaper from the master bath, and Bunny had expressed a wish for a stained-glass window in the design.
Tyler had laughed at Charlie's efforts, stuffing hundred-
dollar bills into her purse and telling her to go buy Bunny
a housewarming gift. By that time his verbal abuse and

false accusations had beaten most of the heart out of her, but she'd surprised herself by ignoring his disparaging comments and continuing with the project. After all, she'd been an expert in stained-glass art in college, and she still had the knack for design, the technical skill and the creative desire. It had been an anchor in the growing storm of her disintegrating marriage.

Now Charlie traced the outline of the glass unicorn's curled horn. Bunny had once said she'd even be willing to pay for such a piece. There was a lean-to at the rear of the garage that Charlie could use as a studio to finish the panel. If Bunny still wanted it, she'd give it to her with the information that other pieces could be commissioned— for a price. If Charlie knew her young Charleston society matrons, what one had, they all must have. Maybe, just maybe, a Charlotte Kincaid original could become the newest fad.

She turned the scrap of wallpaper over, reading the name and number she'd scribbled there aeons ago. Before her courage could desert her, she sat down on the side of the bed and reached for the phone.

"Hello, Bunny? How are you? It's Charlotte. I'm fine, just fine." Charlie reached behind her and rubbed the unicorn's horn again for luck. "Listen, Bunny, I've got a surprise for you...."

"WHAT WERE YOU and Hector conniving over today?" Milady demanded.

Charlie looked up from a copy of *American Artist* she'd borrowed from the Natchitoches Parish Library and smiled at her grandmother's truculent expression. Milady didn't like to be in the dark about anything going on at Evening Star. Or about anything else for that matter.

Despite her age, she maintained an active social life of letters, phone calls, bridge club and charitable works.

"We weren't conniving," Charlie said, gracefully tucking her slacks-clad legs beneath her. They sat in the parlor after another of Sudie's wonderful suppers, watching television and relaxing before bed. "He was helping me crate up my glass to send to Bunny Morrison."

Charlie felt a warm glow of satisfaction and pride at that statement. It had taken her almost a week of constant work, all of her remaining supplies and all but thirty dollars of her funds. The tips of her fingers were in shreds from glass slices, and she wore strips of white adhesive tape as her battle medals, but the unicorn was finished and on its way, along with her hopes.

"Well, it was just the prettiest thing I ever saw," Gina gushed. She wrapped her long, taupe-lacquered nails around the highball glass and took a tiny sip of her after-dinner Scotch. "Didn't you think Charlotte did a nice job, Howard?"

"Hmm?"

Gina raised her voice over the drone of the television, addressing the man slumped low on the cordovan leather chair and ottoman. "I *said,* didn't you like Charlie's little glass window?"

"Real nice."

Gina made a moue of distaste and waved an airy hand. "You know men, Charlie, they aren't interested in anything but hunting and gambling and whoring."

"Regina! I don't like that kind of language in my house!" Milady's pale eyes shot sparks. Miss Scarlett, who'd been dozing on the sofa next to her, opened one protuberant black orb and pulled her lips back in a halfhearted snarl of agreement.

"Well, it's the truth." Gina propped her shapely bare feet on the low coffee table and adjusted the legs of her orange silk lounging pajamas, her expression petulant. "They just don't understand about class."

Charlie laughed softly. "That's a fairly broad statement, wouldn't you say?"

Gina gave a long-suffering sigh. "I'd have thought you, of all people, would agree with me. It wouldn't be surprising if you were off men altogether after the way Tyler treated you."

Charlie paled. "What do you mean?" she asked carefully.

"Well, not giving you a cent, that's what. Honey, I think you need to go see my lawyer about that."

Charlie relaxed. For a moment she'd been afraid Gina had somehow gotten a whiff of the particulars of her breakup with Tyler. There were some things just too humiliating to reveal even to family.

"I told you it was my choice," she said. "I don't want anything from Tyler."

Milady gave a disgusted snort. "Shortsighted as always, Charlotte. How do you expect to support yourself? You're pretty enough to snag another husband, I guess, but just about useless for anything else."

Stung, Charlie shut the magazine with as much dignity as she could muster. "I'm trying to drum up a few commissions right now, Milady. It might be slow at first, but if I can establish a name for myself—"

"That's just dabbling. Nothing more than a glorified hobby."

"And I'm going to have lunch with Becky Gilchrist tomorrow. You remember her? She married Wylan Turner."

"I remember she was a little mealymouthed hussy," Milady grumbled, stroking the spiky ruff encircling Miss Scarlett's throat.

"Becky was one of my very best friends!" Charlie protested, shaking her head. "You are downright irascible tonight!"

"My arthritis is giving me a twinge or two," the old woman muttered.

"Oh, you poor thing," Gina cooed in sympathy. "Did you take your tablets like Dr. Melford said?"

"That quack! And don't you start in on me, Regina! I'll take what medication I see fit. Now what about Becky Turner?" she demanded of Charlie.

"Becky works at the university. She thinks there might be something opening up part-time in the art department for the summer session."

"Teaching a bunch of snotty-nosed kids, I'll wager. Charlotte, I meant you for better things," Milady said.

Charlie took a deep breath, striving to control her temper. She knew it wouldn't do any good to argue with Milady, but neither was she going to let her grandmother change her mind. And besides, arguments couldn't be good for the old lady. As always, Charlie was the peacemaker.

"Sometimes you have to do what you can, Milady," she said quietly. "And I want to try. Nothing may come of it, anyway."

"Well, I've got a wonderful idea!" Gina chirruped brightly. She took a final swallow of her drink and set it down, the ice cubes tinkling against the sides of the glass. "While you're waiting for all this to happen, you can help me come up with the decorations for the Spring Cotillion. I'm chairman of the decoration committee, you know. Won't that be fun?'' She beamed expectantly at Charlie.

Charlie blinked, taken aback. There were too many painful memories associated with that annual event. She was gradually coming out of the nightmare, breaking out of the hard shell of pain like a chrysalis. But she still felt too emotionally fragile to face all the old faces again so soon, her wings of newfound independence still too wet for full flight. Her disastrous meeting with Luke Duval had merely affirmed that.

She licked her lips. "Ah, Gina, I don't think—"

"Now don't you go and tell her no," Milady ordered. "This is just the thing to get you back in circulation again."

"But I don't want—"

"Sounds like an excellent idea to me," Howard said, rising from his chair and stretching, hands over head. "Just the ticket to pull you up out of the dumps, Charlotte."

"I don't think I'm...um, quite ready for something like that yet," Charlie said unsteadily.

"Well, never mind, then," Gina said, her orange-tinted mouth forming a hurt pout. "I thought I'd be doing you a favor. Just because I need a little help, I don't want you to feel *obligated*."

"Nonsense! Of course, Charlotte will be glad to help out!" Milady said. She fixed her gaze on Charlie, frowning. "After all, helping a member of the family is the least she can do. Isn't that right, Charlotte?"

Charlie wondered how a tiny woman like her grandmother could dominate her so easily. With just a look she'd managed to make Charlie feel like the most ungrateful freeloader in the world. What did you call someone who refused to pull her own weight?

Parasite.

The ugly word whispered in Charlie's brain, and with it the echo of Luke's taunting laugh. She looked up to find three sets of eyes watching her.

"All right." She'd been ganged up on, she knew, but fighting all three of them didn't seem worth the effort. "I'll be glad to help you any way I can, Gina."

"Oh, wonderful!" Gina bubbled. "Isn't that wonderful, Howard?"

"Jim-dandy." He offered his arm to Milady. "Could I see you to your room?"

"Thank you, Howard. You're a good boy," the old lady said. "I confess all this squabbling has made me a bit tired tonight."

Gina and Charlie both rose to press the obligatory kiss to Milady's wrinkled cheeks, then she and Howard made slow, stately progress out of the parlor. Miss Scarlet yawned and stretched, then trotted off in their wake. Gina immediately began to babble animatedly about her ideas for the cotillion.

"And I think it would be just darling to have little rosebuds and hearts, and maybe one of those tinkly fountains...."

Charlie sank back down into her seat and prepared for the siege, half listening to Gina's glorious plans.

The sooner she was able to come up with a method of supporting herself, she thought sourly, the sooner she could stop being the pushover of the family.

Suddenly, waiting for Bunny and her friends to come through with commissions wasn't enough. There were some very nice gift shops in Natchitoches that might be willing to take some pieces on consignment. She'd just have to raise the funds for new supplies somehow so that she could get started.

Shuddering, she listened to Gina's ideas about lavender cupids and vowed to begin the very next day.

CHAPTER THREE

"EAT IT AND SHUT UP."

Luke scowled at the plastic cup of yogurt and granola his petite secretary/assistant had just plopped down in front of him amid the organized chaos of his office desk. "You call this food?" he demanded.

Rachel Aubert propped her fists on her sweetly curvaceous hips, thrust out the magnificent bosom scarcely concealed by her white lab coat and glared back at him like an exasperated Shirley Temple. Her cornflower-blue eyes snapped and her short blond curls bobbed as she pointed at the concoction. "I call it nutrition. You know better than to skip breakfast."

She made it sound as if such an oversight was the first step on the road to nuclear destruction—which in Dr. Luke Duval's case might well be correct.

"But—"

"I said eat!"

"Yes'm." Duly chastened, Luke picked up the white plastic spoon and dug in.

"Grouchy as an old bear lately," Rachel muttered, fiddling with the clasp of her dainty gold watch. "You *know* your metabolism has to be coddled! No consideration for the people who have to work here..."

"All finished." Luke dropped the spoon into the empty cup. His tone was meek. "May I go to work now?"

Rachel beamed, her pearly smile lighting up her diminutive features. "Now isn't that better?" she cooed, giving Luke's broad shoulder a motherly pat.

Luke stretched back in his old leather office chair, nearly reaching the packed bookshelves behind him, and grinned. "No one would believe me if I told them what a bully you are."

Rachel dimpled and fastened her watch clasp with a snap. "It's purely self-defense, I assure you. You've been in such a foul mood all week! Darn!" The watch slid from her wrist and hit the floor.

Luke swept up the gold linked bracelet and passed it back to her. "I've had a lot on my mind. Sorry."

Luke inwardly grimaced at his own words. Yeah, he'd had a lot on his mind ever since his run-in with Charlie Kincaid. Damn the woman! Seeing her again, touching her—it had been a mistake, because knowing her for what she was didn't lessen the ache that centered low in his belly every time he thought of her. And he'd been thinking of her entirely too often, waiting for the word to come from the street or from down at the co-op that she'd left again for parts unknown. Only she hadn't.

Remembering their explosive meeting, he was ashamed of some of the things he'd said and done. But sometimes there was no accounting for what a man would do when he was hurt and angry, and his anger had festered for nine years. He'd just wanted to make it plain he'd wised up to her female tricks. Now, if only she'd go back to Charleston, he'd call the score even and get on with his life. He was just sorry that Rachel had caught all the fallout from his uncertain temper these days.

"You can come up with any excuse you want, Luke Duval," Rachel lectured in a starchy, no-nonsense voice, "but the reason you're so cantankerous is all those empty junk food calories you consume, not to mention the sugar and preservatives. And when you forget to eat at all—" She broke off with a mock shudder, refastened her watch and reached for a stack of phone memos.

"I'll try to do better, I promise," Luke said solemnly, but there was a distinct twinkle in his eye.

"You do that!" Rachel laughed. "And I'll keep an eye on you, too. After all, what are friends for?"

Their laughter mingled in an easy camaraderie of long standing, and Luke smiled fondly at Rachel. There had been a time when they'd been "involved," but that was long past. It hadn't been much of an affair as affairs went—merely two lonely people searching for companionship—but when the fire of passion died, they'd found to their delight they'd become friends in the meantime. Luke knew it was generally assumed they still had a "thing" going on, especially when he'd lost his last assistant and offered Rachel the position, but he couldn't help what other people assumed.

Sometimes he wondered if it bothered Rachel that their names were linked by the Natchitoches gossip-mongers, but since he was as likely to be at her place for dinner as his own, he supposed it was inevitable. And it gave them both a kind of smoke screen while they discreetly dated others. Besides, despite the fact that Rachel looked about as sweet as a sugarplum, she was the best damn assistant he'd ever had.

"You've got a full clinic this morning, so we'd better get cracking," Rachel informed him, suddenly all efficiency. "Here's your calls for the afternoon, and Howard Montgomery wants you to take another look at his Thoroughbred's leg."

"Hell." Luke grimaced as he rose to his feet. At Rachel's questioning look he hastily explained, "I thought we had that under control."

"Well, Mr. Montgomery's still worried, so you'd better get out there as soon as you can. And also, Rob Thompson called and said to remind you you're supposed to help him this evening at the East Park Country Club."

"Damn!" Luke scraped a hand through the tawny mane of his hair in exasperation. "I forgot all about it. How'd I let myself get volunteered for that, anyway?"

"I don't know, but Rob told me not to let you try to weasel out of it. Cousinly duty, he called it." Rachel's watch slipped off her wrist and fell to the floor again. "Oh, horsefeathers!"

"Why don't you get that thing fixed?" Luke asked, picking it up again.

"I've been meaning to, but I just haven't had time."

"You're going to lose it," Luke warned mildly. "Let me drop it off for you at Peyton's, okay?"

Rachel smiled her gratitude. "You don't mind?"

"No problem. I'll pass right by." He dropped the watch into his shirt pocket and opened the door leading to the examining rooms and kennels. The cacophony of yips and barks from their animal patients and the sharp odor of disinfectant filled the office. "Come along. Duty calls."

The morning clinic was full, but Luke didn't forget his promise to Rachel. Later, on his way to make calls at several outlying farms, he made a detour down the brick-cobbled main street of Natchitoches. The avenue was bordered on one side by a row of businesses, many of them bearing a lacy fretwork of cast-iron balconies and railings in keeping with the Creole heritage of the city. On the other side a steep bank fell away to the narrow channel of Cane River-Lake, the remnants of what had once been an oxbow curve in the Red River. Now it was completely cut off from the river, but the lake was still the center of the "oldest city in the Louisiana Purchase." In the summer the lake sported water-skiers and fishing boats in abundance. And this portion of the riverbank below Front Street was most famous as the site of the annual Christmas Festival where hundreds of thousands of colored lights lit up the city for the month of December.

Luke parked his truck, then strode down the sidewalk toward the understated entrance of Peyton's Jewelers. He'd have to get a move on if he had any chance of being finished in time to help Rob with the preparations for the upcoming country club cotillion. His cousin ran his own electrical service, and someone had talked him into helping with the lights and sound system. Luke wasn't above lending Rob a hand now and then, but it was more than ironic that he'd gotten himself involved with the poshest event in the entire parish—an event he'd attended only once himself and that had left his life in shambles. Scowling at the memory, he pushed open the glass door of the jewelry store and came face-to-face with Charlie Kincaid.

She paused with her hand on the chrome handle of the door, her gray-green eyes wide and faintly startled. "Oh! Excuse me."

Doesn't she own any normal clothes? Luke's first thought was rife with annoyance, but it wasn't clear if it was due to this unexpected meeting or the sharp twist of something primitive that stabbed him in the gut at the sight of her.

Dressed in a svelte green silk sheath and high heels that showed off the shapeliness of her slim legs, Charlie was a picture of cool sophistication. Her lips gleamed with a peachy gloss, and her vibrant red-brown curls were arranged in a calculated tousle that made a man's hands itch with the urge to touch. The bones under her skin looked as fragile as porcelain, and she was as delicate and feminine as a portrait on an antique cameo. Now that he considered it, maybe it wasn't what she wore, but how she wore it, with flair and elegance that put other women to shame and made him feel gross and uncivilized in his heavy boots and faded jeans. The feeling raised his defensive hackles.

"Been shopping, princess?" Luke's assessing gaze took in her empty hands, and his half smile was nearly a sneer. "What's the matter? Didn't they have any rocks here big enough to suit you?"

Her features stiffened, and she tucked her narrow envelope clutch tighter under her arm. The little smile she gave him was cool and haughty. "I'm...just browsing today, Dr. Duval. Excuse me, please."

"By all means." His tone was mocking as he held open the door. "I wouldn't dream of detaining you. I don't suppose we'll have the pleasure of your company around here much longer, anyway."

A spark of irritation kindled in the depths of her green eyes. "Really, Lucas, this role of tin-star sheriff is growing extremely tiresome. The next thing I expect is for you to order me to get out of town before sundown!"

"Now there's an idea," he drawled.

"Save your breath." Her soft mouth compressed with anger. "Your bad manners never impressed me."

"Honey, I wasn't being polite. I was trying to avoid a showdown."

Her soft, incredulous laugh was laden with disdain. "You have an exalted estimation of yourself, Lucas. You were never that important to me, and you certainly aren't now. I'm home to stay, and your nasty manners aren't reason enough for me to leave."

He frowned, and his voice was a husky growl. "Then maybe I'll have to provide you with a few more."

"I'm not nearly so gullible as I was nine years ago." Her expression grew thoughtful. "All this effort makes me wonder, though."

"Wonder what?"

A small feline smile appeared on her lips. "What's really the problem, Luke? Didn't *you* ever get over *me?*" With this parting volley she sailed out the door.

Damn! Luke ground his teeth. She hadn't changed a hair. But what else did you expect from a simpering miss whose greatest concern was the size of a man's bank account and whether his blood was blue enough? He stalked up to the glass counter, dug into his shirt pocket for Rachel's watch and slammed it down in front of Jim Peyton, the store's portly, middle-aged owner who'd been watching their exchange with interest. Jim took one look at Luke's glowering expression and hastily smoothed his own features into lines of polite inquiry.

"What can I do for you today, Luke?"

"Rachel's watch. The clasp is loose. Can you fix it?"

Jim gave Luke an odd look, then pushed his horn-rimmed glasses up his nose and examined the bracelet. "Sure. It'll be ready tomorrow."

Luke was already regretting his abrupt tone. It wasn't Jim Peyton's fault that seeing Charlie invariably put him into a mood to bite his nails—tenpenny ones, that is. Luke managed a weak grin.

"Fine. I'll tell Rachel." He glanced back over his shoulder through the store's glass door, but Charlie had disappeared down the street. "Missed a sale there, eh,

Jim? Didn't you have anything that pleased Her Majesty?''

Jim dropped Rachel's watch into a small manila envelope and scribbled busily on the flap. "Huh? Oh, nothing like that. Actually, Ms. Kincaid wasn't buying. She was selling."

"What!"

"Oh, yes. Several very nice pieces. A diamond ring, a sapphire brooch and such. Of course, I couldn't give her their full value...."

The front door swished, and the jeweler glanced up, surprised to find he was talking to himself.

HECTOR PARRISH'S NEPHEW was a slender young man of about eighteen known as Pigeon. Luke was fairly certain that if Pigeon had another Christian name, the family had long since forgotten it. While Hector was an absolute genius with engines and mechanical things, he had no notion of what it took to handle animals, but with Pigeon it was just the opposite. That was why Howard Montgomery had hired him as a groom on Luke's recommendation when he'd bought his first racehorse. Now Pigeon slowly walked the huge roan known as Kingdom's Bobby around the paddock at Evening Star while Luke propped himself against the fence and watched.

"He's still favoring that right knee, Pigeon," Luke muttered, his eyes narrowed.

"Yassir, that's what I told Mr. Howard," Pigeon said, shaking his head. "He ain't going to make a runner outta this one."

"We haven't given up yet. Keep up the treatment. If he doesn't respond soon, we may have to consider surgery," Luke said, chewing his upper lip. "You can turn him out now, Pigeon. I'll check on him again in a day or two."

Pigeon grinned, showing broad white teeth in his dark face, and led the horse away. Luke turned to Hector, who'd been silently watching the proceedings.

"Howard isn't going to like this," Luke commented to the older man. The roan's injury stubbornly refused to heal properly, and Luke's professional frustration was showing. He hated to admit defeat on anything, but especially on such a beautiful piece of horseflesh as this one.

"He sets great store in that pony," Hector agreed. Pulling a red bandana from his pocket, he mopped his damp face and the bald spot on the back of his grizzled gray head. "You doin' the best you can, Doc. What you need is to set a spell in the shade and have a glass of lemonade."

Luke had to admit the idea had great appeal. He was hot and dirty and smelled of blood, disinfectant and horse. He cast a quick look at the distance of the sun over the horizon, decided he was so late already that another few minutes wouldn't matter to Rob, then grinned at Hector. "That wouldn't happen to be Sudie Mae's homemade lemonade, would it?"

"Shore is."

Luke laughed. "Then start pouring."

Minutes later, sitting in the cool, dark confines of the barn on an overturned feed bucket, Luke let Hector pour him a second glass of the tart-sweet beverage from a battered thermos. They sipped in companionable silence— Hector, because he was taciturn by nature and he and Luke had been friends for quite some time; Luke because he was lost in his thoughts.

Something didn't add up, and it had been bothering him all day. Like a sore tooth that you couldn't help touching, he'd gnawed at the reason for Charlie's visit to

Jim Peyton's establishment. What would possess a woman like Charlie Kincaid to part with her jewelry, and for less than it was worth, at that? Was she just so unsentimental, or even vindictive, that cold hard cash was more appealing than anything given to her by an ex-husband? Surely a woman who enjoyed the best of material things would be loath to part with such obvious displays of wealth, no matter who had provided them. It didn't make sense.

Luke drained the last of his lemonade from the quart jar he'd used as a drinking glass, then set it down in the straw-strewn dirt between his battered boots. "Quite a bit of excitement here at Evening Star now that Miss Charlie's back for a spell, I guess."

"Yep."

"She's going back to Charleston soon?"

"Nope."

Luke chewed on that for a moment. "Can't think what she wants to stay around here for."

"Can't you?"

"She's bound to be missing her society friends."

"Not so's I can see." Hector bent over, forearms to knees, his own quart jar dangling between his careworn but still skillful fingers.

Luke made a little sound of disgust. "She won't be satisfied with the life around here for long."

"You lay off, son," Hector said sternly. "That little girl, she needs a resting place. It takes a lot out of a woman to miscarry a baby like that."

Luke looked at Hector in shocked silence. The image of Charlie, her slender form tortured by painful spasms, made his throat so raw that he had to swallow hard. When he finally spoke, his voice was a hoarse whisper. "I didn't know."

Hector nodded. "She don't say much, not even to Sudie, but she was in the hospital a long time."

"God!" Luke's voice shook and his hands clenched into fists. "Is she all right?"

"Just hurtin' here." Hector touched his chest over his heart. "You come home to your own folks when you feel like that."

"Yes." Luke stood up abruptly. "What about her husband? Will they work things out?"

Hector shrugged. "It ain't my place to say. But Sudie, she ain't got a kind word for that man. No, sir, not when he ain't give our Charlie not one red nickel to live on after all she's been through!"

Suddenly the little scene in Peyton's Jewelry made sense. The way Charlie held her purse in such a tight grip, the proud, imperious tilt of her chin—all a facade. Luke felt lower than a snake's belly.

"That sorry, low-down..." He cursed Tyler Frazier and himself in one breath.

Hector nodded, his black eyes shining with contempt. "Rich folks can be mighty mean sometimes. What if Miss Charlie hadn't had her grandma to take her in?"

Luke couldn't bring himself to feel very charitable toward Margaret Montgomery. She'd made it quite clear nine years ago he wasn't good enough for her precious granddaughter. At least the old woman had the decency to welcome Charlie home. That was certainly more than he'd done.

Charlie Kincaid was home, sick and probably broke, and all he'd done was make a complete ass of himself! Remorse twisted through him, heavy and scalding. Evidently Charlie hadn't had it as easy in Charleston all these years as he'd supposed. All right, so she'd hurt him way back then, playing with him as if he was one of her pretty boys, then tossing him casually aside when someone of her own class came along. He hadn't exactly been an angel, either, letting his anger get the better of him, showing her with a little stage-dressing of his own that *no one* called the shots for Luke Duval. It seemed damn childish, looking back now, but the way he'd behaved toward Charlie recently wasn't any better. Damn it! And it was certainly no way for a thirty-four-year-old man to act.

It was time he had a little compassion for Charlie Kincaid. Knowing some of her troubles, the least he could do was stay clear of her. She didn't need any more grief, least of all from an old flame with a chip on his shoulder.

Luke cleared his throat and bent to pick up his medical bag. "I guess it's a good thing Charlie had all of you, Hec. Tell Sudie I still think she makes the best lemonade in the state, will you?"

"That I will," Hector replied. "You come back soon, you hear, son?"

"Sure. See you, Hec." Luke flashed a halfhearted grin, but he knew he would be avoiding Evening Star—and Charlie—from now on.

CHARLIE SMOOTHED the crease in her taupe linen trousers, automatically checked the pins in her intricate chignon, and picked up her portfolio and purse from the foyer table. The sound of raised voices coming from the den made her pause uncertainly. Usually after supper the only sounds heard in the old house came from the television set or the creaking of the century-old floorboards, certainly not from the raised voice of her own grandmother! Charlie and Gina were on their way to a meeting of the decorations committee at the club, but like a moth to a flame, Charlie was inexorably drawn to the archway

into the den to witness the spectacle of Margaret Montgomery in an icy rage.

"You needn't take that attitude with me, Howard,"
Milady snapped, glaring through her gold-rimmed reading glasses at the red-faced man who was obviously holding on to his own temper with some effort. "Nothing
means more to me than Evening Star—nothing! I won't
sit back and let you drive it to ruin with these wild ideas
of yours."

"I've done all right for the place so far, haven't I?"
Howard demanded hotly. He stood like a reluctant sup-
plicant before the sofa where Milady was enthroned, and
his resentful words blared like a brass trumpet. "Without your constant interference I could do even better.
Having to come to you with hat in hand every time I need
something—well, it's humiliating, that's what it is!"

"I'll remind you just who you're working for, young
man." Milady's spine was ramrod straight against the soft
cushions. "You've been amply rewarded."

"Is that what you call it?" Howard's face turned an
even darker beet-red as Gina joined Charlie in the doorway, and looking up, he realized he had an audience. His
jowly face was florid with rage, but he controlled his voice
when he spoke again. "If that's all my devotion to you
and this place means, Milady, then you can think about
doing without my services at all!"

Turning on his heel, he stormed out of the room,
brushing past his wife and Charlie with barely a glance.
The redhead's concerned frown puckered her smooth
brow, and she rushed to Milady's side.

"Now don't you fret," Gina said in a soothing tone,
taking one of Milady's veined hands between her own.
"You know Howard doesn't mean the things he says when
he's upset. I'll speak to him."

Milady jerked her hand free of Gina's. "Don't use your sweet talk on me. I'm not in my dotage yet, and I'll decide what's done here on Evening Star. I know how to handle your husband even if *you* don't."

"Milady, you shouldn't get so worked up," Charlie said worriedly. "It can't be good for you."

"You all probably wish me in my grave, anyway." Milady made an impatient gesture at both Gina's and Charlie's murmured dissent. "Well, I'm not done for yet. Oh, I'm tired of the lot of you! Help me up, girl. I'm going to my bed. It's the only place around here where I can find some peace."

Gina dutifully gave the old woman her arm. As soon as Milady was on her feet, she irritably brushed off Gina's hands, made a brief good-night and left Charlie and Gina standing rather nonplussed by the abruptness of her exit.

"My God, she's getting more cantankerous every day," Gina said with a long-suffering groan. "Just like Howard. And I'm getting damn tired of playing Henry Kissinger between the two of them, I can tell you."

"Do you think Howard meant what he said?" Charlie asked anxiously.

Gina's artfully plucked brows arched. "You mean about leaving? Of course not," she said carelessly. "He's put too much into this place to leave it now. They have these spats about twice a month." She adjusted the appliquéd front of her coral sundress, picked up her matching straw tote from the hall table and gave a little laugh. "Usually on the first and the fifteenth, if you catch my meaning. Don't worry. Milady seems to thrive on bedeviling Howard. Come on. We're going to be late."

Moments later they were speeding toward town in Gina's white Cadillac. Charlie sank down in the luxurious white leather seat and wondered if she'd done Milady a disservice leaving her to Gina's and Howard's tender mercies all this time. If tonight's fracas was any indication, the relationship was a rocky one, and Charlie felt a sudden surge of guilt. Although Milady was as spry and sharp as the proverbial tack, she was still an old woman. Her golden years should be ones of ease and leisure, not constant acrimony.

Perhaps Milady had been wrong in her determination to hold on to Evening Star. She could have sold it for a tidy profit years ago and lived well anywhere in the world. Even as she formed the thought, Charlie smiled. Milady would never do that. The dark loamy earth of her birthright was as much a part of her as her gray eyes, and Charlie had to admit that she felt the same way. No matter that she hadn't visited after her marriage, she'd always known that Evening Star was *here* if she needed it. More times than she'd like to remember, that knowledge had sustained her in the face of Tyler's rages.

When Gina parked in front of the clubhouse at the country club, Charlie felt a moment's uncertainty. Nothing seemed to have changed. The golf course still fell away into the darkness of lush, rolling fairways behind the long, impressive edifice the same way it had the night she'd made her own promenade at the cotillion, the night Luke Duval had made it abundantly clear he didn't want her. Shaking off the miasmas of the past, Charlie followed Gina into the building and down the hall to the large, well-lit room that Gina planned to transform into a romantic twenties-style ballroom with Charlie's help.

There was a great deal of activity going on, and a score of male and female volunteers working at assorted tasks. Charlie wasn't quite prepared for the barrage of greetings their arrival produced, but she did her best to hide her shyness behind a cool smile—which froze on her face when she caught sight of Luke Duval perched on top of a ladder, stringing electrical wire into the rafters. She barely stifled a groan. Not Luke again. Not twice in one day! The fates were certainly having a heyday at her expense.

"What's *he* doing here?" Charlie asked Gina, her voice too soft to be heard over the chatter of conversation.

Gina followed her gaze, then gave Charlie a puzzled look. "The vet? He and Rob Thompson agreed to do the wiring."

Charlie glanced at the gangly, black-haired man with the homely face and kind brown eyes holding the base of the ladder. "Rob Thompson? I don't know him."

"He's the electrician we used when we rewired the house last year. He moved here a few years back from Texas with his little boy. Michael, I think the child's name is. Someone told me the vet set him up in business. A Duval cousin or something like that."

"How...how nice," Charlie said weakly.

"Oh, yes, that vet is as nice as they come." Gina giggled. "You can ask almost any unattached female in town. Luke Duval has dated just about all of them. Say, didn't you once have a yen for that guy yourself?"

"A yen?" Charlie forced a laugh. "Really, Gina, that's carrying things a bit far, don't you think?"

"I wouldn't blame you if you still did," Gina purred, her copper-colored gaze playing over the long-legged male in question. "There aren't many men on this earth who can do justice to a pair of jeans the way Luke Duval can. Makes my mouth water. Oh, there's Macy!"

Gina dragged Charlie over to meet Macy Gideon, the cotillion chairperson, and immediately demanded Charlie show off her proposals. In minutes they were surrounded by an interested crowd made up of debutantes' parents and boyfriends exclaiming at the scope and sophistication of her Art Deco theme and corresponding sketches.

"Don't you just love it?" Gina gushed, bending over Charlie's portfolio spread open on a table of sawhorses.

"It's perfect," Macy agreed

"And I know where to borrow the potted palms!" someone added excitedly.

"My grandfather's got a gazebo..."

"We could build a backdrop..."

"The high school has a mirror ball..."

Step by step, suggestion by suggestion, the plans fell into place.

Thankfully Charlie got caught up in the enthusiasm, but she never quite lost her uneasiness over Luke's presence. After the day she'd had—the degrading experience of disposing of her jewelry to get a stake, then fencing verbally with Luke, and finally realizing that Milady's situation wasn't ideal—the thought of having to tackle Luke's hostility again was more than she could stand.

After promising to paint the backdrops the following day, she was at last able to slip out of the circle of committee members. Gina was still holding court among a group of admirers that included the club's tanned and muscular golf pro, and she ignored all Charlie's signals that she was ready to leave. Heaving a sigh of annoyance, Charlie stepped out into the relative privacy of the hall to wait. She was bending over the water fountain to get a drink when she felt a presence. She knew who it was without even turning around.

"Lost your string of admirers, princess?"

Charlie wiped the droplets of water from her mouth and steeled herself for the impact Luke always made on her. When she turned, her face was serene. "I don't know what you mean, Doctor."

He crossed his arms over his broad chest, stretching the red fabric of his knit shirt over his shoulders, and gave a little snort of disbelief. "Men flock around you like geese, and you don't know what I mean."

"Up until now," she said pointedly, "I've always been able to fend off any unwelcome advances."

A reluctant laugh escaped him at this barb. "You have, have you?"

"Yes. I've had plenty of practice at it." Her eyes were suddenly bleak, and she turned away.

He caught her arm. "Wait, Charlie. I want to talk to you."

"I'd rather not," she said stiffly, not looking at him. "Nothing you can say is of the slightest interest to me."

"Damn it, Charlie! I'm trying to apologize!"

She looked up, her eyes wide and startled. "What?"

"Last week and...and this morning. I guess I shouldn't have been so hard on you."

Charlie's mouth trembled, but she tugged her arm free of his grasp and looked at him with hard disdain. "When were you anything else?"

Luke swallowed. "Yeah. But I didn't know you'd been sick."

All the color washed from her face. "Sick?"

He made a helpless gesture. "Ah, your, er... miscarriage. I'm sorry."

"Is this another tidbit of gossip from down at the co-op?"

He looked uncomfortable. "Actually, Hector told me."

"Doesn't anyone respect a person's right to privacy anymore?"

"Hec was just looking after you, that's all," Luke protested.

She was angry now, furious. "What else did he tell you, Lucas? Did he tell you the real reason I was in the hospital? You might as well know it all. I'm sure everyone else will soon! I didn't stay in the hospital so long because I lost my baby. I had what Milady so delicately terms a nervous breakdown."

There was a little sharp sound as he took a breath. "Charlie?"

"Do I look a little mad, Luke?" she asked, breathing hard. "I was for a time, you know. Is that what you wanted Hector to tell you?"

"No." His throat worked, and he reached for her. "No."

Charlie backed away from him, her chin high with defiance. "I'm doing quite well, thank you, if people will only mind their own damn business! Is there anything else Hector said I should know about?"

"Only that Frazier hadn't given you a cent. Look, Charlie, if you're pressed for funds, I can help—"

Her eyes blazed with a green fire. "Damn you! I'm not for sale no matter what you think!"

Luke shoved his fingers through his hair in agitation. "Hell, I didn't mean it that way!"

"I don't care how you meant it!" She was shaking so hard she could barely speak, but her warning was clear. "You stay away from me, Luke Duval! I can accept your hate, but I'll be damned if I'll accept your pity!"

CHAPTER FOUR

"THIS REALLY BRINGS back memories, doesn't it?" Becky Turner asked, her engaging grin creasing her fair, freckled face. She selected a plastic-wrapped slice of angel food cake from the cafeteria line in the NSU Student Union while Charlie dubiously eyed the selection of salads.

Choosing the one that appeared the least wilted, Charlie grimaced at her redheaded friend. "I'll say. Nothing's changed in nine years—including the food."

Becky giggled and carried her loaded tray to the cashier. "Come on now, Charlie, it's not that bad!"

"How would you know?" Charlie shot back with a laugh that lifted her shoulders beneath the raw aqua silk of her unstructured suit jacket. "You eat anything. And drat your hide, Becky Gilchrist Turner, you never gain an ounce!"

Becky's carroty curls bobbed, and her expression was smug. "I know."

After accepting her change from the bored cashier, Becky led Charlie toward a table next to a long window. Since the university was between its spring and summer sessions, only a few other diners were scattered among the tables filling the high-ceilinged area. Becky unloaded her hamburger, fries, coleslaw, cake and malted milk, then flashed Charlie another grin. "There is justice in the world. Since the Lord didn't make me beautiful like you, the least He can do is keep me skinny."

Charlie laughed softly and poured low-cal dressing on her salad. She took a sip of her diet drink while eyeing Becky's coltish, tomboy figure beneath her sedate shirt-waist dress. No one would guess slim-hipped Becky was the mother of two preschoolers. Ignoring the pang of sorrow over her own lost infant, she smiled brightly. "The only other person I've ever seen eat as much as you is—"

"Luke Duval," Becky said around a mouthful of burger. She dabbed daintily at the corner of her mouth with a paper napkin. "We used to have some great times hanging out in here, didn't we?"

Charlie picked up her fork and stabbed viciously at the inoffensive mound of lettuce in her salad bowl. "Yeah. Great."

Since that humiliating night at the country club, Charlie had promised herself not to waste another thought on Luke Duval, but it was easier said than done. Becky was right. Old memories haunted the campus.

Luke had walked her to classes between these aging redbrick buildings, driven her to the Watson Library in his battered old truck, kissed her for the first time on the riverbank below the intramural softball fields. Then she'd floated in a cloud of foolish happiness; now she was merely annoyed at the evidence of her past gullibility. Becky's impulse to reminisce didn't improve her mood.

"Do you remember when we all went fishing and the mosquitoes nearly carried us off? Wylan was covered with so many welts his mom thought he had the measles!" Becky said, giggling. "I thought Luke was going to drown you in calamine lotion, he was so upset."

"It's no wonder some people say Louisiana's state bird is the mosquito," Charlie joked weakly.

Becky nibbled contemplatively on a catsup-drenched french fry. "Gosh, we were so young then. And who could have guessed I'd end up with Wylan!"

"You look happy."

"I'm delirious with it—most of the time." Becky picked up another fry and shrugged philosophically. "We've had our ups and downs, but who doesn't these days? Not that it's always smooth sailing, with my work, Wylan's auto-parts business expanding and the girls always into something, but I know I'm very lucky." She broke off, grinning. "Sounds pretty tame next to the high society doings you're used to, I suppose."

"No. It sounds lovely." Charlie's voice was a bit wistful.

"Well, for ordinary folks I guess we do okay. The rest of the gang has, too," she said. "Buford and Sally just bought the gas station at the south fork, Madge is working as a lab tech in Dallas and Bobby's in Shreveport. Of course, you know Luke has the veterinary business in his back pocket in this town, and he's still hell on wheels with the ladies."

"I would have thought he'd have settled down by now," Charlie admitted carefully. With one finger she traced the circle of condensation on the table left by her glass. "There's no one, er...special?"

"I guess he's having too much fun." Becky shrugged. "Of course, they say he and Rachel Aubert have had a thing going for a while."

"Who's Rachel Aubert?" Charlie asked around a sudden involuntary constriction in her throat.

"The blonde who works for him at the clinic. Petite, fabulous figure. She's cute and friendly. I like her. I really don't know what Luke's waiting for. Maybe he's just not the marrying kind."

"Maybe not."

Becky's pale blue eyes were suddenly serious. "Look, I know it's hard for you, but I just wanted to say I'm sorry—about you and Tyler, I mean."

"These things happen," Charlie said, shrugging. For a moment she'd thought Becky was referring to her and Luke. She could almost laugh at herself for being so sensitive about something that was ancient history—at least to everyone else. But she was touched by Becky's concern for her. "I'm all right, you know."

"I don't mean to pry, of course, but is there any chance you and Tyler—?"

"No!" Charlie tried to soften the harshness of her tone with a slight smile. "None at all."

"Oh." Becky blinked and swiftly changed the subject. "By the way, Mother tells me your cotillion decorations are just fabulous."

"I hope everyone likes what we've done," Charlie said. "Is your sister excited about making her debut tomorrow night?"

"Not as much as Mother!" Becky laughed. "All the to-do is about to drive everyone batty. Daddy mumbles under his breath about the expense, and Audrey and her boyfriend loftily discuss this 'anachronistic Southern custom,' but, of course, she wouldn't miss it for the world...."

Charlie hid a wry smile behind another bite of salad as Becky rambled on. While some people like Becky felt awkward about the subject of Charlie's divorce, there were others whose avid curiosity led them to probe what was still in many ways an open wound. Like Bunny Morrison when she'd called to thank Charlie for the stained-glass unicorn.

"Really, Charlotte," Bunny had gushed through the telephone line, "I had no idea you were hiding so much talent! It's absolutely perfect, and lately whenever Trey and I entertain, everyone ends up in the bathroom admiring your handiwork!"

"Sounds crowded," Charlie teased, inwardly jumping up and down with delight.

Painting backdrops for free and assembling scores of inexpensive stained-glass novelty sun-catchers for the local shops had kept her busy, but the remuneration would be minimal at best. Bunny's patronage was just the kind of exposure she needed to secure larger projects. Surely it was only a matter of time before some of her other friends decided they wanted a similar attraction in their own homes. A nudge in that direction wouldn't come amiss, however.

"Listen, Bunny," Charlie continued, curling the spiral of telephone cord around her index finger, "I enjoyed working on your project so much, and I've got some time on my hands here, so spread the word for me, will you? I'd be willing to work on selected original commissions. Ask Lizabeth especially. I saw their house plans, and the kitchen window that will overlook their pool is just crying out for something unique."

Bunny sniffed. "Unique? Lizabeth Worley wouldn't know unique if it hit her square on her button nose. But I'll be sure to mention it. If anyone could use a little of your taste and style, it's Lizabeth."

"Now, Bunny, let's not be catty," Charlie chided gently.

Bunny's high-pitched giggle grated over the receiver. "You were always such a spoilsport, Charlotte! I don't know why I miss you so much."

"It's nice of you to say so."

Bunny's tone became sly. "And I know someone else who's missing you."

"Who?"

"Tyler." Bunny's voice fractured as she hurried to fill the dead silence emanating from Charlie's end of the wire. "I saw him at the Richardsons' party. He just looked— well, lost without you, Charlotte."

"I'm sure Tyler isn't pining away." There was no mistaking the sharp, bitter inflection in Charlie's words.

"I know it isn't any of my business, but what really happened between you two? I mean—"

"You're right. It isn't any of your business," Charlie interrupted. "You can tell the gossips that the divorce suit cited 'irreconcilable differences' and let it go at that, Bunny."

"Well, all right. You were always a bit of a loner, so I guess it's not surprising you're going to play your cards close to your chest on this." There was rueful disappointment in Bunny's tinny voice. "Tyler's not talking, either."

"Well, that's certainly satisfying to know!" Charlie snapped. "Did you grill him, too?"

"Everyone's interested, that's all. Tyler tries to be his usual charming self, but he's not accustomed to the cold shoulder he's getting from your friends—myself included."

Charlie laughed outright at this obvious ploy. "Now I'm supposed to fall on your neck out of gratitude and spill my guts, right?"

"That was the general idea," Bunny agreed cheerfully.

"Bunny Morrison, you're incorrigible!"

Now Charlie smiled to herself, remembering Bunny's unrepentant cheekiness. She took a final bite of her salad while across the table Becky continued her nonstop chatter, and the smile disappeared, because while she was waiting for the commission that would make her career, she had to have a real job. No one was going to call her a parasite again.

When her friend paused for breath, Charlie asked the question that was foremost in her mind. "Becky, were you able to find out about any job openings for me?"

"You're lucky I work in Personnel," Becky said. "I heard just this morning that Mrs. Hazelton in the Fine Arts Department is going to have surgery at the end of the week. It would be a temporary position, and I don't know what the duties are exactly, but I know there are some kids' activities and—"

"It doesn't matter. I'll take anything," Charlie said eagerly.

Becky gave her a curious look, but instead of commenting, dug into her purse for a bundle of papers. "I took the liberty of bringing you all the application forms. If you get over to the Fine Arts Department right away, maybe they'll hire you on the spot."

"You're a doll! I'll do it now." Charlie began to gather up her purse and tray.

"Hey, wait till I finish my cake and I'll go with you," Becky protested.

The hunk of white cake in front of Becky looked more like a dried sponge than something edible. Gray-green eyes sparkling with humor and excitement, Charlie smiled at her friend. "Leave it. If I get this job, I promise I'll make you a ton of my famous Mississippi mud pie."

Becky scrambled up. "Then what are we waiting for?"

"UNCLE LUKE!"

A stocky five-year-old dynamo raced across the asphalt parking lot of the Duval Animal Clinic and flung himself into Luke's welcoming arms.

"Hey, Mikey! What's the good word, tiger?" Luke said, swinging the black-haired boy skyward and laughing as he squealed with pleasure.

Blue eyes and dimples completed Michael Thompson's charms, and now he looped his arms around Luke's neck and grinned beguilingly. "Have you locked up yet, Uncle Luke? I want to see the animals. Can I, huh? Dad says we might be too late. Are we?"

Luke looked up as Mikey's father, Rob, climbed out of his white van with the Thompson Electrical Service logo on the side. The clinic was on a main road on the outskirts of Natchitoches, and the tall pine trees lining the property cast long shadows across the parking lot.

"I think something can be arranged," Luke assured the boy. "Rachel's still inside, and I'm sure she'll give you a quick peek. Tell her I said it was okay to show you the raccoon with the broken leg."

"Awright! Neato!" Mikey squirmed out of Luke's arms and was headed for the entrance in a flash.

"Hurry back, Michael," Rob called, sauntering to Luke's side. "These people are ready to go home."

"Okay, Dad!" Mikey flung over his shoulder.

Luke leaned against the tailgate of his brown pickup, crossed his denim-clad legs and tipped his baseball cap to the back of his head. The June heat still rose in waves from the pavement, and a sheen of moisture covered both men's upper lips. "Well, cuz? Had a busy day?"

"Can't complain." Rob shrugged his massive shoulders and shoved his hands deep into the pockets of his khaki work pants. "In fact, things have been so good I'll be able to pay a little extra on the note this month."

Luke snorted. "Why put pressure on yourself like that? I'm not worried about it."

"I know that, but I'm going to all the same. The chance you gave me to open the business meant Michael and I could be together. Roughnecking and having to leave him with Celia's mother all the time nearly killed us both." Rob's brown eyes grew almost black at the mention of his ex-wife, a boozy, bed-hopping aspiring model who'd deserted both husband and nine-month-old son and never looked back.

"Hell, Rob," Luke drawled, "I just knew a good investment when I saw it. Look, I spent most of the day in surgery, and I'm ready for a cold one and some chow. You and Mikey want to join me?"

"You don't have any . . . er, plans?" Rob glanced in the direction of the clinic.

"Nothing special."

Rob's homely features relaxed. "Then, sure. Mikey said something about McDonald's, but maybe we can talk him into pizza instead."

Mikey's excited piping issued from the front of the building, interspersed with softer feminine syllables. The little boy skipped out the front door, dragging on Rachel Aubert's hand.

"Hold it, sport!" she said, her blond curls bobbing with her laughter. "I've got to lock up."

Neatly attired in dark slacks and pale blue lab coat, she wrestled with an enormous set of keys for a moment, selected one, then deftly locked the door to the now-darkened clinic and dropped the ring into her oversize hobo bag. Then she took the youngster's hand again and walked toward Luke and Rob.

"Who's your boyfriend, Rachel?" Luke teased.

Mikey dissolved into giggles, his bright blue eyes sparkling at Rachel. "He called me your boyfriend!"

Rachel ruffled the boy's straight black hair. "I'd be lucky to land a heartbreaker like you, Mikey. If I were just a few years younger, sport, you'd have to watch out."

"Say, Rachel," Luke said, "we're thinking of going out for a bite of something. Want to tag along?"

Rachel cast a swift glance at Rob, who hadn't said a word since her appearance.

"It won't be much fun for the lady, Luke," Rob blurted suddenly. "I have to go by the country club." Shuffling his big feet, he mumbled something further about a final systems check. His craggy face was suffused with a deep, bashful color under his tan.

"Oh, that's right," Rachel said a shade too brightly. "The cotillion is tomorrow night, isn't it? I'm sure you've got lots of work to do."

"We still have to eat," Luke pointed out, puzzled at his cousin's abrupt manner.

"Well, while there's nothing I'd rather do than go out with three handsome eligible bachelors," Rachel said, "I'm afraid I can't. Remember I promised my mother I'd drive to Robeline tonight and spend the weekend?"

"Oh, yeah. It slipped my mind. Some other time then," Luke said easily, draping his arm around her shoulders and giving her neck an affectionate squeeze. "Tell your mom hello for me."

"I certainly will." Rachel smiled and ran her fingers lightly down Luke's stubbled cheek. Stepping out from under his arm, she flicked Rob another quick look, then gave Mikey a friendly mock punch to his chin. "See you later, sport. Next time you come by I'll let you help me feed our patients."

"Okay!" Mikey beamed, waving as Rachel strolled toward her car. "Thanks, Miss Rachel!"

"At least one of the Thompson boys knows how to treat a lady," Luke remarked, narrowing his amber-brown eyes at Rob. "Cripes, Rob! What a sourpuss you are. Don't you like Rachel?"

Rob scowled at his cousin. "Most of us don't have your way with women."

"Right." Luke gave a wry, self-deprecating chuckle.

Way with women, was it? If Rob only knew what a damn mess he'd made of his last talk with Charlie Kincaid. God, what a jackass he'd been! The thought of what Charlie had been through made his gut twist with remorse. The least he owed her was another apology for the things he'd said. He'd promised himself to stay away from her, but his guilt ate at him, making him restless and edgy. He might never be able to make things right, but he had to try for his own peace of mind. A thought struck him.

"You say you've got to go by the country club this evening?" he demanded.

Rob nodded. "Yeah. It won't take long to make a final check while the committee finishes decorating."

"Everyone will be there?"

"I guess." Rob shrugged, looking puzzled.

"Tell you what," Luke said, clapping his cousin companionably on the shoulder. "You pick up the pizza tab and I'll give you a hand at the club. Deal?"

"Pizza!" Mikey exclaimed. "Awright! And I want to help, too."

Rob laughed and grinned, a father's love shining in his eyes. "You heard the man, Luke. A deal it is."

CHARLIE SURVEYED the country club ballroom and felt a warm pleasure and pride flow through her. Gina's volunteers had taken Charlie's ideas and transformed them into this sumptuous reality of mauve, violet, silver and

gray. The backdrops for this year's cotillion were light but
sophisticated, the small stage on which each debutante
would appear in turn a bower of Art Deco irises and lil-
ies. All that was lacking now was soft lights, music and the
banks of fresh flowers that were to be delivered the next
day. She almost wished she'd be there to see it.

"This is definitely the prettiest theme we've ever had,"
Gina said at Charlie's side.

Macy Gideon agreed with a slightly harried smile.
"You've both done a fine job. Now you can relax and
enjoy the party. On the other hand, *I've* still got to get
through another day of nervous mothers. I've got to run.
Are we all through here?"

"Mr. Thompson is supposed to check the lights one last
time," Gina answered. "He should have been here by
now."

"I'll go outside and wait for him," Charlie offered.

"You're an angel," Gina said. "Send him in when he
gets here and I'll bring the car around front. You know
how testy Milady gets when anyone's late for supper."
Gina linked her arm through Macy's. "Now, sugar, have
you told me what you're going to wear? And is Edgar
going to wear a tux this year? I swear Howard is giving me
fits about his, but I told him . . ."

Charlie smiled to herself as she walked to the front
door. The decorations were perfect, and she'd had an
agreeable interview with the dean of the Fine Arts School
that afternoon. While she hadn't exactly been hired on the
spot as Becky had foretold, Charlie knew she'd made a
favorable impression. And why not? Her credentials were
more than adequate. She shoved her hands into the
pockets of her aqua jacket and crossed her fingers. It
would be hard to be patient until next week, but the dean

had made it clear no decision regarding the temporary position would be made until then.

Charlie reached the main entrance just in time to help a small black-haired boy push open one of the heavy double glass doors.

"Thanks!" The little boy grinned, showing a dimple and the remnants of Italian red sauce on his round, tanned cheek.

"You're welcome," Charlie said, smiling back. "Are you looking for someone?"

"No, ma'am. I'm holding the door for my dad," he said proudly. "Oops! Here he is."

Puffing, the child tugged on the heavy door again. Charlie hid her smile and added her efforts. The door swung open just as Rob Thompson appeared on the top step of the covered portico, carrying a heavy tool kit.

"Thanks, Mikey," he said, and nodded to Charlie. "Evening, ma'am."

"Hello, Rob," Charlie answered with a smile. She liked what she knew about the laconic electrician, having met him occasionally during the long hours spent painting backdrops. "Is this your son?"

"Yes, ma'am. This is Michael."

"How do you do, Michael?" Charlie said, bending down to shake the boy's hand. "I'm pleased to meet you."

"You can call me Mikey," he said. "Everyone does. Me and Uncle Luke are going to help Dad tonight. But first we had pizza and root beer and everything!"

Charlie drew back with a sinking sensation in the pit of her stomach. "How...how nice."

"Maybe Ms. Kincaid doesn't care for pizza," Luke said, standing on the threshold with a cardboard box of light bulbs in his arms.

Charlie felt her features grow stiff, even though her heart hammered in her chest at the sight of Luke in his short-sleeved western shirt. It irritated her that she had no control over her response to his magnetism, but she'd die rather than show it.

"I love pizza," she said, defiant and defensive at the same time. As though seeking support, she touched Mikey's shoulder. "I always order mine with extra pepperoni and anchovies. How about you, Mikey?"

"Anchovies? Ugh!" Mikey made a face and shook his head vehemently. "I like hamburger pizza best. But I can't eat as much as Uncle Luke. He ate almost a whole one by himself."

Charlie pasted a sugar-sweet smile on her lips. "Then if your Uncle Luke gets a tummy ache in the middle of the night, it's no more than he deserves." She pointed in the direction of the ballroom. "Gina and Mrs. Gideon are waiting for you, Rob."

"Right. Come on, Mikey," Rob said, and ambled off, the little boy trailing adoringly after him.

"I'll be along in a minute," Luke called after him, his tawny eyes never leaving Charlie's face.

"Excuse me," Charlie said coolly, but Luke continued to block the door, his wide shoulders nearly filling the space between the metal frame.

"I want to talk to you," Luke said, his voice gravel rough.

"No." She shook her head almost as vehemently as Mikey had, and the mahogany highlights danced in her hair. "I prefer not to listen to any more of your insults and insinuations. Get out of my way. I'm going home."

Luke stepped out of the doorway, setting his box aside on the floor, then held open the glass door for her. With her chin tilted at an imperious angle Charlie sailed past him out onto the portico. The late-evening heat was still stifling, even though the sun was just disappearing behind the tops of the trees on the first fairway. She caught her breath at the temperature, then stopped breathing altogether when Luke's large hand closed around her wrist.

"Hold up a minute," he said, his jaw pulsing. He tugged her to the side of the porch out of the path of traffic. "Damn it, I've got something to say!"

"I'm not interested in anything you could possibly say to me, Dr. Duval," Charlie said between gritted teeth.

He released a breath that was pure exasperation. "Why do you have to make it so hard?"

"Me?" Her voice was incredulous.

Raking a hand through his sun-streaked hair, he tilted his head to one side and favored her with a truculent expression. "You make me feel like a damn fool."

"I can hardly take credit for something for which you have an abundance of natural talent," she purred, her gray-green eyes wide and guileless.

His snort of laughter surprised them both. "You're still able to take me down a peg or two, aren't you? Hell, yes, you make it hard! Miss Society Girl who's always in control of the situation, able to whip ruffians like me with a single flick of that razor-edged tongue while looking as cool and enticing as a mint julep on a hot day."

"Is there a point to this?" she asked tightly.

"Don't get your feathers ruffled. I swear I never knew a woman so ready to take offense at a compliment!"

Her eyebrows arched. "Oh, is that what it was?"

"Damn it, Charlie! If you'll just let me say my piece, I'll retire from the field, bloodied, but with at least a portion of my pride."

Charlie licked her dry lips and glanced away. "W-what is it you want to say?"

"I want to say I'm sorry. I made some unwarranted as-
sumptions, and I said some things I'm truly ashamed of
the other day. You didn't deserve that kind of hostility,
especially after everything you've been through."

He hesitated for an instant at the flicker of raw pain
that chased across her face and without conscious intent
reached out and caught both her hands, needing to touch
her so that she would understand his sincerity.

"I hope you'll find it within yourself to forgive me,
Charlie, and—good God! What have you done to your
hands?"

He rolled her hands palm up and stared in horror at the
cross-hatching of fine cuts that mutilated the soft skin of
her fingers and palms, some merely scratches but others
deeper, almost like incisions.

"It's nothing, really." She tried to tug free, but he held
her firmly.

"Nothing! You look as though you've been playing in
my scalpel tray! Did you do this working on this damn
cotillion? Don't these people have any sense? You're not
physically strong enough to manhandle scenery. You
could really hurt yourself. Someone should take care of
you—"

"Luke! I said it's nothing." She broke into his tirade,
a bit mystified at his angry outburst. "And it has nothing to do with the decorations. It's an occupational haz-
ard...."

Still frowning, his thumbs rubbed over her palms,
brailling the ribbons of fine scars. "You're working in
glass again?"

Charlie nodded, feeling a bit breathless at the astute-
ness of his guess and the warm patterns he was tracing on
her sensitive palms. "A girl has to make a living somehow," she said flippantly.

"I see."

And Charlie thought he did, too clearly. Would he laugh at her feeble attempts toward independence, taunting her with the fact that it was too little, too late? But he surprised her.

"You're working on a commission basis?"

She nodded uncertainly. "I'm making an attempt. It will take a while to build a name...."

"Not as long as you think, I'll wager." A crooked smile slowly lit his face. "You're talented enough to pull it off."

"I hope you're right. If I don't cut off a finger in the process," she joked wryly, unnerved by his unexpected support of her endeavor. "I'm not nearly as clumsy as I was at first, but every time I slice a finger I tell myself nothing worthwhile is totally painless."

Luke lifted her abused hands, staring at them strangely. His fingers tightened around hers, and something flared within the golden depths of his tawny eyes that took Charlie's breath away.

"You could be right," he murmured. "Charlie—"

A strident blast of a car horn made Charlie jump guiltily. Gina's white Cadillac waited in the driveway. She tugged her hands with a kind of rising panic. "There's Gina. I've got to go."

He didn't release her. "Wait, Charlie, there's a lot that hasn't been said yet."

"You said enough."

Her heart hammered in her chest. She was frightened of him, and of herself, and of the nearly overwhelming awareness they'd shared for a single blinding instant. Luke had shown himself capable of humility, kindness and concern, and Charlie was afraid of her weakness, her susceptibility to this gentle version of Luke. She couldn't fall for him again. She couldn't!

Gina tooted impatiently from the driveway, and Charlie jerked her hands free, babbling, "I accept your apology. Thank you for that. I've got to go."

She nearly tripped in her haste down the steps, lurching on the gravel driveway to catch herself on the chrome handle of the Cadillac's door.

"Don't think you can run away, Charlie," Luke called after her.

She jerked her head back, casting him a startled glance as he watched her from the porch. His lips tilted in a lopsided half smile that was all arrogant charm and blatant masculine self-confidence.

"We're going to talk, honey," he said. "And it might as well be sooner than later. I'll see you here tomorrow night."

Charlie allowed herself a small smile. With a toss of her curls she opened the car door and climbed in. She sank into the white leather upholstery, barely attending to Gina's chatter, and her smile grew even wider.

Luke Duval thought he was so smart! Well, she'd give almost anything to see his face when he realized she hadn't jumped to do his bidding. Not only was she not attending tomorrow night's cotillion, but now a string of wild horses couldn't drag her there!

CHAPTER FIVE

"WHAT DO YOU MEAN you're not going?"

Charlie looked up from the paper pattern of templates she was carefully laying out on jewel-toned shards of glass and frowned at the slight figure of her grandmother silhouetted in the doorway of her studio. "What? Going where?"

Milady stamped over the threshold of the lean-to and wrinkled her nose at the conglomeration of old paint buckets, broken yard tools and leaky water hoses that lined one wall. A single bulb on a dangling electrical cord illuminated the countertop along the other wall that was Charlie's workbench, now spread with rolls of copper leaf and lead solder, paper patterns, glass cutters, boards, hammer, nails and myriad panes of colorful glass.

"Don't be impertinent with me, missy!" Milady snapped. She looked with distaste at the dusty accumulation, tucking the hem of her cool cotton wrapper-styled dress out of reach of several gossamer cobwebs. "You knew very well I'm talking about the cotillion."

"Oh, that." Charlie turned back to her project.

"Yes, that. Gina just told me, and she's very upset."

Charlie raised her head again, pushing back the weight of heavy curls from her perspiring brow with a little sigh. The lean-to wasn't air-conditioned, and the warmth of the June afternoon raised the temperature inside to broiling levels. A movement behind Milady caught Charlie's eyes. "Don't let Miss Scarlett come in here!"

Milady snatched up the rotund dog, her attitude huffy and indignant. "You needn't vent your spleen on my pet, Charlotte. She can't hurt any of your precious playthings!"

With another sigh Charlie set down her patterns and slid off her stool. "I just don't want her hurt, Milady. There are glass slivers on the floor that could cut her pads."

"Oh." Somewhat taken aback, Milady's gray head bobbed in understanding.

"We girls have to stick together, right, Miss Scarlett?" Charlie asked, letting the dog sniff her fingers before— cautiously—scratching her peaked ears. For once Miss Scarlett bore the ministrations without so much as a growl, and Charlie felt subtly vindicated.

"My point exactly," Milady said, returning to her topic, as stubborn as a dog with a bone. "Gina and I both want you to go to the cotillion."

Charlie wiped her sweaty palms on her fashionably faded jeans. "I helped with the decorations, didn't I? There's no reason I should attend the actual event. Besides, there are just too many memories."

"Pshaw! I don't hold with that drivel," Milady said in a scathing tone. "I'd never have believed my own granddaughter was such a coward. All you're doing is hiding out, first at that fancy hospital, now at Evening Star."

"That's not true." Charlie was surprised that her voice was unsteady, and she fought to make her tone even and reasonable. "I've lived with other people's expectations long enough, so if I choose not to attend this function, then that's my right."

"You can't hole up like a wounded animal, Charlotte. Certainly people are going to be curious about you and Tyler, but that's no reason to become a recluse!"

"My decision has nothing to do with Tyler." Charlie's lips twisted wryly. That was certainly the truth!

Her grandmother's expression was exasperated. "Well, then you're making even less sense than I thought. Listen here, girl, you've got to show this town what you're made of—and that's good strong Montgomery stock!"

"I don't have to prove anything to anyone but myself."

"You're being deliberately obtuse, Charlotte," Milady said in disgust. "We've already discussed this. You've got to get back into circulation, and the cotillion's the perfect place to start."

"Why?" Charlie laughed softly. "The last thing I'm looking for is a husband."

"That's certainly shortsighted! The only thing you're trained for is being married. I know this isn't Charleston, but there are plenty of fine, marriageable men in this town. No one in Tyler's league, of course, but there are some suitable bachelors." Milady's blue eyes gleamed slyly. "You might even reconsider Luke Duval now that he's so successful."

Charlie felt herself go cold inside. Milady had been so adamant in her disapproval of Luke all those years ago that this turnabout was chilling. "I can't believe you actually mean that," she said hoarsely.

"Why not?" Milady's cackle of laughter echoed off the bare rafters. "He really showed me! Never thought he'd amount to a hill of beans, and now look at him—a big fine house and a thriving practice. You could do a lot worse. Of course, he'll never admit it, but I did him a big favor back when you were so smitten with him."

"Favor?" Charlie croaked.

"Where do you think he'd be today if you two young pups had kept on seeing each other? Certainly not where he is!"

"Luke never lacked determination," Charlie countered.

Her grandmother made a disparaging gesture. "He'd never have made it through school at all with a young wife to support, and maybe even a couple of howling babies. Of course, he might not have had that problem with you, would he?"

Charlie gasped at the careless cruelty of Milady's words and felt the sting of tears behind her eyes. "Does it give you pleasure to say such hurtful things to me?" she asked shakily.

"Somebody's got to wake you up out of that dreamworld of yours," Milady retorted. She gestured to the fragments of glass on Charlie's worktable. "No one's going to take this hobby of yours seriously, and I won't always be around to pick up the pieces for you. I'm an old woman, and I want to see you settled before I die."

"Don't try to make me feel guilty, Milady. It won't work anymore." Charlie's words were low and tight, her anger barely held in check.

It was useless to remind Milady that her opposition to Luke Duval had played a part in Charlie's rash and disastrous decision to marry Tyler Frazier. But she'd been taught to respect her elders, so the heated words she longed to fling at Milady remained in her mouth unsaid but scorching. Jerking the beaded chain attached to the light bulb, she plunged the workshop into semidarkness, ending the discussion.

"Come on," she said. "It's too hot in here for you."

"I've lived in Louisiana all my life, young lady, and most of it without the benefit of air-conditioning!" Milady returned sharply.

"It's too hot for Miss Scarlett, too."

Grumbling, Milady turned, carrying the dog, and Charlie followed her out the door and carefully locked it. Brilliant sunshine beat down on them, and the air was laden with the smell of parched earth as they walked toward the house.

"I don't want to discuss this anymore, Milady," Charlie said wearily. "I'm not hiding out, but I'm not putting myself on display, either. I'll go to church or shopping or wherever you want, but I'm not going to the cotillion tonight. Besides, I don't have anything to wear."

Milady set Miss Scarlett down and smiled slightly. "Don't worry about that, Charlotte. I sent Gina to Alexandria last week to pick up a dress for you, and Sudie's pressing it right now."

Charlie came up short, her mouth open in stupefaction. Totally serene, Milady continued up the path.

"Don't be too late coming in," Milady ordered. "You really must do something about your hair."

With an inarticulate sound of frustration, Charlie whirled and stomped down the driveway. Her progress was punctuated every few yards by a puff of white silt as she kicked one unfortunate dirt clod after another into oblivion.

"WHAT YOU DOING hidin' out in here, Miss Charlie?"

Charlie straightened up from her slouched position in the cockpit of the Stearman and smiled wryly at Hector Parrish. "I'm sulking, Hector."

"You been fighting with your grandma again?" Hector leaned into the cockpit, his gaze automatically running over the familiar controls.

"I could never fool you, could I?"

Hector's wide grin showed perfect white teeth the envy of men half his age. "Since you was knee-high to a cricket, you been comin' out here whenever there's an upset in the house."

"I know I should have more sense, Hector, but she makes me so angry sometimes!"

"Your grandma's just trying to do what she thinks is right for you."

"What *she* thinks. It's as if I'm still six years old." Charlie patted Hector's arm at the frown that creased his lined brow. "Don't worry. I'll figure out how to deal with Milady someday. And sitting in Daddy's crop duster still makes me feel better."

Hector's face lit up. "You want to crank her up, Miss Charlie?"

"Could I? Just for a minute?" Charlie's expression was suddenly as eager as Hector's.

"Shoot, you could take this baby up for a spin if you wanted to. She's running like a top," Hector said proudly. "Course the landing field may be a bit bumpy 'cause no one's cared about it since your daddy—"

"Oh, I'm not feeling that ambitious today," Charlie interrupted with a laugh, "but if we could just start her up, for old time's sake...."

Charlie's ears were still ringing with the roar of the Stearman's powerful engine when she mounted the porch stairs half an hour later. She and Hector had coaxed the old plane into life with as much gusto and pleasure as two kids with a new toy, and Charlie's annoyance with Milady had evaporated with the old rituals that she and her father had once shared.

Charlie paused at the door to dump the white silt out of her aerobic shoes, and her expression turned pensive. Milady was certainly abrasive, but Charlie had to admit deep down that the old woman might have a point. Evening Star was her refuge, but she couldn't let it become her crutch.

Of course, Milady couldn't know that her refusal to attend the cotillion had more to do with Luke's promised continuation of their conversation than with any real timidity over facing a large gathering of curious townsfolk. Avoiding Luke's unsettling presence right now was common sense, not cowardice, wasn't it? She wasn't hiding out at Evening Star any more than she'd been hiding out in the Stearman's cockpit this afternoon. It was just that sometimes it was just as the old adage said—discretion was the better part of valor.

Reassured, Charlie nodded to herself, picked up her shoes and strode barefoot through the foyer, only to hesitate as a telephone began to ring in the small study off the den Howard used as an office. Charlie knew it was a private business line, but no one else was about, so on impulse she entered the book-lined room and picked up the receiver.

"Hello?"

"Howard Montgomery."

"Just a moment. I'll—"

"Charlotte? Darlin', is that you?"

Charlie caught her breath. This was a moment she'd known was inevitable, yet had been dreading. Shivering, she squeezed her eyes closed and forced an even tone. "Hello, Tyler."

"Darlin', I can't tell you how good it is to hear your voice. How are you?"

"It's a bit late to be concerned about my welfare now, isn't it?"

"Oh, you're peeved at me because I didn't come to Long Pines to visit. But, darlin', you know the doctors advised against it."

"Many times I wished you'd come—"

"Oh, darlin', I wanted to..."

"So that I could tell you what I really think of you, Tyler. How is Valerie these days?"

"Now, Charlotte," Tyler said in an aggrieved tone, "you're jumping to conclusions again. I told you she didn't mean anything to me. Valerie's a disturbed woman. I had no idea she'd confronted you with her delusions. How could you believe her lies?"

"Don't!" Charlie's stomach lurched, and she fought back nausea. The sincerity and sadness in Tyler's mellow voice made her question herself just as it always had. But she wasn't going to allow him to manipulate her this time. "It doesn't matter now, anyway."

"But it does. When they served the divorce papers I was shocked. But more than that, darlin', you hurt me. It was too fast. You should have given us some time to work things out before taking such a drastic step."

"It wouldn't have done any good."

"Charlotte, this doesn't sound like you at all," he protested. "You're still not well, are you? They warned me not to rush things, and here I've gone and upset you. I'm truly sorry, darlin'. Look, we'll talk again, but right now could you run and get Howard for me?"

Suspicion narrowed Charlie's eyes, and her hand tightened on the receiver until her knuckles were white. "What do you want with Howard?"

Tyler's charming laugh trickled down the telephone wires, faintly mocking. "Business, darlin'. Just because we're having a few difficulties, doesn't mean I intend to break off all my dealings with the Montgomerys. After all, Howard and I were friends long before he introduced us."

"Don't delude yourself, Tyler. We are not 'having difficulties.' We are divorced."

"These things have a way of working out, darlin'. You know your place is with me. Think of our life here in Charleston. How long do you think you can stand that one-horse town? You'll be bored to tears."

Charlie sucked in an angry breath at Tyler's unflinching arrogance. He was as blind to his own faults as he'd ever been. And she was human enough to wish she could knock him off his high horse at least once.

"You don't give us enough credit," she said. "As a matter of fact, my life is very full here. I'm working again, you know."

"Howard keeps me informed. I'm glad you've found something therapeutic to fill your time for now. I do care about you, darlin'. You're always in my thoughts."

Charlie's cheeks burned with resentment. She felt violated knowing he'd kept tabs on her through Howard. Their relationship was over, no matter what Tyler wanted to believe, but she understood his motives. He'd always been concerned with appearances, the shiny red exterior of the apple more important than whether the core was rotten and wormy. If he really believed she'd agree to a reconciliation just to save his face before Charleston society, however, then he was the one who was crazy. It was a matter of pride to appear strong and collected in the face of her ex-husband's patronizing attitude.

"It's been quite revealing chatting with you," she said, "but I really must run. Tonight's the cotillion, you know, and I mustn't be late."

Tyler chuckled. "Ah, you must really be hard up if you can settle for such provincial pleasures."

"Sometimes it's not the event itself. It's the company," she murmured. "I'll tell Howard to call you."

Resisting the urge to slam the receiver home, Charlie gently laid it in its cradle, then looked up to find her grandmother watching her from the doorway.

"Changed your mind, have you?" Milady asked archly.

"No..."

"Of course, Howard will tell him if you don't go."

A series of emotions worked Charlie's features: exasperation at the predicament her pride had gotten her into, realization that her grandmother was right about Howard's reporting back to Tyler, trepidation at the thought of meeting Luke again, reluctant admiration at Milady's luck and deviousness.

Milady held out an arm over which was draped a delicately figured silky dress the color of butterscotch. Her gray eyes sparkled with triumph as she raised one silver brow in mute inquiry.

Charlie blew out an aggravated breath and stepped forward. "Oh, for heaven's sake! Give me the damn dress!"

I KNEW THIS WAS A MISTAKE.

The music, conversation and laughter of cotillion night flowed around Charlie. On the dimly lit dance floor young women in white ball gowns danced with their handsome escorts. Charlie caught a flash of Audrey Gilchrist's cascade of carroty curls among the group. Once she, too, had experienced the heady excitement of a cotillion presentation, had danced to "The Tennessee Waltz" with her head full of dreams, only to have those dreams dashed by Luke Duval and a dark-eyed girl in a scarlet dress. Even after all these years the memory was still painful, and Charlie quickly turned her attention elsewhere.

On her left Gina, elegant in emerald satin, chatted animatedly with Louise Bewley about a new designer-boutique in Shreveport. Gina had hardly sat out a single dance this evening, no thanks to Howard, who was ignoring his wife in favor of a glass of bourbon and earnest conversation. He and Louise's husband, Ken, Edgar Gideon, and Jim Peyton were discussing Thoroughbred handicapping and Sunday's card at Bossier City's track, Louisiana Downs. Even as Charlie watched, Harry Humphries, the tanned and smiling golf pro, claimed Gina again, and she swayed off with an apologetic smile for Louise and a flirtatious flutter of lashes for Harry.

"You and Gina did a wonderful job with the decorations," Louise said, turning to Charlie and reaching for her wineglass in one motion. The plump brunette wore a strapless black sheath and a fashionably short gypsy haircut.

"Thank you." Charlie wet her lips and smiled. "I enjoyed the work, and I loved making things beautiful for the girls."

"They'll always remember tonight. I know I've never forgotten my debut," Louise said, her carmine-tinted lips curving in a nostalgic smile. "How about you?"

"It's hard to forget a night that changed your life," Charlie agreed obliquely.

"Gina tells me you're a working artist now. That some of your things are hanging in the most elite homes in Charleston."

"Gina exaggerates."

"And you're too modest!" Louise said with a laugh, waving an admonitory finger in Charlie's face. "I know your work is fabulous—and fabulously expensive."

"Quality is always worth paying for, but my panels are competitive."

"Is that right?" Louise's expression was hopeful. "I'd like to see them sometime."

"I have a few small things in Boudreaux's Gift Shop, and I'm working on a larger display piece right now. I'll be glad to show it to you as soon as I'm finished, Louise. Of course, most people prefer to select a custom design to reflect a wallpaper motif or illustrate a hobby or perhaps a favorite scene."

"You know, I've been after Edgar to bump out a bay window in our breakfast area," Louise said thoughtfully. "Would you consider designing something for us?"

"I'd be glad to," Charlie replied, pleasantly surprised. Perhaps her appearance tonight wasn't a total loss after all. Then a sudden solidly male presence behind her chair made her change her mind again.

"Hello, Louise, how's the kitten?" Luke asked, his large hand resting along the back of Charlie's chair. In an expertly tailored dark suit, with his sandy brown hair combed ruthlessly into order, he was almost a stranger, and a distinctly masculine and disturbing one at that.

"Hi, Luke. Sheba's just fine. Amy adores her," Louise added with a bright smile.

"Every little girl should have a kitten," Luke agreed easily. "Say, Charlie, how about a dance?"

"Oh, I couldn't leave Louise," she protested weakly. He towered over her, and she was acutely conscious of his size, his warmth and his piny after-shave.

"Don't be silly!" The other woman laughed aside Charlie's excuse and scraped back her chair. "Besides,

I'm going to check out the buffet. I heard someone say the tiny shrimp-pies are divine."

Luke stood looking down at Charlie, his lean features set in faintly mocking, fully challenging lines. Charlie stifled an inward sigh and lifted her chin. She'd known she couldn't avoid Luke all evening. It had been against the odds that he'd be tied up helping Rob all night, even though she'd wished—pettily, she admitted—that the band would have at least one or two minor electrical problems that would keep the technical crew tied up.

"Come on, Charlie," Luke urged softly, one corner of his mouth twitching. "For old time's sake."

Charlie's chin went up another notch. She'd said the same catch phrase to Hector earlier in the day, but it hadn't made her heart pound like this. Whatever Luke's motives for seeking her out, she knew he wouldn't be satisfied until he'd said his piece. Silently she gave Luke her hand and allowed him to lead her onto the dance floor just as the band struck up a medley of golden oldie ballads.

It felt strange having her in his arms again, Luke thought.

Tentative. Familiar. Wonderful and terrible.

Their feet moved in slow patterns, and he splayed his palm against her back, feeling the silky material of her dress move over her silkier skin. She stared stonily at the starched white front of his shirt.

"You're terribly quiet," he murmured.

"It's my nature."

"Relax, Charlie," he chuckled. "I'm hardly likely to eat you alive in such a public setting, although it's heartening to see you've finally stopped running away from me."

She sniffed disdainfully. "Some things never change, including your exaggerated opinion of yourself."

"You look too beautiful to be in such an irritable mood. What's the matter, Charlie? Too many memories for you?"

"You should know." She tossed her head, looking up to meet his eyes for the first time, and Luke's breath hissed at the pain he saw shining in their gray-green depths.

"I would have thought cotillion night was a happy memory for you," he said hoarsely. "Wasn't that the night you decided to marry Tyler Frazier?"

"I don't remember."

His hand tightened around hers, and there was the residue of old bitterness and insecurity in his voice. "You can fool yourself, but don't try to kid me. That night no one could measure up against the golden boy."

You could have, if you'd only wanted to, she thought.

Her throat tightened with tears. What good were useless recriminations now? It only brought back the hurt. She stopped dancing, but Luke refused to let her pull away.

"Let me go." Her voice was husky. The other dancers eddied around them like water past a stone. "I refuse to discuss my private life with you."

"Why? I'm curious, you know. After all, you got everything you wanted when you married Frazier—wealth, prestige, the perfect home, the adoring husband. You threw a lot away when you left him."

"You have no right to judge me," she managed. "You made it clear what you wanted that night."

"I suppose so." He shrugged. "And you did, too. Life on Frazier's pedestal was great while it lasted, huh, Charlie?"

"You couldn't be more wrong." Charlie met his gaze, and her eyes glittered with unshed tears. "It wasn't a pedestal. It was a prison."

Luke went utterly still, and Charlie broke free, nearly running through the dancing couples toward the ladies' room. Once through the door to the ladies' lounge, she ignored the feminine chatter, fleeing down the long line of stalls and out through the locker room on the other side, taking the exit that opened onto the tennis courts.

Her heels tapped across the concrete, the court markings only faintly visible in the reflected light of a streetlamp. Her chest hurt with the effort she made to hold back her tears. Finally she slowed her furious pace and dropped to a convenient bench located in the shadows on the far side of the courts to gather her composure.

She breathed deeply, inhaling the warm, flower-scented air, and her thoughts flew back to that other night....

IT WAS HER FIRST cotillion, and the spangled night, the sweet odor of gardenias and the orchestra's romantic music swirled around her. It didn't even matter that the man she danced with wasn't the one she wanted. She could close her eyes and pretend.

In her virginal white lace dress and the long kid gloves of a debutante, she felt almost like a bride. And maybe soon that was just what she'd be.

No, her thoughts weren't on the solemn, courteous young man who waltzed her in lazy circles around the floor of the country club ballroom. That was for her grandmother. He was an old family friend, an acquaintance of Cousin Howard's, his South Carolina lineage distinguished enough to suit the old lady even for this important event in her granddaughter's life. It was a pleasant nuisance, a moment's distraction, the last thing she could do for the Grand Dame before the ultimate defiance. Nineteen was old enough to know her own mind, wasn't it? They'd just have to accept it.

Tonight, she thought, drifting in a rosy haze of anticipation. No matter how late, no matter if the stars were disappearing in the birth of a Louisiana dawn, she'd find a way to go to Luke. He'd been angry about the cotillion, hadn't understood the importance of it to her family, but she'd make it up to him. All their harsh words would be forgotten when she told him she'd be his wife.

Lord, she loved him. She shuddered slightly, dizzy from the dance and the images that pressed behind her eyelids. Her heart actually hurt with the swelling volume of her love, and the thought of holding him, loving him as they'd both wanted but had denied for so long made her thighs weak with desire and her blood race with fever.

Soon, she promised herself.

"I thought this was an exclusive event," her partner murmured in her ear.

"Hmm?" She opened her eyes reluctantly, feeling a bit guilty about her neglect. He was really very nice, after all, and deserved more of her attention. "In what way?"

He nodded in the direction of the door. "Those derelicts."

Her curious gaze followed his, and then she stumbled, stunned, snagged by a pair of golden brown eyes.

"Oops, sorry!" her partner muttered, pulling them out of the circling crowd. "Clumsy of me. Are you all right?"

She couldn't speak, nodding only, arrested by those lion's eyes.

What was *he* doing here? Dressed in a shiny, ill-fitting suit that couldn't disguise his broad shoulders or the narrowness of his hips, meeting her astounded gaze with challenge in the set of his strong chin.

"You know them?" her escort asked.

Startled, she noticed for the first time the others in the laughing group, so obviously out of place at this aristocratic gathering in their cheap finery, but either ignoring that fact or flaunting it intentionally. Her gaze slipped to the sultry brunette with the melting Spanish eyes clinging like a leech to the arm of her sandy-haired companion.

Again she nodded, swallowing. "From college."

The blond young man at her side gave a little disparaging snort. "They'll let in anyone with the price of a ticket these days." His blue eyes narrowed. "You sure you're all right?"

"If I could just have something to drink? Punch or...?"

"Coming up," he said cheerfully, turning toward the loaded refreshment table. "Stay right there."

She couldn't have moved if her life had depended on it, for *he* was coming toward her now, the only silent and implacable face in a crowd of merrymakers. Disentangling himself from his crimson-gowned companion, he threaded through the crush until he stood before her, looking down at her with mockery in his eyes.

"Having fun, princess?"

"What are you doing here?" Her voice was a whisper.

He shrugged. "Thought it'd be fun to see how the other half lives."

Her glance flickered to the girl behind him. "Who...?"

"Oh, that's Carmen." He let his gaze spill over the crowd. "Is this shindig really as dull as I think it is?"

"Let's dance." Carmen appeared at his side, her scarlet lips pouting prettily.

He draped a possessive arm over Carmen's shoulders, pulling her close, fitting her against his side. "Anything you want, honey."

Smiling, he caught Carmen's chin, dropped his head and sealed her pouting mouth with his own. It was no mere peck, but a lengthy kiss, and the stricken girl watching saw their cheeks flex with an intimate exchange of tongues that sickened her. When he raised his head, Carmen wore an insipid look and smudged lipstick.

"C'mon, honey, let's dance," he said thickly, turning away. Carmen purred and snuggled even closer, her dark eyes ablaze with feline triumph.

"Luke!" It was a cry of pain. Looking back over his shoulder, he saw her mouth the silent question. "Why?"

"Come on, princess, did you think I'd waste my time on a snobby little girl too scared even to invite me up to the big house for Sunday dinner?" He gave another careless shrug. "I got tired of waiting for you to grow up, so I found myself a real woman." He smiled into her white face, and his soft laugh pierced her like a blade. "See you around."

Shattered, she watched him melt into the crowd while her world collapsed around her. But she was too well brought up to cause a scene; the horror of that had been inbred in her. A lady always knew how to handle a crisis, no matter what. Numb, she let the coolness of shock and despair flow through her, silently accepting the punch cup pressed on her by her convivial partner, sipping and nodding as though her heart hadn't just been ripped from her body. After a while she became aware of her escort's persuasive voice then, slowly, the sense of his words.

"You really mean it? Could you make me the happiest man on earth?"

Disinterested, she looked at him, the gray-green of her eyes fathomless and unreadable. Her companion took her blank look and pale face for amazement. Like a clumsy puppy, he stumbled over his words in his eagerness.

"It's fast, I know, but the families...and we're perfect together...make everyone happy..."

And that was really all that was left to her now, she realized suddenly. Duty and obedience to family...and pride.

"Yes." The word broke into his feverish speech. "Yes, Tyler. Perhaps we should think about getting married."

CHAPTER SIX

"CHARLIE?"

She jumped at the sound of her name, and the reverie faded from her mind, like turning off a bad television drama that had no interest nor connection to the person she'd become.

In the darkness footsteps crossed the tennis courts toward her in tempo with the barely audible strains of music that drifted from the main building. Knuckling away the damp evidence of her tears, she swiveled on the bench, keeping her back turned. There was no need for her to ask who it was.

"Go away, Luke."

"Are you all right?"

"Can't you take a hint? I don't want to talk to you anymore." With her face averted she felt rather than saw him sit down beside her on the wooden bench.

"I'm sorry I made you cry."

"Who says I'm crying?" she flared.

Without answering he reached in front of her and dropped a folded white handkerchief into her lap. Angrily she picked it up, blotted her face and tossed it back to him.

"You love being right, don't you?" Her voice was bitter.

"About what?"

"About me. Spoiled rich girl, got what she deserved."

"I thought so. Now I'm not so sure."

"So gallant!" she sneered. "What is this? Don't tell me you're turning on the famous Duval charm just for me?"

"Charlie, stop."

"Well, why not?" Her voice rose. "After all, I'm the one who got away, even if I was a wet-behind-the-ears kid nine years ago. Maybe that's the reason you can't let things rest."

"Is that what you think?"

She shrugged, shaking back her hair, and stared heavenward at the scattering of stars across the dark sky. "Everyone's been quite eager to tell me what a ladies' man you still are. 'Hell on wheels' is what Becky called you."

He snorted. "That's hardly what I'd call flattering, but if you're wondering about my sex life...yeah, over the past few years I've been getting enough."

"Goody for you."

"What else did Becky tell you?"

"That you and someone called Rachel seem to be an item."

"Rachel's my receptionist." His words were flat, but then his voice dropped. "You aren't jealous, are you, princess?"

Charlie jumped to her feet. "Don't call me that!"

Luke caught her hand to hold her back, blocking her path with his body. "Touched a nerve, did I?"

"I knew you could be brutal," she said with scathing contempt, "but I didn't realize you were the kind of heartbreaker who *likes* to see a woman cry."

His free hand came up to thread through the tangle of mahogany curls at her temple, and his tone was silky. "Did I break your heart, Charlie?"

Her breath caught. "Leave me alone!"

Bending his head, his words became a gravelly rasp. "God help me, I don't think I can . . . because you surely broke mine."

His mouth covered hers, smothering her whimpered protest, gentling her with the warm and mobile persuasion of his lips. Pulling her close, he held her as if she were made of the most fragile and precious porcelain imaginable. But beneath his iron constraint was a power that radiated into her core, melting her resistance, burning away her resentment. In an instant there was only sensation, and Charlie was drowning in it.

The pressure of his mouth, the faint rasp of his beard and the musky scent of his skin made her dizzy. She was off balance and clutched at Luke's lapels to stay on her feet, leaning into his embrace, unable to think. He peppered light kisses along the lower curve of her lip, then caught its fullness gently between his teeth, nibbling hungrily.

There was a similar hunger growing deep within Charlie, and when he trailed kisses down her throat, it was an instinct older than time that made her arch her neck to allow him access. His hands moved restlessly on her shoulders, down to cinch her waist, then to cup the gentle flare of her hips, pulling her closer into the cradle of his thighs and the proof of his desire.

"Damn you, Charlie," he muttered. "See what you can still do to me?"

She gasped and shuddered, overwhelmed by the electric arc of mutual passion that seared them like summer lightning. Luke took outrageous, unrepentant advantage, swooping to recapture her mouth, plying her deepest secrets with his rapacious tongue. Wildfire raced through Charlie's veins, and her moan of need was matched by Luke's answering groan.

He pulled back slightly, his breath harsh in his throat, and gazed with wonder down into her hazy expression. "My God, we're as good together as we ever were."

"No!" Panic exploded in Charlie's head, banishing desire in a rush of humiliation. Frantic, she tore free of his embrace, her breasts heaving and her lungs laboring for air.

Luke reached for her. "Charlie..."

"Don't touch me!" She backed away, her fists clenched, the ache of tears in the throaty quality of her voice. "Is this your idea of revenge? To prove to yourself what a slut I am by using your highly touted sexual expertise on me?"

"It's not like that."

"Isn't it? Humiliating me isn't enough for you. You want me to pay over and over, as if I were the only one to blame! Well, I'm not going to let you do it. I've paid for my mistakes, and you aren't going to punish me anymore."

He was dumbfounded. "Punish you? Charlie, listen to me—"

"Why should I?" She was haughtiness personified, her chin tilted at an imperious angle, her eyes glistening in the darkness. "So you can tear another chunk out of my heart and then laugh when I throw my life away?"

"That's enough!" He caught her upper arms, controlling her easily, then froze, pierced through by the sight of a single crystal tear spilling down her cheek.

"God, I hate you!" She spit the words as though they were flavored with wormwood. "I hate you for what you did to me, but most of all for what I did to myself!"

Luke felt something twist inside his chest, but anything he might have said died on his lips at the cold, implacable set of her exquisite features. She looked pointedly at his hands. He opened his palms, and she stepped free, walking away from him into the darkness without a backward glance.

Luke fought back a terrible urge to laugh—at himself, at life—but there was nothing humorous in the despair that clawed like a demon at his heart. Everything was suddenly clear. For nine empty, restless years he'd lied to himself. He'd never gotten over Charlie Kincaid, and after holding her tonight, he knew he never would.

He was desperately, hopelessly, eternally in love with a woman who hated his guts.

"A MAN IN LOVE is a miserable creature."

"Huh?" Luke glanced up from a chart and frowned at Rachel's teasing countenance. The crisp odor of disinfectant filled the clinic, empty now of the morning's array of pet owners, and a single forlorn howl echoed from the direction of the kennels.

"I said, a man in love—"

"I heard what you said." He leaned over the counter and dropped the clipboard onto Rachel's desk. "What about it?"

"Ooh, what a grouch! Here, have some nourishment." She pulled a chocolate bar from her desk drawer and shoved it at him.

"No thanks. I'm not hungry."

A flash of mock alarm crossed Rachel's piquant features, and she tugged absently at a springy blond curl at her temple. "Golly, this is more serious than I thought. Lunchtime and the incredible eating machine isn't interested? All right, come clean. Who is she?"

"Who is who?"

"You've been so surly all week, I figure it has to be woman trouble. Come on, sonny, tell Mama Rachel all your problems."

Luke laughed. "You're a loon, you know that?"

"And you're dodging the issue."

"That's because there is no issue."

Rachel's cornflower eyes were bright with skepticism. "Oh, yeah? What about—"

"Hey, Uncle Luke!"

Mikey Thompson burst through the clinic's front door. He wore red shorts and a T-shirt that sported the latest cartoon craze, a quartet of martial arts experts who just happened to be turtles. Skidding to a halt in front of Luke, Mikey hopped impatiently from one tennis shoe to the other as his father followed him into the clinic.

"Is he ready, Uncle Luke?" Mikey asked, his voice high with excitement. "Can I take him home now? Can I?"

Luke grinned. "Well, I don't rightly know. Miss Rachel, is the patient ready?"

"I was just going to check on that," Rachel answered with a fond smile. She slipped from around her desk and headed down the corridor. "Be right back!"

"Oh, boy, oh, boy!" Mikey caroled.

Rob Thompson smiled indulgently and dug his hands into the back pockets of his khaki pants. "I couldn't hold him off any longer. Mrs. Andrews said he's been a little wild today."

"I can imagine," Luke said with a laugh, thinking of the grandmotherly baby-sitter who kept Mikey for Rob during the summer. He went down on one knee before the boy, his expression serious. "Do you think you're ready for this, Mikey? It's a big responsibility, you know."

"Yes, sir!"

"There's someone here who wants to see you, sport," Rachel said behind them, then set a small black-and-white bundle down on the tiled floor.

Sporting a jaunty red ribbon bow around his neck, the mongrel puppy instantly bounced into the boy's out-stretched arms, sniffing and licking and wiggling and wagging his tail madly in pure delight. Bowled over, Mikey squealed and giggled, then wrestled with the over-joyed animal.

"Love at first sight," Rachel remarked, smiling. "You've got a smart pup there, Rob. He thought of a thousand ways to get out of his bath while I was trying to groom him."

"Ah, thank you for taking so much trouble with him, ma'am," Rob said, rocking awkwardly on his heels.

Rachel's head didn't reach the top of Rob's broad shoulder, but she faced him with mock belligerence, her hands on her hips. "Don't you 'ma'am' me, Robert Thompson! I'm not your maiden aunt!"

"No, ma'am, I can see that," he gulped. His gaze dropped for the briefest of instants on the womanly full-ness of her bosom before he realized that he'd repeated the offense, and his long cheeks flushed brick-red under his tan. "Excuse me, ma'am . . . er, sorry! Ah, Michael, pick up that dog. We've got to go!"

"Okay, Dad!" Mikey scrambled up, holding the pup, a smile as big as Texas on his face. "Thanks for finding him for me, Uncle Luke. I'll take good care of him. I promise!"

"I know you will, partner." Luke ruffled the boy's black hair. "And don't forget to bring him back in for the rest of his shots in a few weeks. Have you decided what you're going to call him yet?"

"How about... Pardner! Like the cowboys say it." Mikey was pleased with his inspiration.

"Sounds good to me," Luke replied. "What about you, Miss Rachel?"

"Perfect, I'd say." She smiled briefly and retreated behind the chest-high counter.

"Let's go, Mikey," Rob said gruffly, holding open the glass door. He gave a brief wave that included everyone in the room.

"Why don't you and Mikey come over Sunday afternoon?" Luke suggested. "It's warm enough to swim off the dock, or maybe we can take the boat out."

Rob's gaze bounced between Luke and Rachel, and he shifted his feet uncomfortably. "We'll have to see how things go," he mumbled.

"Aw, Dad!" Mikey protested. "I wanna go!"

"I said we'll see, okay?" Rob jerked his head. "Let's get a move on, hotshot."

"Okay." Struggling with the squirming puppy, Mikey followed his father. "See ya later, Uncle Luke!"

The door closed behind the Thompsons and peace returned to the waiting room—except for the strident rattle of clipboards and irritated shuffling of papers coming from Rachel's desk. Luke rested his forearms on the counter, one eyebrow raised inquiringly. "So what's eating you all of a sudden?"

"Your cousin!" Rachel's rosebud mouth compressed mulishly. "What's the matter with that man, anyway? I'm friendlier than a used car salesman, and all I ever get is the cold shoulder from him. Why doesn't he like me?"

"Hey, easy! Rob likes you just fine. He's just not accustomed to dealing with pretty women. Gets him all tongue-tied."

She sniffed disdainfully. "Pretty, huh? Don't try to soften me up with your sweet talk, either. The man's impossible."

"Look, his ex-wife did a number on him. Cut him some slack, okay?"

"It's no never mind to me," she said airily.

"He's really a great guy once you get to know him." Luke rubbed his jaw thoughtfully. "Maybe you ought to come over Sunday evening, too. Give him a chance to get over being shy around you."

"You trying to play matchmaker or something?" she asked suspiciously.

"Of course not. Just a friendly get-together. We'll throw some steaks on the grill. Maybe I'll ask some other folks, too."

"Well . . ."

Luke's mouth twitched. "Besides, I'll need someone to help with the cooking."

Rachel laughed. "The ulterior motive revealed at last! All right, but don't think you're putting anything over on me. And remember, if you meddle in my love life, then I get to meddle in yours. Which leads me back to the question of the day. Who is she?"

Luke groaned. "Now don't start that again!"

"I know you well enough to—" The phone rang, and Rachel broke off, lifting the receiver to speak quietly and efficiently to the caller.

Luke breathed a sigh of relief at the reprieve. Rachel had a tenacious curiosity, but Luke was still feeling too emotionally raw to discuss Charlie Kincaid. He lifted the day calendar from the counter and walked to the window to review his afternoon appointments, but his thoughts turned unerringly to Charlie.

Since he'd been blasted by the realization that he still loved her, his head had been spinning in place like a squirrel on a treadmill. Never in his life had he felt so helpless. Should he do the noble thing and leave her alone as she'd asked? That was what love was all about, wasn't it, doing the selfless thing? His heart plummeted at the notion. He'd been unforgivably cruel to her on more than one occasion, and she hated him, never wanted to see him again, and yet...

And yet Luke couldn't forget the sweetness of her response. Whether she'd admit it or not, the physical attraction was still as strong and potent as ever. That counted for something. Surely there was some hope, some fine thread of connection that could be rewoven into the fabric of a relationship.

It wouldn't be the same bright flame of first love that had fired them so long ago. Too much had happened; they'd both become different people. But maybe that was good. He was now in a position to offer her things he never could have then. All he had to do was make her see it could work again between them. Somehow to mend the fences...

God, he wanted her! In all the many aspects of intimacy—heart, mind, body and soul. And he'd be good to her, better than Tyler Frazier had ever been. It was simply a matter of determination, and timing, and persistence.

Nodding slightly, Luke felt the strength of his resolve surge through him. He'd take it step by step, wooing Charlie Kincaid with all his skill and daring until he *made* her love him again. But first he had to convince her to see him so that they could finally clear the air about what had gone wrong nine years ago.

The opportunity came sooner than he expected. Rachel hung up the telephone and looked up from her desk.

"You'll have to postpone lunch," she announced. "That was Charlotte Kincaid. She's bringing in her grandmother's dog. They think Miss Scarlett's dying."

CHARLIE HUNG UP the phone and turned back to her distraught grandmother. "It's all right, Milady. The receptionist said to come right now."

"Look at her! She can't breathe!" Milady bent tearfully over the cardboard box resting on the kitchen table. Miss Scarlett lay prostrate inside it, obviously in acute distress. "I knew something was wrong when she wouldn't eat last night."

"Now, Miss Margaret," Sudie Parrish soothed, patting Milady's still-erect back, "don't get yourself upset. I'm sure Dr. Luke can help her."

Howard Montgomery leaned against the kitchen cabinet and frowned. His face was flushed with the heat of the day, and his boots were dusty from a morning's work supervising in the fields. It was obvious he'd come in expecting a cool lunch and not a crisis with a group of hysterical women.

"I don't want to upset you, Milady," Howard said, wiping his neck with a damp dish towel, "but I think it may already be too late."

Milady's lips trembled. "If only I'd found her sooner. But she hid in my closet, and I...I..."

"It's no one's fault," Charlie said, lifting the box.

She'd been working in her studio when she'd heard Sudie's call, and she still wore jeans and a baggy T-shirt, with her hair scraped back in a scraggly ponytail. Although facing Luke Duval again after their last argument was something she would rather have avoided, this was an emergency. Firmly she quashed her nervous trepidation, admitting to herself that there was no one else she'd trust with Miss Scarlett, who was really a member of the family.

"Come on, Milady," Charlie urged. "Gina's gone to play tennis, but we can take your sedan."

"That might not be a good idea, Charlotte," Howard said cautiously. He bent solicitously over Milady and gently cupped the old woman's thin shoulders. "We've got to be realistic about this, my dear. Miss Scarlett's a very old dog, after all. It might be more merciful to end her suffering."

Milady drew a slow, shaky breath. "Yes, I know."

"I don't think you need to put yourself through this," Howard added. "Let Charlotte handle it. I'd go myself, but if I don't get that crew on the beans in the north quarter, we're going to lose the entire crop, so—"

"I understand," Milady said, patting his hand. "You're a dear boy, Howard, and you work too hard."

"Why don't you let Sudie fix you a cup of tea with a little touch of something in it?" Howard suggested. "You'll feel better if you rest a bit, and Charlotte can call you from the vet's office as soon as she knows... anything."

Milady stood, reached inside the box and laid her hand against Miss Scarlett's heaving side. She looked at Charlie, then squared her shoulders and shook her head. "No, I couldn't let Charlotte handle it alone."

"Nonsense," Charlie said gently. "Of course I'll go, but don't give up on Miss Scarlett yet. Why, she's as tough as you are, Milady!"

"Here, I'll carry her to the car," Howard offered, relieving Charlie of the box and leading her toward the back door.

Charlie gave Milady an encouraging nod, grabbed her purse and followed Howard to the garage where they loaded the ailing animal into the back seat. Howard leaned through the window as Charlie started Milady's aging but well-maintained sedan.

"Take my advice and don't prolong this," he said. "A long, drawn-out struggle to keep this old dog alive isn't worth it."

"Let's allow the doctor to decide," Charlie replied stiffly. "Miss Scarlett is really the only thing Milady cares about besides Evening Star."

"I know that." Howard looked a bit hurt. "And it's Milady I'm thinking of. She's going to take it hard, no matter what. Better to get it over quickly rather than place her under too much stress."

"I see your point, but I don't think you're giving Milady—or Miss Scarlett—enough credit. I'd better go. They're waiting on me."

Howard watched her as she backed out of the garage, and Charlie wondered if he was annoyed. After all, he was accustomed to having his wishes carried out for the most part. Despite their complaints, Milady and Gina usually deferred to him, but Charlie just couldn't make herself agree that putting Miss Scarlett to sleep was the only solution. As she sped toward town, she hoped that she was right.

A short time later Charlie carried the box holding Miss Scarlett into the front office of the Duval Animal Clinic. The petite blond at the desk jumped up and hurried around the counter to help.

"Oh, you must be Ms. Kincaid! Come in. I'm Rachel Aubert."

"Charlie Kincaid," Charlie replied, a bit taken aback by the unassuming friendliness of the other woman.

Rachel's smile was genuine and open, her blue eyes soft with kindness. And, as Becky had intimated, she was what the boys in high school used to call "stacked," with a full, curvy figure and the kind of bustline Charlie had always dreamed of having.

Rachel peered into the box and made sympathetic noises. "Oh, the poor thing. Let's take her back to the examining room. Luke's on the phone, but he'll be right with you."

Charlie followed her into the clinic proper, trying to ignore the pang of vague bewilderment. So this was the type of woman Luke was involved with. Well, she couldn't fault him, for she found herself responding involuntarily to Rachel's warmth, too. *Maybe I ought to congratulate him on his good taste,* she thought sourly.

They entered a small, meticulously clean room with a stainless-steel examining table. A counter with sink and shelves above ran the length of the rear wall and sported neat stacks of chrome equipment, including a microscope, and rows of tobacco-brown medicine bottles. Charlie slid the box onto the table and stroked Miss Scarlett but got little response from the panting dog.

"Sorry to keep you waiting, Charlie," Luke said, striding into the room. He twisted the knobs on the faucet and began to briskly wash his hands. "How's the patient?"

"Not good." Charlie bit her lip. "Milady's very upset."

Drying his hands on a paper towel, Luke turned, his gaze raking Charlie's disheveled appearance. He almost smiled, for she looked very young and approachable, not at all the cool socialite, but those observations were for another time, and he clamped down on everything but the need to behave professionally.

"Let's see," he murmured, tossing the towel into a wastebasket. With the utmost care he lifted Miss Scarlett out of the box and began his examination.

Charlie watched anxiously, acutely aware of the strength and gentleness in Luke's powerful hands. "Is...is there any hope?"

Luke glanced up, surprised, and then smiled suddenly, a grin that dazzled Charlie with its charm and compassion. "Sure. Quite a bit, in fact. Looks like pneumonia, but it's nothing a round of antibiotics won't fix. I know your grandmother sets great store in her pet."

"Oh." Charlie felt the tension drain out of her in a rush, leaving her weak, and she answered Luke's smile with a tremulous one of her own. "We were afraid she'd have to be put down, and I didn't know how I'd tell Milady."

"We're not to that point yet, but I'm going to have to keep her for a few days."

"Yes, of course."

Luke nodded and gave Rachel instructions, then took the hypodermic she filled and gave the dog an injection.

"Rachel, if you'll put Miss Scarlett in a kennel, we'll keep an eye on her until the crisis is past."

"Absolutely." Rachel picked up the dog and smiled at Charlie as she headed toward the kennels with her burden. "Don't worry about her, Charlie. She'll probably perk right up now. That's what they usually do."

"Thank you." Rachel left, and Charlie took a deep breath, pushing the loose tendrils of her ponytail away from her face. "Thank you, too, Luke."

"That's what I'm here for." He washed his hands again, then folded his arms and looked at her intently.

"Er, yes." Charlie gave a soft, nervous laugh. "Sometimes I think Milady finds it easier to show affection to that dog than she does to people."

"It's not so unusual."

"Well, if you can help Miss Scarlett, I'll be very grateful."

"Grateful enough to let me take you to lunch?"

Startled, Charlie's eyes widened, and she cast a brief glance in the direction Rachel had taken, then back to Luke. "Ah, I don't think that's a good idea."

Luke followed her glance, frowning, then his expression cleared. "I want you to know something."

"What?"

"Rachel and I aren't having an affair. A long time ago, yes, briefly. But not any longer. We really are just good friends."

Charlie flushed and she looked away, anywhere but the mocking, tawny eyes that seemed to be able to read her mind. "It's none of my business."

"It's as much your business as you care to make it." Luke stepped around the examining table, closing the distance between them, and his voice was a low rumble in his chest. "Look, I don't blame you for being wary, especially after last Saturday night, but you know how I get when I don't eat."

"Yes, I know." A half smile played over her lips.

"Then take pity on me. After all, I'm going to cure your grandmother's dog. So feed me, and..."

She looked up with a question in her eyes. "And?"

Luke took a deep breath. "And I'll tell you a story about a girl named Carmen."

"MILADY TOLD you *what?*"

"That you were already engaged to Tyler before the cotillion."

"But that wasn't true!"

Luke's jaw worked. "I see."

They sat at a tiny table in the rear of Lasyone's Meat Pie Kitchen on Second Street waiting for their orders. In front of them tall tumblers of iced tea sat gathering dewdrops of condensation while lemon wedges floated in the beverage like bright yellow smiles. Charlie noticed the liquid was the exact shade of amber as Luke's eyes. She looked away, and her voice held a tremor.

"You thought I'd been playing games."

"Yeah."

Charlie shook her head sadly. "No, I wasn't. I thought you understood why I had to go to the cotillion with Tyler, but then when you came...with that girl, and said the things you did..."

Luke stared at a far corner of the room. "It was staged. To salvage my pride. I figured if I showed up with a tart like Carmen, it'd show you nobody could treat Luke Duval that way! Your grandmother made it clear I couldn't offer you the kind of life you needed, that you'd already decided what you wanted by choosing Tyler."

"And you believed her." Charlie swallowed hard.

Luke rubbed his palm down his jaw in a tired gesture, then leaned on his forearms with his hands clasped in the middle of the table. "Hell, Charlie..."

"No, don't say it." She placed her hand atop his folded ones. "I believed her, too. When she told me I shouldn't have expected better treatment from a man like you."

"Like me?"

"Poor, arrogant, out to get what you could—in short, a man just like my father." Charlie laughed without humor. "Oh, Luke. We weren't ever in Milady's league!

While we were trying to figure out a relationship she was fighting for a life. *My* life. Can't you see? She thought I'd be throwing away everything important on a 'no-account' just like my mother. No wonder she was ruthless. No wonder she practically pushed me into Tyler's arms."

Luke frowned. "She manipulated us. Damn it, what gave her the right?"

"Don't be angry."

"My God, Charlie! We loved each other! Can you forgive her?"

She shrugged. "Love was her motive, too. At least I can understand. And things were kind of rocky with us then. It probably didn't make any difference in the long run."

Luke turned Charlie's hand over, studied her scarred and scratched palm, then laced his fingers with hers. His voice was quiet. "But it was a 'road not taken' for us."

A smile slowly appeared on Charlie's lips. "You still read Frost."

He nodded. "There's another line I like— 'Something there is that doesn't love a wall, that wants it down.'"

A small, puzzled pleat creased her brow, and she shook her head, confused. "What . . . ?"

"The wall that's been between us for nine years, Charlie. I want it down."

"Maybe it already is." She sighed. "All those hard feelings, and no one was to blame. It's good to know the truth and put the past behind us. I can't hate Milady. And I can't hate you."

Luke's hand squeezed hers. "Do you think—" he cleared his throat "—perhaps there's another chance for us?"

She drew back, tugging her hand free, and her eyes were suddenly green and startled. "That . . . that's too much to expect."

"Charlie." Luke's husky tone was earnest. "We've always had something special."

Studying her tea glass, she sluiced the moisture off its side with her finger, then shook her head. "No, Luke. I'll be glad if we can be friends again, but as for anything else...I'm not the same green girl you once knew. I don't believe in love anymore."

The disillusionment in her voice hurt Luke unbearably. God, what had her life been like to bring her to this? A fierce protectiveness washed through him, but instinct made him hold back, knowing that she wasn't ready to accept any protestations of devotion from him now. But she would be. If not today, then tomorrow, or the day after that.

"Friends, huh?" He smiled at her, an easy grin that crinkled the corners of his eyes. "The kind of friends that share an occasional lunch?"

"Sure."

"Talk on the phone once in a while?"

She laughed softly. "Yes, of course."

"Maybe go out to a movie sometimes?"

"Well . . ." She looked up as the waitress brought their orders, a selection of spicy fried meat-filled pastries for which Natchitoches was famous accompanied by a side dish called dirty rice. She picked up her fork and showed Luke a dimple. "We'll have to wait and see about that."

"More walls, Charlie?" He brushed his knuckles down her cheek in a brief caress, then quoted softly, "'Before I built a wall I'd ask to know what I was walling in or walling out.'"

CHAPTER SEVEN

"IS THAT WHAT I think it is?" Becky Turner demanded.

Charlie stood in the carport of Becky's ranch-style house and offered her friend a large, aluminum foil-covered pan. "Uh-huh."

"Mississippi mud pie?" Becky's blue eyes lit up.

"Yep."

"You got the job!"

"Yes!"

Becky let out a high squeal of delight and eagerly drew a triumphantly grinning Charlie through her back door. She hastily cleared a rag doll and the sports section of the *Sunday Times* off her country-blue kitchen counter to make room for Charlie's pan. "Tell me about it! When did you hear? How soon do you start?"

Charlie set down the sinfully rich concoction of chocolate, cream cheese, pecans and whipped topping, laughing at Becky's infectious enthusiasm. "Just today. I saw the dean at church this morning, and he gave me the unofficial notice. They're going to call me tomorrow, and I start this week!"

"Charlie, that's wonderful! But I certainly didn't expect my reward so soon."

Charlie shrugged. "Milady's having Sunday dinner with Reverend Wilkinson, and Howard and Gina went to the races with some of Howard's business friends, so I shooed Sudie out of the kitchen and had some fun."

"Oh, do tell!" Becky teased. "Charleston's 'hostess with the mostest' actually sullied her very own lily-white hands with manual labor?"

Charlie placed her fists on her hips, flattening the gathers of her mint-colored seersucker sundress in mock belligerence. "I'll have you know I'm a very good cook! We only hired a chef for large affairs. Of course, if you don't believe me, I can always take this pie to Miss Scarlett who's convalescing at the animal clinic...."

"Don't touch that pan!" Becky threatened, laughing. "You know I can't wait to dig in. And congratulations! We'll practically be working together. Wylan, did you hear?" she called into the adjoining den.

Wylan Turner sat up on the sofa where he'd been indulging in a Sunday afternoon snooze to the drone of a televised baseball game. Through the sliding glass doors Charlie could see the Turner's two blond daughters, Regan and Angela, playing in a sandbox in the fenced yard.

"Hiya, Charlie." Wylan, a comfortable-looking man with thinning sandy hair and the first evidence of a middle-aged paunch, stifled a yawn and then grinned. "Good news, huh?"

"Thanks to Becky," Charlie began. The wall phone pealed and Becky grabbed it, waving Charlie on into the den to visit. After a moment Becky called Charlie to the phone.

"He wants to talk to you," Becky said with a mischievous twinkle.

"Who?" But Becky only looked mysterious as Charlie took the receiver. "Hello?"

"All right, I'm not taking no for an answer this time," a deep voice said.

"Luke?" A curious weightlessness curled in the pit of Charlie's stomach, an annoying sensation she'd been unable to control during the past several days whenever Luke called to report on Miss Scarlett's progress.

"Uh-huh. Becky tells me congratulations are in order."

"Yes, they are," she replied proudly. "I'm going to be working in the children's summer art program at the university."

"Then it's high time for a celebration. And I don't want to hear any more of your lame excuses about why you can't come to a simple cookout."

Charlie flushed. Even though she and Luke had come to an understanding, she wasn't exactly certain what being his friend entailed. He'd casually mentioned an afternoon barbecue, and she'd just as casually declined, because if there was one thing of which she was certain, it was that one misstep with Lucas Duval and she was likely to find that she'd fallen, as Sudie liked to say, "out of the frying pan and into the fire." But even with these reservations, her protest was weak. "But, Luke—"

"Becky and Wylan and the kids are coming," he interrupted. "They're going to pick up some extra ice for me. Why don't you ride with them? There'll be some other people here you'll enjoy, too. Come on, Charlie, it's perfectly harmless. What are you scared of?"

"Not a thing!" she snapped.

His chuckle was low and husky. "Then prove it."

"How can I refuse such a charming invitation?" she said with haughty sarcasm.

"I love it when you're snooty."

Despite herself, Charlie laughed. "You bring out the worst in me, Luke Duval!"

"That's a matter of opinion, sweetheart. I'll see you shortly then?"

What harm could it do? Charlie asked herself. Spending the afternoon alone at Evening Star suddenly held no appeal. Besides, it would do both her and Luke good to prove to themselves they'd broken the habit of going for each other's jugular vein at every opportunity.

"Yes," she said, "I'll be there."

Many hours later Charlie sat on the edge of Luke's wooden dock watching the sun sink into Sibley Lake in an explosion of magenta- and plum-colored sky. Two-year-old Angela Turner sprawled bonelessly in Charlie's lap, sound asleep, exhausted by the sun and fun. Pleasantly weary herself, Charlie sighed with contentment.

It had been a wonderful afternoon. Rob Thompson and his son were there, as well as Rachel Aubert, the Turners and their girls, and two other young couples, the Johnsons and the Moores. The children swam off the dock or paddled around in the shallows, and Luke had given everyone a ride in his powerful bass boat. Mikey had caught a string of white perch off the point, and there had been generally a lot of running and shrieking over the wooden decks and up and down the slope of a pine-covered hill that was Luke's backyard.

Charlie had enjoyed a regular female gabfest with Rachel and Becky as they helped out in the kitchen, and she found herself liking Rachel, with her wisecracks and perpetually sunny disposition, more than ever. Even old Bertell Dickson had dropped by just in time to partake of the steak supper Luke prepared on the grill and to quiz Charlie about all her activities and Milady's health.

"So here you are."

Charlie looked up at Luke and smiled, placing a finger across her lips. He wore faded cutoff shorts with raveled hems and a thin knit shirt that showed off the fluid lines of his muscular chest. Nodding, he sank down beside her, hanging his bare legs off the edge of the dock and leaning back on his elbows.

"She's worn out," he said, gazing at the little girl Charlie cuddled so protectively.

"Positively exhausted by all the fun," Charlie agreed softly, inhaling the pleasantly musty odor of sun-warmed male skin. "It's been a lovely day, Luke. I'm glad I came."

"Me, too." His smile widened, and he wagged a foot back and forth over the water. "And all I had to do was bully you unmercifully to get you here."

"I'm a slow learner sometimes, but I eventually get it right." Her lips curved sardonically. "I'd almost forgotten what it was like being around real people, folks without pretensions who don't give a darn about the latest designer labels."

Luke plucked a faded blue thread from the ragged edge of his shorts. "I guess this is a far cry from Charleston."

"Thank God."

She glanced at Luke, then let her gaze travel up the bank to the wide expanse of his house with its natural cedar siding and acres of glass overlooking the water. The adults sat in scattered groups on the deck indulging in desultory conversation, and Mikey and Regan played with Luke's own dog, a well-mannered chocolate Labrador called Hershey.

"It's beautiful here, and peaceful," she said. "You've got a lot to be proud of, Dr. Duval."

"Thanks."

He wanted to tell her it was all for her, that everything he'd done for the past nine years had been either consciously or unconsciously with her in mind, but he knew it was still too soon. It pleased him enormously that she liked his house. He imagined Charlie living here with him, and in his mind the structure that had been a good buy, but merely a roof over his head, became a home, complete with African violets on the windowsills and panty hose over the shower rod. The fantasy made him smile.

Charlie caught her breath at his smile. Why did he have to be so blatantly male, so utterly dazzling in his attraction to her? To hide her involuntary reaction she bent her head, nuzzling the damp tendrils of candy-fluff hair at Angela's temple.

Luke went still, drinking in the tender sight. Charlie's hair framed her face like a dark halo as she kissed the sleeping child. Something tight hurt in his chest, turning his voice hoarse.

"You make a perfect Madonna." He saw the flash of pain darken her eyes to flat gray before she looked away, and he sat up, cursing under his breath. "I'm sorry, Charlie. I didn't mean to remind you—"

"Do you think I ever forget?" She shook her head. "I wanted children, but I'd nearly given up hope. It was a miracle that I got pregnant at all, considering. Not that anything would have saved my marriage at that point."

"And you hoped it would?"

Charlie lifted her gaze, and her eyes were stormy. "No. But I still wanted my baby."

Clumsily Luke put his arm over her shoulders and tried to offer sympathy. "You're still young enough—"

For an instant she relaxed against him, soaking in the comfort. With her cheek against his chest her voice was muffled. "That's not something I think about anymore."

They were silent for a long moment, then Charlie straightened, resettled Angela more comfortably and put on a determinedly cheerful smile. "Besides, being unofficial aunt is lots of fun. I noticed Mikey thinks the world of his Uncle Luke."

Luke allowed her to replace the emotional distance between them, grateful that she'd shared what she had. It was a step in the right direction, but he was careful not to push too fast, even though his impulse was to pull her into his arms and shelter her from any possible hurt. Instead, he raised one knee and hooked an elbow around it.

"Yeah, Mikey's a great kid."

Charlie glanced up the hill toward the wide deck. "His father doesn't seem too happy at the moment."

Luke followed her look. Rachel was just disappearing inside with a tray of empty glasses, and Rob was stuffing used paper plates into a garbage bag and glowering in the direction of the dock. Luke wondered briefly why his cousin wore such a ferocious scowl, then shrugged. "Maybe he's got indigestion from all that mud pie he ate."

"No one ever got sick from my dessert!" she spluttered, laughing indignantly. "Maybe it was *your* incinerated steak. Don't you know what rare means?"

"Anyone who'll eat bloody meat has to be part cannibal." He made an English butler face and sniffed disdainfully. "Totally uncivilized."

Before Charlie could frame a retort, Becky called from the deck that they were ready to go. Luke scrambled to his feet, then steadied Charlie's arm as she did the same, shifting Angela so that the child's head lolled on her shoulder.

"Do you want me to take her?" he asked.

"No, I don't mind." They began to meander back up the dock. "Thanks again for inviting me," she said.

"Since this was what I'd call a fair success, how about accepting another invitation? Say, maybe a movie at the Parkview?"

"Isn't that pushing our luck?" A worried crease appeared between her brows, and she bit her lip. "I...I don't know where you expect something like that to lead."

"Nowhere. Anywhere. Hey," he chided, "we're old friends, remember? And you need to loosen up a little. I simply enjoy your company. Forget the movie if it makes you uncomfortable."

She looked relieved. "Okay."

Luke squelched his frustration and tried another tack. "By the way, Miss Scarlett is well enough to come home."

"Oh, that's great! You really are a miracle worker."

"With all due modesty, I agree. You know she's got heart trouble, so the pneumonia was tricky. I've got to take a look at Howard's colt tomorrow evening, so I'll bring her out to Evening Star when I come."

"That's too much trouble."

"No trouble." He hooked a thumb in his waistband and grinned. "But to show your appreciation, afterward you can ride with me to pick up an ice cream or something."

Charlie laughed uneasily. "You're certainly determined, aren't you? I would have thought you'd be reluctant to face Milady's wrath again after everything."

Lady, you don't know the half of my determination, he thought, then shrugged. "I can let bygones be bygones as well as you can. And besides, I've got Miss Scarlett in my corner this time."

"Don't tell me you're smitten with that ugly mutt!"

"Ladies of every species love me. You'll see," Luke promised with a grin. "And I'll see *you* tomorrow night."

They had reached the deck by this time, and Luke saw that Charlie didn't have a chance to protest his plans as Becky and Wylan gathered up their girls, said a quick goodbye and whisked Charlie off to collect her car from their house. The party quickly broke up after that, and amid the flurry of goodbyes Luke barely had a chance to offer Rachel a quick thank-you before she bustled off as well. Rob and Mikey, both barefoot and with T-shirts pulled over their bathing trunks, were stacking folding chairs on the deck, so Luke went inside to check the kitchen, only to find Rachel had taken charge in her usual competent fashion, leaving him little to do in the way of KP.

Whistling softly, Luke investigated the depths of his refrigerator, looking for a couple of long-neck beers for himself and Rob. Despite Charlie's wariness, he was chipping away at that rock wall of hers. In his estimation the fact that he'd so neatly arranged to see her again the next day deserved a toast. He heard the whisper of the sliding glass door and Rob's heavy tread.

"Say, cuz, how about another beer?" Luke asked over his shoulder.

"You can keep your damn beer!" Rob growled. "Where the hell do you get off treating that little girl like that?"

Luke turned and set the bottles down on the kitchen's central island, his expression mirroring his surprise. "Who, Charlie?"

"No, not Charlie!" Rob roared. With a vicious swipe of his bare foot he kicked the door of the refrigerator closed so hard that it rocked the appliance back and forth. "Honest to God, Luke, if you weren't my best friend I'd beat the crap out of you!"

Honest bewilderment clouded Luke's features. "Hold up, buddy! I'm not following you."

"It's a poor excuse of a man who casts after another woman while he's still got one dangling on the line."

Luke scowled, his own anger building. "If you're talking about Charlie and me—"

"Hell, yes, I'm talking about you and Charlie. Damn it, man! You've got no right to treat Rachel that way."

"Rachel?"

"It about broke my heart to see Rachel watching you paw another woman. You've got no class at all." Rob's angry tone held a wealth of disgust.

"Rachel?" Luke repeated, then broke into a crooked grin and began to laugh.

Rob's face darkened, and he started around the island, his hands clenched into fists. "By God, I *will* beat some sense into you!"

Luke sobered and held up a placating hand. "You've got it all wrong, buddy. Rachel and I aren't involved. Haven't been for ages. How the hell could you have missed that?"

Rob's brown eyes narrowed suspiciously. "So why was she watching you like a hawk this afternoon?"

"Because she's been dying to find out who's been driving me crazy lately."

"Charlie Kincaid?"

"Yup."

"But I thought . . . that is, you and she . . ."

"Yeah, we've got some history to overcome, but I'm working on it. I'm nuts about that woman, always have been, and she loves me, too, only she doesn't know it yet."

A flush crept up Rob's neck, but he held on to his belligerent air. "Are you sure you and Rachel aren't . . . ?"

Luke leaned back against the counter and took a sip of his beer. "Positive. It's real interesting, though, the way you charged to Rachel's defense like a white knight just now. Yes, sir," he drawled, "real interesting."

Rob's cheekbones turned brick-red. "So if you and Rachel aren't going together, you won't mind if I ask her out sometime?"

"Hell, no! Rachel's a free agent. In fact, I'll give you my blessing."

Rob stuffed his hands into the back pockets of his swim trunks, fidgeted, then reached for the other beer. "Yeah, well, that's all right, then."

"I wondered what was holding you back. Got a hankering for her, do you?"

"She's about the sweetest little gal I've ever seen."

Luke snorted. "Much you know! Just wait until she starts ordering you around. Talk about bossy!"

Rob took a deep swig of beer and then stared morosely down at his bare toes. "I'm probably just daydreaming. Why would a classy lady like Rachel have anything to do with a tongue-tied oaf like me?"

"Only one way to find out. Give her a call. You may surprise yourself."

"Yeah, well, we'll see." Rob grimaced dubiously, set the bottle down and walked toward the door. "I'd better take Mikey home. Thanks for dinner."

"Anytime. And Rob?"

"Yeah?"

Luke's grin was teasing, but his warning was serious. "You'd better be nice to Rachel, or next time *you'll* be answering to *me.*"

TWO WEEKS AFTER Luke's cookout Charlie walked out of the air-conditioned Fine Arts building and into a wall of heat that made her catch her breath. Summer was in force with a vengeance, crisping the entire area with cloudless days and temperatures that were more like August than June. Farmers down at the co-op were already whispering the dreaded word "drought," and Charlie knew Howard worried and listened keenly to every weather report. Blinking against the brilliant blue sky, she noted a hazy buildup to the west and mentally crossed her fingers, hoping today would be the day the cycle of summer showers began.

Hitching her tote bag in her grimy fingers, Charlie walked down the building's steps. When she reached the sidewalk, a low wolf whistle froze her in her tracks.

"Hey, gorgeous, can I carry your books?"

Charlie smiled to herself and tossed her head in a superior manner. "Not even if you're on the honor roll, buster. Cutting class again, Duval?"

"Only for you, baby." Luke grinned and fell into step with her, giving her his best James Dean heavy-lidded leer. "Wanna go to the library and neck?"

Charlie spluttered with laughter. "We never!"

He looked disappointed. "Are you sure?"

"Yes!" She tried to feign indignation, but the smile that hovered on her lips made it impossible. "What are you doing here, anyway?"

"Your grandmother's car is in the shop, right? I figured you could use a ride home."

"Thanks, but I was going to get a lift from Becky."

"I told her I'd take care of it."

"You did, huh? Rich veterinarians don't have to work, I guess."

"Self-employed veterinarians can sometimes arrange their hours to suit their convenience." He shrugged, lift-

ing broad shoulders under a checked cotton shirt. "I can
give Howard's colt another look while I'm at it."

"Well, since you put it so graciously..."

"Just what I like—a sensible woman. Come on, I'm
parked in a no parking zone."

"Always the rebel!" she laughed as he hustled her toward the parking lot.

In the past weeks Charlie had found herself on the re-
ceiving end of a lot of Luke's attention. Oddly he never
quite seemed to ask, so she never had the chance to say no.
They'd been out for ice cream and taken several drives
together. It had been his pickup truck that had delivered
her completed demonstration stained-glass window to
Boudreaux's Gifts. She'd even tagged along once for a
very interesting few hours while he made a couple of veterinary calls.

He was always doing nice, rather unexpected things for
her. One day he'd dropped by the campus with sack
lunches, and they'd watched the softball teams practic-
ing while they ate croissant sandwiches and lemon cook-
ies he'd bought at a Front Street tearoom. Another time
he'd whisked her to his house to solicit decorating advice
about drapes and carpeting in the guest room, listening
with rapt attention as she discussed the merits of loden
green versus raspberry.

It was all rather disconcerting, she thought as Luke
opened the door of his brown truck for her. He helped her
inside the cluttered interior, grumbling good-naturedly.

"I wouldn't be risking a ticket if you'd take the Mercedes, you know."

"I told you how I felt about that."

When Milady's old sedan had developed alternator
problems, he'd pressed her to take his second vehicle, a
Mercedes coupe, for the duration. He'd been annoyed

when she hadn't accepted his offer, but she'd come so far on her quest for independence that it was a matter of principle.

"So how was class today?" he asked as he started the truck.

Charlie shuffled a crumpled pile of candy bar wrappers into a ball and stashed it under her feet. "Hectic. We're letting the kids try different media. It was clay today."

"I guessed that." He checked the traffic, smirking slightly. "That smear on your nose is a dead giveaway."

"What?" Hastily Charlie sat forward, inspecting her face in the rearview mirror. Sure enough, there was a dab of white on the bridge of her nose. She lifted the hem of her oversize T-shirt and scrubbed vigorously at the spot. "You might have said something sooner!"

He chuckled. "You've changed a lot, Charlie. In the old days you'd never let anyone see you this way—mussed and somewhat less than immaculate."

"What a bore I must have been back then." She gave up on the smear, sliding back in the seat with a resigned shrug. "I love this job, even if it's only part-time. Grungy goes with the territory, so you'll have to get used to the new me."

Luke's tawny brown gaze swept her critically, taking in the well-laundered blue jeans and grimy shirt, the bandana holding back her unruly curls, the mouth that was bare of all lipstick. Returning his attention to the highway, he remarked, "Actually, you've never looked more beautiful."

There, he's done it again, she thought with a jolt, knocked her off balance with a careless comment. "Th-thank you," she stammered.

Luke kept his eyes on the road. "You're welcome."

If he hadn't been so absolutely casual and offhand, Charlie would have sworn she was being courted ever so subtly. As it was, she decided that Luke was simply sincere in his desire to cement their newly re-formed friendship.

And that's what I want, too, she assured herself, despite a tendency she'd recently discovered to think about Luke's lean body, his skillful hands, his sensual mouth—especially that!—at the most inopportune times. His casual touches were friendly but sexless, nothing to warrant the outrageous, lustful reactions they elicited from her traitorous body. It was an annoying fact that she was a healthy young woman whose needs had been ignored for far too long, but this relaxed and caring friendship that she and Luke now shared was too precious to her to risk for the sake of mere sex.

Damn it.

She pushed her windblown curls from her face and the pang of regret out of her head. After all, only a fool would want further complications just when things were finally coming together for her. She cast around for a safe subject.

"So how is Howard's horse doing?"

"Fairly well. I've had Pigeon blister that bowed tendon a couple of times."

"Do what?"

He laughed. "Blister the area with a compress of red mercury and iodine. It brings the red blood cells and antibodies to the injury and promotes natural healing."

"Ugh. It sounds terrible."

Luke turned off the main highway onto the lane leading to Evening Star. "It's usually effective. We've also been swimming him." He pointed across a distant paddock at a stock pond. "It looks like we're just in time. Want to see?"

"Sure." She hung on to the door handle as Luke turned his truck in through a gap, then jounced it over the bumpy pasture toward the pond. "Howard's talking of hiring his own trainer, you know."

"Thoroughbred horse racing is a tricky business. I hope he knows what he's doing," Luke commented.

"He's already got quite an investment with the five horses he owns, and there's talk of more to come. If he gets the trainer he wants, he says he's going to plow up a soybean field and build a training track right here on Evening Star so he can oversee things personally."

"Howard his big ideas," Luke said dryly, then brought the truck to a halt on the pond levee. He cocked his head, frowning up at the hazy sky. "Is that thunder I hear?"

"I hope so," she replied, plucking at her shirt. "A storm would cool things off, not to mention the crops need it."

"Don't get your hopes up. It's probably miles away. Ready to see some equine water therapy?"

Charlie nodded and they climbed out, waving to Pigeon who had Kingdom's Bobby on a long lunge line at the water's edge.

For the next fifteen minutes Charlie sat on the truck hood and watched Pigeon put the roan through his paces, leading him in and out of the water, forcing the animal to swim to exercise the injured tendon gently. Afterward, Luke and Pigeon examined Kingdom's leg, and Charlie had to laugh when the horse gave a great shake of his mane and tail, soaking both men with the spray. She was still laughing when Pigeon led him away.

"Well, that's one way to cool off!" She rocked backward on the hood of the truck, holding one knee and giggling. Luke climbed up the bank toward her, running a hand through his tawny brown hair and wiping his damp face with his shirtsleeve.

"Woman, you've got no respect for a professional at work!" His grin was lopsided. Placing both hands on her waist, he lifted her from the hood, and his hands lingered as he gazed down into her upturned, laughing face. Something flickered in the depths of his lion's eyes. With a groan he cupped her face in his big hands and kissed her gently with exquisite tenderness.

He drew back, and Charlie's eyes were as dark and green and unfathomable as the water in the pond's deepest end. "Why...why did you do that?" she whispered.

"Because I needed to." He bent toward her again.

"Lucas, don't." She turned her head aside. "You're changing things."

"Change is inevitable."

"There have been enough changes in my life lately."

He sighed and let the tips of his fingers trail along the delicate line of her jawbone. "You can't deny what's between us, Charlie. You know I want you. We've both been vibrating like plucked strings since the day you came back to town."

"Don't push me!" She pulled away, her eyes flashing. "Milady, you, Tyler—everyone knows what's best for me but *me*. I'll let you know when—or even if—I'm ready for things to change, and if that doesn't suit you, then you can quit hanging around here all the time."

"Still a prima donna at heart, aren't you?"

His words hurt her, but stubbornly she clamped down tightly on lips that trembled, and turned to climb back into the truck. She'd die before she showed him he could still wound her so easily.

Luke slammed her door with more force than necessary, then stalked around the front of the truck and slid into the driver's seat. His jaw flexed with irritation. "All right, have it your way—for now."

He reached for the ignition key, then hesitated. Stretching across to punch the button to the glove compartment, he removed a small white paper sack and tossed it carelessly into her lap. "Here. I've been meaning to give you this."

"What is it?"

"Just open it?"

Curiously she opened the sack, removing a small tissue-paper-wrapped bundle. Peeling the thin tissue back, she uncovered the cold glitter of gold and gems, then gasped as recognition slammed into her like a juggernaut. Tyler's offerings filled her hands like something incredibly obscene. Stunned, she looked up at Luke and felt the hot rush of tears.

"Damn you, Luke!"

CHAPTER EIGHT

"THAT'S A HELL of a fine thank-you."

"Is that what I'm supposed to say?" Charlie hissed. She crammed the jewelry back into the bag. "I thought we'd come farther than this."

"Farther than what?"

"Than *this!*"

She threw the sack at Luke, and it crackled against his chest, then rolled to the littered floorboards. Neither one of them made a move to pick it up. Her voice was scathing.

"Time to up the ante, is it, Luke? A little something to sweeten the pot?"

"No, of course not." His expression was rife with puzzled frustration. "Hell's bells! I was trying to do you a favor by getting your stuff out of hock before Jim Peyton had a chance to sell it."

"Why should I want it back?" she demanded bitterly, dashing the tears from the corners of her eyes. "They're nothing but ugly reminders of what a failure I am."

"You're not a failure."

"You don't know anything about me!" she flared. "For all your talk of wanting me, you don't have any idea who I am."

"Then tell me."

She laughed, but it was a harsh sound. "All right, but don't blame me if you don't like what you hear. According to my husband, if I hadn't been so inadequate in every way, including in bed, he wouldn't have been forced to seek satisfaction elsewhere, and there would have been no reason for him to buy me expensive baubles to appease his conscience. It's such a hardship for a man to have such an absolutely worthless wife, unable to do the least thing right.''

"You didn't believe that crap, did you?''

"You hear anything often enough and you'll begin to believe it. I was raised to please, you know. Self-doubt has always been my tour de force.'' Her eyes grew dark and as gray as sheet ice. "But the thing of it was, I could never please Tyler. It took therapy for me to realize how sick our relationship was, that he was abusing me and I was taking it like a spineless fool.''

Luke made a low sound like a growl, and his hand closed over her wrist. "He hit you?''

She shook her head. "He never laid a finger on me. In some ways I wish he had. Then maybe I would have come to my senses sooner. Instead, I let him destroy all my self-respect with his rages and his jealousies. Do you know what he told me after my miscarriage?''

Luke shook his head.

"He said it was a blessing since the baby probably wasn't his, anyway.''

Luke bit out an expletive, and his hand tightened. "And you get angry with me!''

"What makes you any different?'' She jerked her arm free, and her voice broke. "You both think you can buy what you want.''

"Now wait just a minute!''

"I told you before. I'm not for sale! So keep Tyler's trinkets, or give them to charity, or throw them into the lake, because I certainly never want to see them again!''

"All right, I will," he said.

"Good!" she shot back, and with that, grabbed her tote bag and scrambled out of the truck.

"Where the hell do you think you're going?" Luke thundered.

"For a walk. To the moon. Anywhere, as long as it's away from you!" Charlie flung the words over her shoulder as she stormed across the grassy pasture.

Cursing, Luke cranked the vehicle, then sent it speeding after her. He hung out of the cab window, paying no attention to the potholes that violently bounced the truck on its springs. "Get back in here, woman! I was only trying to help you out—"

"I don't need your help!" She whirled around to glare at him. "Can't you get that through your thick head? I can stand on my own two feet, so don't do me any more favors!"

"All right, fine!" he shouted back angrily, and stood on the brakes. "Suit yourself, Miss High and Mighty. We'll see what stubbornness gets you."

He reversed the truck so hard and fast that the rear wheels spun, then careened across the pasture, through the gap and headed back to town. Charlie was too upset to care.

By the time she walked through the pastures and up the long lane to the house, Charlie's temper had wilted with the oppressive heat. On some level she knew Luke's actions might well have been motivated by a desire to please her, but the jewelry was a symbol of a past that continued to dog her footsteps in spite of all attempts to put it behind her. All the old feelings of helplessness and inadequacy had come flooding back, filling her with an impotent rage. Damn them all! She was through being manipulated and used.

The cool interior of the house was a blessed relief, and Charlie set her tote bag wearily onto the oak kitchen table just as Gina glided into the kitchen.

"They're at it again." She pursed her orange-tinted mouth and gave a long-suffering sigh.

"Who is?" Charlie fixed a glass of ice water and drank thirstily.

"Howard and Milady. Can't you hear them? Howard just told her the south section's beans failed." Gina cocked her head, inspecting Charlie inquisitively. "Gracious, sugar, you're a mess! Where have you been?"

Charlie shoved her fingers through her disheveled locks, realizing she made a poor comparison with Gina's cool appearance in her crisp peach jumpsuit, but didn't care. Her mind settled on more urgent matters.

"You say we've had a crop failure?"

"Isn't it awful? If we'd had just a little more rain . . ." Gina shrugged. "The cotton still might make it, but the soybeans are a write-off. We'll have to refinance, of course, but that's nothing new."

"There must be something we can do." Charlie hurried toward the sound of raised voices, and Gina trailed along behind her.

"You can't blame me for the weather," Howard was saying as they entered the book-lined study.

Milady stood beside the shuttered window inspecting several papers she held in her veined hands. "No," she snapped, "but I can certainly blame you for overextending us with your high-falutin' notions, young man! I don't know why I let you talk me into horses, of all things. Miserable, smelly, *stupid* animals."

"The horses are my investment. I've taken nothing out of Evening Star for them. Besides, we're no worse off now than we've been in the past," Howard grumbled, his hands jammed into the pockets of his khaki pants and his mouth a mutinous line. "Things will work out by harvest. They always do."

"You'd better hope they do, or the lending institutions will own this place and we'll all be out on the street!"

"Is it really that bad, Howard?" Charlie asked from the doorway.

Her cousin whirled around, his brown eyes startled. He was quick to regain his composure and his usual jovial manner. "It's nothing to worry your pretty head about, Charlotte. Your grandmother likes to dramatize the situation, that's all."

Milady sniffed and tossed aside the papers. "And your cousin likes to turn a blind eye to the risks involved."

Howard spread his thick hands, palms upward in appeal. "Look, losing one crop isn't going to ruin us. Besides, it's still not too late to reseed the acreage with a grain crop like milo. We can have Grant's Dusting Service do it by air. It'll cost us, but it'll be worth it in time saved if we can still make a fall harvest."

"It doesn't have to cost that much, Howard," Charlie interjected. "I can do it for nothing."

"What!"

Ignoring both Milady's and Howard's startled exclamations, Charlie explained. "In fact, I don't know why I haven't thought of this before. I could be doing all of the dusting for us. Daddy taught me everything he knew about flying 'low and slow.'"

"I absolutely forbid it! The very idea!" Milady pressed her hand to her thin chest.

Charlie's mouth flattened into the same determined line as her grandmother's. "I have to start pulling my weight around here, don't I? I refuse to live like a . . . a parasite! And admit it, given the amount of insecticides, herbicides and defoliates we use, I can save Evening Star a lot of money this way."

"You know, she's got a point, Howard, honey," Gina said, arching her plucked brows.

"Well..."

"No!" Milady said. "It's too dangerous."

"Nonsense," Charlie said, becoming more and more excited with the idea. "My rating is current and Hector's kept the plane in wonderful condition. It's important to me that I do this. It's a way I can contribute, don't you see? And I know Daddy wouldn't object to the use of his plane, wherever he happens to be at the moment."

There was a sudden and complete silence in the room. Charlie frowned. When she looked at Howard and Gina their eyes wouldn't meet hers, but slid away to rest accusingly on Milady, whose features were as pale and still as marble. A premonition trilled along Charlie's spine.

"What is it?" she asked, glancing between the three.

Howard swallowed. "Charlie, my dear girl—"

"I'll tell her," Milady interrupted brusquely. Her pale gray eyes were expressionless. "The only way I know to do this is to come right out and say it, Charlotte. Your father's dead."

A fist slammed into Charlie's chest, expelling all her breath on a soundless gasp. "What?"

"Heart attack. A veteran's hospital in California notified us."

Charlie felt Gina's hand on her shoulder in silent comfort, urging her into a chair. Her thoughts were numb, and her brain spun with vertigo. "When?"

Milady's gaze never wavered. "Six months ago."

It took a moment for that to sink in. When it did, her light-headedness vanished in a rush of disbelief. "Why didn't you tell me?" she croaked.

"I didn't think you were strong enough at the time," Milady said.

"*You* didn't think!" Charlie lunged to her feet, her breath coming in sharp, rasping gasps. "Oh, God! How could you do this to me? I knew you hated Roy Kincaid, but I had no idea you could be this vindictive. Do you hate me so much?"

That startled Milady. "Charlotte, I don't hate you."

"I was never so sick I couldn't have stood the truth. Damn you! Damn all of you!" Her cry was raw and anguished. "I had the right to bury my own father!"

She ran from the room, and they heard the back door slam.

Gina looked at her husband. "I'm ashamed of us."

"I know what's best for my granddaughter," Milady replied stonily. "If she's upset now, just think what the news would have done to her then."

"She's a grown woman," Gina said with a stubborn pout. "I wouldn't blame her if she packed her bags and left for Charleston again."

"Maybe the best thing," Howard muttered under his breath.

"She'll be all right," Milady said, but there was a thread of uncertainty in her reedy voice. She frowned suddenly, listening. "What on earth is that racket?"

"Lord have mercy!" Sudie's sharp cry rang from the rear of the house, bringing everyone on a run.

"What is it, Sudie?" Howard demanded.

Sudie pointed through the French doors. "I'm gonna kill my man Hector for sure! It's gonna storm, and Charlie's done took off in her daddy's old plane!"

ESCAPE.

There was nothing so exhilarating. If you flew high enough, and fast enough, and long enough, you could almost outrace all pain, disillusionment and fear. Almost.

A patchwork of green and brown fields floated beneath the Stearman. Charlie's ears throbbed with the deafening roar of the engine, and hot wind blew in her face. She functioned automatically, operating flaps and ailerons, checking gauges, trying to keep the rending talons of grief at bay.

Daddy.

There had never been enough time to tell him how much she loved him. Now there never would.

A flash to the east jerked Charlie to complete awareness just in time to see another forked tongue of lightning streak through a plum-colored thunderhead. Roy Kincaid's smoke-roughened voice echoed like the distant thunder within the recesses of her head.

Only a dummy forgets about the weather, Charlie.

I didn't forget, Daddy.

I don't waste time with Sunday-school pilots, baby. When you fly, it's for real. You don't get second chances.

I know that.

So quit mooning around and set this bucket of bolts on the ground, girl.

"Yes, sir, Daddy," Charlie said aloud, and banked the aircraft in a wide turn. No matter how far you ran, there was no escaping some realities, and she might as well face them at Evening Star.

She nearly didn't make it.

Gusting tailwinds made her struggle with the throttle while silver sheets of rain fell to the right and left and angry navy blue and purple storm clouds roiled on all sides. Just when she thought she'd have to find a handy stretch of highway to land the Stearman, Evening Star came into view. Praying she wouldn't have to fight a crosswind, Charlie eased the buffeted airplane lower and lower, finally lining up with the ancient landing field.

Her landing wasn't anything to be proud of, not with all the bumping and bouncing the Stearman did before it finally settled to the earth, but Charlie wasn't proud. It was enough to be safely home. Thunder was her fanfare as she taxied toward the old barn hangar, lightning her spotlight in a day gone as dark as midnight.

She killed the engine, reaching for the tarp that would cover the open cockpit just as the first slash of rain hit her cheek. Scrambling out, she felt hard hands lift her and looked up to find Luke's stern face, his sandy hair plastered dark and wet against his brow. She didn't question his presence. It was enough that he helped her to secure the tarp while the wind tore at her hair and icy rain soaked her clothes.

"Come on!" he shouted over the howl of the elements.

"The chocks!" Bent over to protect her face from the worst of the stinging spray, Charlie retrieved the heavy wheel chocks from beside the barn. She and Luke pushed and kicked them into place, and puddles that had appeared almost like magic began to dance with a barrage of pea- and marble-size hail. Luke grabbed Charlie's hand, and they dashed for the safety of the dim, dry barn.

The storm beat a muffled tattoo on the tin roof. Charlie gasped for breath and wiped at the water streaming down her face, shoving back the sodden tails of her wet hair with an impatient hand.

"Thanks," she said. "I thought you left."

"Sudie had Rachel call me on the CB. She thought somebody ought to be around to pick up the pieces."

Luke pulled his fingers through his hair, pushing it straight back from his brow in a teenage hood's pompadour. His expression was thunderous. "Haven't you got a lick of sense? You scared those people to death pulling a fool stunt like this!"

"*Those people* don't give a hoot in hell about me."

Abruptly Charlie turned away. She snatched an empty cotton feed sack from a pile on the half wall separating two hay-filled stalls and blotted ineffectually at her soaked clothes. "My dad..." She choked to a stop, shivering violently.

Luke came up behind her, closing his hands around her upper arms, rubbing back and forth to warm and comfort her. Thunder boomed and lightning cracked over their heads as the storm built to a crescendo. "I know. God, I'm sorry, Charlie."

"He never even knew about the baby...and now they're both gone."

"Not gone," Luke murmured. "You have to believe they're someplace good...together."

Her breath caught on a silent, convulsive sob of pain and grief. "Oh, Luke..."

He turned her, and she fell against his chest, weeping. Luke rubbed her shoulders through the soaked cotton knit of her blouse, murmuring soft words of comfort. Her hands twisted in his shirt, hanging on as though Luke were the only steady rock in a sea of despair.

"It's all right, sweetheart," he said, his own voice raw. "Cry all you want."

"Hold me, Luke," she shuddered, pressing her cheek into the hard wall of his chest.

"Yes."

"Don't let me go."

His fingers caressed the tender nape of her neck under her wet hair. "I won't."

"I didn't mean what I said before. You were being kind, and I said such awful things...."

"It's all right."

"You're the only one I can count on." Desperately her hands climbed up his chest to link around his neck.

"I'm here for you, Charlie." Luke gazed down into her tear-drenched eyes, then bent his head and softly melded his mouth to hers. It was a kiss of comfort and atonement, and he caught the soft hiccup of her breath and made it a part of himself.

She murmured against his lips, a hungry, needful sound, and moved even closer, pressing a hand against the side of his chest. The coin of his nipple, puckered with the chill, poked through the thin cotton shirt into her palm. Luke sucked in a harsh breath, and in an instant's lightning flash the kiss changed and deepened, exploding into something altogether different.

Tongues met and parried, bodies pressed urgently, and mutual groans struck deep harmonic chords of desire. Charlie gave herself up to the demand of the blood thundering through her veins, needing Luke, wanting him. In the shadows of loss she craved a reaffirmation of life, and Luke was all that was strong and vibrant and *alive*.

Somehow she was pressed between the wooden stall and Luke's lean body. His knee was bent and the top of his rock-hard thigh rode between the notch of her legs. She arched against his heat, and her tongue met his, giving him fire for fire, demanding just as he was demanding.

Luke pulled back, his breath harsh in his chest, his amber eyes hooded. He took in her soft features, her dazed expression, the tremulous quiver of her voluptuous lower lip. Her damp shirt slicked close to her body, delineating the lacy wisp of her bra and the outline of the distended nipples beneath it, no more impediment to his avid gaze than if she were naked.

"You know where this is leading." His voice rumbled low, but it wasn't a question. She nodded, and her tongue flicked out to capture the flavor of him that lingered on her moist lips. He stifled another groan, shifting as his body rode him hard. "If we don't stop now, there'll be no turning back."

"No."

"No?"

She reached for him. "No turning back."

Luke's control broke. He groaned and pulled her hard against him, seeking her lips in a hot, wet, breath-stealing kiss. It was a moment for exultation, for savoring her surrender, but his need for her, so long denied, overrode even that luxury. The air crackled and sizzled with a charge of passion more potent than the electrical fireworks filling the skies outside, and vaguely Luke knew that there was indeed no turning back, not from a physical union and, whether Charlie realized it or not, not from its emotional consequences.

Luke slipped his hand beneath the tail of her shirt, briefly caressed the slender curve of her waist, then boldly filled his palm with the weight of her breast. His mouth moved across her cheekbone, then explored the delicate shell of her ear. She shivered uncontrollably, arching her back and pushing her breast into his palm as though seeking his warmth.

"You're cold," he said.

"Not really."

Her fingers plucked at his shirt buttons, freeing them from the stubborn holes, then tugging his shirttail from the waistband of his jeans. When his shirt hung open, she pressed her palms against the washboard of his rib cage, then trailed her fingertips through the soft bramble of sandy hairs that lightly sprinkled his beautifully muscled chest.

With a low sound of impatience Luke reached for her shirt hem, then whipped it over her head, tossing the garment into the pile of hay behind them. His breath caught at the sight of her, her skin glowing like ivory in the dim light. With hands that trembled visibly he unhooked the front clasp of her bra, pushing aside the lacy undergarment to reverently stroke the velvety underside of her breasts and rub his work-roughened thumbs against the rosy crests, budded now with her arousal.

"You're beautiful," he said, his voice thick.

Charlie shuddered and swayed against him. A heaviness centered low in her belly, an ache that pulsed and grew with each touch, each caress until she was nearly mad. Somewhere deep inside, in a part of her she'd never dared examine too closely, she'd known that Luke could do this to her, could render her helpless with desire and totally out of control.

Perhaps she'd feared that loss of control on a subconscious level; perhaps she'd always held a part of herself back because of it. Certainly she'd never experienced anything so devastating with Tyler. Maybe he'd sensed that he'd never really touched her core. Cold, he'd called her, never blaming her lack of response on himself, using it as an excuse for his escapades. But she was anything but cold under Luke's expert caresses. She burned with need, a sexual hunger that raged unchecked, forcing her to trust him and making her forget all her insecurities and fears in a desperate desire to touch and be touched.

With a boldness she hadn't known herself capable of, she reached for Luke's belt buckle, slipped it free, then fumbled with the stiff metal button at his waist. Finally there was a soft metallic rasp as she slid his zipper down and caressed the hot, hard length of him through his briefs. He stiffened and groaned, then captured her mouth again, plunging his tongue deeply to drink of her essence. His hand splayed in the small of her back, then slipped underneath the waistband of her jeans, sliding beneath the thin silk of her panties to cup her bottom intimately.

"Oh, God, Charlie," he murmured, "you're killing me."

Her heart thumped madly in her chest, and she gasped for air. "Lucas, please..."

He swallowed, glanced up, then flung down the stack of feed sacks piled on the stall divider to cover the mound of prickly hay. With infinite care he lifted her, then placed her on the improvised bed, following her down. The weight of their bodies crushed the dry stems, releasing the crisp, golden odor of new hay.

"This isn't the way I wanted it," he said, his tone as rough as emery paper. He slipped off his shirt and reached for the fastener of her jeans.

"What do you mean?" She gasped as he stripped her, leaving nothing but the unfastened bra hanging wantonly from her shoulders.

He kicked off his boots, his tawny eyes gleaming as he looked at her. He laid a possessive, predatory hand against her middle, his thumb hooking into the shallow indentation of her navel. "When I thought of this, of you and me, I always pictured you on satin sheets."

He bent his head, lightly kissing where his hand had rested. She gasped and arched in reaction, then groaned and thrashed when his mouth moved, boldly capturing and suckling the sensitive tip of her breast.

PLAY THE "LUCKY 7" SLOT MACHINE GAME!

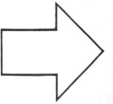

NO COST! NO OBLIGATION TO BUY!
NO PURCHASE NECESSARY!

PLAY "LUCKY 7"
AND GET AS MANY AS SIX FREE GIFTS...

HOW TO PLAY:

1. With a coin, carefully scratch off the silver box at the right. This makes you eligible to receive one or more free books, and possibly other gifts, depending on what is revealed beneath the scratch-off area.

2. You'll receive brand-new Harlequin Superromance® novels. When you return this card, we'll send you the books and gifts you qualify for *absolutely* free!

3. If we don't hear from you, every month we'll send you 4 additional novels to read and enjoy. You can return them and owe nothing but if you decide to keep them, you'll pay only $2.92* per book, a savings of 33¢ each off the cover price. There is **no** extra charge for postage and handling. There are no hidden extras.

4. When you join the Harlequin Reader Service®, you'll get our monthly newsletter as well as additional free gifts from time to time just for being a subscriber.

5. You must be completely satisfied. You may cancel at any time simply by sending us a note or a shipping statement marked ''cancel'' or returning any shipment to us at our cost.

This lovely Victorian pewter-finish miniature is perfect for displaying a treasured photograph— and it's yours absolutely free—when you accept our no-risk offer.

PLAY "LUCKY 7"

Just scratch off the silver box with a coin.
Then check below to see which gifts you get.

YES! I have scratched off the silver box. Please send me all the gifts for which I qualify. I understand I am under no obligation to purchase any books, as explained on the opposite page.

134 CIH ACKR

NAME

ADDRESS   APT

CITY   STATE   ZIP

7	7	7	WORTH FOUR FREE BOOKS, FREE VICTORIAN PICTURE FRAME AND MYSTERY BONUS
🍒	🍒	🍒	WORTH FOUR FREE BOOKS AND MYSTERY BONUS
●	●	●	WORTH FOUR FREE BOOKS
🔔	🔔	🍒	WORTH TWO FREE BOOKS

HARLEQUIN "NO RISK" GUARANTEE

- You're not required to buy a single book—ever!
- You must be completely satisfied or you may cancel at any time simply by sending us a note or a shipping statement marked ''cancel'' or returning any shipment to us at our cost. Either way, you will receive no more books; you'll have no obligation to buy.
- The free books and gifts you receive from this ''Lucky 7'' offer remain yours to keep no matter what you decide.

If offer card is missing write to: Harlequin Reader Service, 3010 Walden Ave., P.O. Box 1867, Buffalo, N.Y. 14269-1867

"I didn't see us that way." Involuntarily her hands came up to clasp his head, her fingers threading through his damp hair.

"You thought about this?" he asked, turning his attention to her other breast. His fingers moved downward to investigate the mysterious triangle of dark hair at the top of her thighs.

"Too many times." Her voice was strangled. "But I...ah!"

He smiled wickedly and continued to fondle her most sensitive places, exulting in her dewy readiness but holding back, denying them both. "You what?"

"I always thought it would happen in your old pickup." Her hands moved restlessly across his back and down the valley of his spine to push fretfully at the stiff denim of his jeans.

"It should have," he growled.

"Yes." She ran a finger inside his loosened waistband, teasing him, tormenting him as he was doing to her. Lowering her lashes, she gave him a slow, seductive smile of blatant invitation. "But wouldn't you agree, better late than never?"

"Damn right." Luke would have laughed if his need hadn't flared out of control in that instant. Shoving down his jeans, he positioned himself between her legs, holding himself on his arms so that he could see her face as he entered her.

Her eyes never wavered from his, as if she, too, wanted to capture and preserve each exquisite moment of their first joining. Slowly, slowly, he eased into her hot, silky depths, feeling the tiny shudders as her body adjusted to his loving invasion. Burying his face in the fragrant curve of her neck and shoulder, he groaned with a soul-deep pleasure. Nothing had ever felt so good or so right as loving this woman.

He feels so good.

Charlie tightened her arms around Luke's neck, savoring the fullness of him. She listened to the harsh, raspy sound of his breath, awash with sensation: the welcome weight of him, the musky scent of his skin, the brush of his beard stubble against her neck. But it wasn't enough. Tentatively she lifted her hips.

Luke's big hands shifted, cupping her buttocks, holding her in position while he thrust and withdrew, slowly at first, then faster and faster. Charlie went wild, her hands touching him everywhere, showering kisses down his strong throat, against the jut of his collarbone, nipping with her teeth at the firm muscles of his broad shoulders.

Without warning Luke pushed her over the edge, and she arched against him and cried out. Waves and waves of pleasure surged through her, unlike anything she'd ever experienced, pitching her headlong through a tempest of his making to lie spent and quaking like a castaway on a distant shore. When the last vibrations faded, she opened her eyes to find Luke's tender smile upon her, and she realized he'd delayed his own completion to guarantee her satisfaction first. Such selflessness in a man was new to her, and with a murmur she pulled his head down for her kiss, inciting him with the seductive undulations of her body to use her for his own pleasure. And he did, in such a way that when he at last shuddered and groaned with his own powerful release, she exploded again and fell with him into that far vale of utter and complete fulfillment.

After a long time, when their racing hearts slowed and they could breathe once again, Luke eased from her. Water dripped from the barn's eaves, and a weak ray of sunshine pierced the interior gloom.

"The storm's over," he said, hitching up his jeans.

"So it is." Color blossomed high on her cheeks.

Luke's mouth quirked in a tender, lopsided smile. Bending, he kissed her quickly, then pulled her to a sitting position. "Which means we're liable to be interrupted at any minute, so to avoid any embarrassment..."

"Yes, of course." She swallowed, bent her head and fumbled with her bra.

Luke dropped her clothes into her lap and brushed away her hands. "Allow me."

He straightened the scanty lace garment, deftly fastening the front catch, then his fingers lingered on the sweet upper swell of her bosom. "Next time we'll try for satin sheets," he murmured, and picked a wisp of hay from her curls.

Charlie gulped and looked away. Scrambling to her feet, she turned her back and pulled on her clothes, supremely conscious that Luke was doing the same. The sodden fabric chilled her skin, but she ignored the goose bumps, running her hands through her hair while she shoved on her tennis shoes. Doubts and reservations assailed her. What had she done?

"You needn't look so alarmed," Luke said behind her.

She whirled around, finding him much too close for her agitated state of mind. "What?"

He brushed her cheek with his fingertips. "There's no turning back, remember?"

Uncertainly she nodded.

"As long as you understand that, then we can take it as it comes, princess. Slow and easy. One step at a time."

She felt a trill of panic. "Luke..."

"Shh." He gathered her into his embrace, and instinctively she snuggled into his warmth. "We're as good together as I always knew we'd be. Don't think I'll let you get away from me this time."

His kiss was tender with the aftermath of passion. When he lifted his head again, her gray-green eyes shone with tears. His expression was instantly concerned.

"What is it, sweetheart?"

"Oh, Luke, I wish . . ."

"What?"

"That you'd been the first for me."

Luke's jaw firmed, and his hands tightened on her. "Just so long as I'm your last."

He took her mouth again, branding her with a kiss of pure possession, staking a claim he dared her to deny.

"Oh, there you are." Howard's voice interrupted them. His portly figure was outlined in the opening of the barn door.

Luke raised his head, but he refused to let Charlie move out of the circle of his arm. "Charlie's safe, Howard."

"I'm glad to see it, but it's you I need, Luke." Howard flicked a disinterested glance at Charlie, but his words vibrated with a strange inflection, excited and despondent at the same time. "Lightning split that oak tree in the big paddock. Kingdom's lying out there under it, dead as a hammer, and I want you to do the autopsy."

CHAPTER NINE

ANGRY VOICES DRIFTED through the dark house. Charlie punched her bed pillow and rolled over onto her side, trying to block out the sounds of Gina and Howard's argument seeping through her bedroom walls. The tension at Evening Star in the week since the thunderstorm had grown like an invisible plague, finally infecting even that usually affable couple.

With a sigh Charlie reached out and turned on her bedside lamp. Sleep was impossible, and guiltily, she knew most of the trouble in the house was her doing. Uncharacteristically she also knew she wasn't going to do anything about it. For once she couldn't hide her injured feelings about the circumstances of her father's death, and she stubbornly refused to be the peacemaker. If other family members felt uncomfortable with the consequences of their actions, then so be it.

Charlie sat up, reached for a copy of *Art News* on the bedside table, then began flipping idly through it, her mind not on the newest acquisition of a Dallas museum, but on the scene that had been played out in Sudie's kitchen a week earlier. As always, Sudie had been sure a freshly brewed pot of herbal tea would be the answer to everything.

"Drink up, chile," Sudie had urged, pouring more of the steaming brew into Charlie's mug. "You don't want to catch a chill, do you?"

Obediently Charlie sipped the tea, a concoction of rose hips and lemon peel, but the hot beverage did as little to dispel the cold numbness of hurt and confusion inside her as had the hot shower she'd taken on returning to the house after the storm and her passionate encounter with Luke. Now, wrapped in a voluminous yellow terry robe, she warmed her hands around her mug and stared into space.

"It doesn't suit you to sulk, Charlotte," Milady said from her seat across the oval oak table. She tipped a small crystal-cut decanter of brandy into Charlie's mug, then added a generous dollop to her own teacup.

Charlie's gray-green eyes focused on her snowy-haired grandmother, her gaze growing smoky with angry resentment. "I have nothing to say to you, Milady."

"Now, sugar," Gina said, frowning as she offered her own cup for Sudie to refill, "you've got to realize no one ever meant to hurt you."

Charlie set her cup down abruptly, splashing brandy-laced tea on the table. Her mouth was tight. "Where is my father buried?"

Gina and Milady exchanged glances. "In a national cemetery in California," Milady finally answered, recorking the decanter.

"Does he have a marker?"

"Ah, there hasn't been time—"

"I'll see to it," Charlie said.

"I'm sure Howard will be glad . . ." Gina began.

Charlie stood up, clutching her forearms as if racked by a chill, her expression harsh. "I said I'll see to it!"

"It's no use getting yourself into a snit about this," Milady said, tapping her nails against the tabletop in irritation. "You've thrown one tantrum already, taking up that old rattletrap of a plane, so don't think of doing anything foolish like running off."

Charlie's mouth twisted. "Now that's an idea."

"Really, Charlie," Gina protested, "you wouldn't leave your home over a silly misunderstanding, would you?"

"Unfortunately I have nowhere else to go." Charlie's tone was icy, her laugh cynical. "Don't worry. I'll be here to reseed those fields for Howard as promised—for the sake of Evening Star."

"See here!" Milady snapped. "I told you I won't have it."

Charlie's voice was soft. "You can't stop me."

Ignoring Milady's outraged gasp, Charlie turned her back to stare out the French doors at the dripping landscape. Howard and Luke were crossing the wind-beaten and rain-bedraggled backyard, and she watched them mount the back steps. A queer thrill raced along her nerves as she looked at Luke. Had she really lain so wantonly in his arms just a short time ago? The men entered the back door, stamping the mud from their feet under Sudie's admonishing eye, but Charlie couldn't meet Luke's questioning glance.

"Howard, honey," Gina said, gliding to her husband's side and sliding her arms around his waist in a comforting hug. "I'm so sorry about Kingdom. Was he really struck by lightning?"

Howard's features were haggard. "Looks that way."

Luke nodded. "All the classic signs. It's a damn shame. He was a fine piece of horseflesh."

"I had real hopes of getting him back into shape in time for a couple of stakes races this fall," Howard said heavily. Gina's bright head cuddled against his swarthy neck. "I guess I need to notify the insurance company."

"I'll call in the autopsy report from my office," Luke offered.

"Can I get you gentlemen something hot to drink?" Sudie asked hopefully.

"I need a bourbon," Howard muttered. "Luke?"

"None for me, thanks. I'm way overdue. I'll phone your insurance agent as soon as I get back, Howard."

"Thanks. I appreciate everything you've done here today." Howard's gaze flicked across Charlie's stiff back.

Luke hesitated, then said reluctantly, "I'll be on my way, then." He nodded to Gina and Milady. "Ladies."

"I'll see you out."

Charlie's words caught them all by surprise. Ignoring the questioning looks, she led Luke out of the kitchen into the wide foyer toward the front door. Luke touched her arm, bringing her to a halt before the hall mirror.

"Are you all right?"

"Sure." She tugged the belt of her robe tighter, sweeping the drying cloud of her whiskey-colored hair out of her face with a defiant toss.

"Here's another question." Luke's mouth curved into a wicked smile. "Are you wearing anything under that robe?"

Charlie's cheeks flushed, but a wave of recklessness made her step closer and run her fingers through the damp hair curling at his nape. "Wouldn't you like to know?"

Rising on tiptoe, she pressed a lingering kiss to his mouth. Deep down she felt a defiant satisfaction that had nothing to do with the sweetness of the kiss, and everything to do with proving to certain people she was her own woman, capable of making her own choices despite what they thought. Kissing Luke showed them all no one would ever dictate to her again. Luke's arms encircled her waist, pulling her closer with frank pleasure, but when he lifted his head, his expression was quizzical.

"Much as I enjoyed that I get the distinct impression it wasn't all for my benefit," he murmured, indicating the audience in the kitchen with a jerk of his chin. "Don't think you're going to use me against your family, Charlie."

A shamed blush heightened her color. How well he knew her already! She'd barely been conscious of such a motive yet, sensitive to her hurt, he knew instinctively what she was trying to do and wisely refused to play her game.

"Can't I kiss you goodbye?" she asked in a small voice.

"Sure, but don't try to put me in the middle. You need to make your peace with Milady and the rest if we're going to go on from here."

"I can't." Charlie tried to pull away, but he held her firmly. Her words were choked. "I can't forgive her."

"Find a way."

She flashed him a resentful look. "You think it's so easy."

"No. But I don't want it getting in our way. We've got enough on our agenda as it is."

"You take a lot for granted," Charlie retorted shakily. "Just because we . . . we . . ."

Luke's strong features hardened. "You're damn right I do. It meant something special to me, and I thought it did to you, too. Or were you only looking for a good—?" He used a gutter word that made Charlie gasp.

"No!"

Luke released her and moved toward the door. "Then grow up, princess. You're not using me to get back at Milady."

Her breath hissed. "Get out!"

"Sure." His tawny eyes blazed. "When you figure it out, you know where to find me."

Now Luke's final taunting words of a week earlier echoed in Charlie's memory, and with a bad-tempered flounce she sent her magazine sailing across the room. It hit the opposite wall with a thump, fluttering to the rug and producing an immediate cessation of hostilities in the room beyond.

For every action there is a reaction, Charlie thought with a brief, sour smile. She propped her elbows on her upraised knees and cupped her chin in her hands in a pensive attitude.

The estrangement between her and Milady had ramifications that affected everyone at Evening Star. She hadn't helped it by promptly using the Stearman to reseed the failed soybean acreage. Milady had laid into Howard for accepting Charlie's help, thus setting off another one of his and Milady's blazing rows. Caught between her husband and Milady, Gina sulkily blamed Charlie for the situation. Sudie's dark eyes mirrored her disappointment at Charlie's unbending attitude toward Milady, but Hector was an ally in her desire to take on all the crop dusting chores, setting the Parrishes at odds, too. And then there was Luke.

Damn him! He hadn't called or dropped by her classes. Stubborn bullheaded man! Where did he get off, asking the hard questions now? Things were too new and confused between them for all the answers to be clear-cut. With a huff of annoyance Charlie switched off the lamp and settled beneath the covers, determined to put him out of her mind. But her recalcitrant body had other ideas, and in the darkness she ached with longing for him, reliving every touch, every kiss.

She knew she cared for him, but whether the feelings that tormented her could be called love was an imponderable dilemma. She wasn't the kind of woman who would give herself lightly, but it was clear the emotionalism of the situation coupled with all their past history had played a part in what had happened between them during the storm. Maybe it was just an explosion that had been nine years overdue. Maybe Luke stayed away now because he regretted making love to her. Maybe she regretted it, too.

Charlie rolled over with an exasperated sigh. And maybe she should stop kidding herself. Whatever the reasons behind their explosive lovemaking, it was clear the chemistry between them hadn't been defused. But what would it take to convince him she hadn't consciously decided to set him against Milady by flaunting their relationship?

Charlie pummeled her pillow. Perhaps it had been a mistake to make love with Luke, but she'd be damned if she'd let their new friendship end on a misunderstanding again. Somehow she'd come up with an excuse to see him, something to soothe his pride while retaining her own, and then make him listen. After that . . . well, then they'd see.

With a groan of pure frustration she buried her face in her pillow and prayed for inspiration.

"SORT OF A PEACE OFFERING," Gina said the following afternoon. She held out her right hand, displaying an opulent sapphire-and-diamond ring for Charlie's inspection. "Howard can be *so* thoughtful sometimes. He knew how I was positively *pining* over this little bauble, and since the insurance settlement on poor Kingdom came in so promptly, he couldn't begrudge me a little something, especially when he's gone and bought three more horses with it, too...."

"It's lovely, Gina," Charlie interrupted. She lifted the other woman's hand so that the ring caught the light pouring through the long French doors in the den. Whatever the couple's argument had been the previous night, Howard had more than made up for it. "I know you'll enjoy wearing such a pretty thing."

Gina spread her immaculately manicured hands to admire the ring again. "It is rather nice, isn't it? But then I deserve an occasional treat, since I gave up a modeling career for that man."

"Do you miss it?" Charlie asked.

"Sometimes. But this is a lovely place to live and there are other compensations. I'm taking Howard out to dinner tonight, and I've got a special thank-you planned for later—" she dimpled "—if you know what I mean."

Charlie sat down on the arm of the den sofa and laughed. "Lucky Howard."

"It always pays to keep your man eager to please, sugar," Gina said with a throaty gurgle. "And take my word for it, a little flirting with someone else now and then goes a long way."

"You're not trying to make Howard jealous, are you?" Memories of Tyler's jealous rages made her frown.

"Not really," Gina said with a laugh. "Howard trusts me. But I can't have him taking me for granted, can I? I'm just keeping him on his toes."

"From the looks of it," Charlie said, indicating the ring with a nod, "it certainly seems to be working well for you."

"You might try it yourself sometime," Gina said archly, then snapped her fingers. "By the way, you had a call earlier. Did you see the message I left you?"

Charlie's pulses jumped. Had Luke finally relented? "What message?"

"Your friend with the ridiculous name called. Let's see...Kitty? Poochie?"

Disappointed, Charlie frowned. "Bunny?"

"That's her!" Gina shrugged and grinned. "She wants you to call her back."

Minutes later Charlie hung up the phone and returned to the den, elation lighting her features.

"So?" Gina demanded curiously. "What gives?"

"Can I borrow your melon-colored sundress?"

"Well, sure. Why?"

"Good news. You're not the only one with something to celebrate tonight," Charlie said. Her eyes sparkled with anticipation. "And I'll be damned if I'm going to do my celebrating alone!"

ALTHOUGH IT WAS NEARLY six o'clock by the time Charlie got to town, the sun was still high above the horizon and Luke's truck, along with several other vehicles, was still parked outside the Animal Clinic. Screwing up her courage, she removed her sunglasses and pushed open the glass door to find Rachel finishing up the last of the day's paperwork.

"Well, hi!" Pleasure illuminated Rachel's cornflower-blue eyes. "Where have you been keeping yourself? Uh-oh, it's not Miss Scarlett again, is it?"

"No, she's fine." Charlie hesitated. "Actually, ah...is Luke around?"

"In the back with Rob Thompson. Talk about a run of bad luck!"

"Who, Luke?" Alarm made Charlie's voice unnaturally high.

Rachel's blond curls bobbed in denial. "No, Rob. He's been in nearly every day this week. First there was this stray collie that had been hit by a car, and then Mikey found a garden snake with a broken tail and nearly had a fit until Luke convinced him it would be all right in the wild, and now someone's given the kid three baby rabbits with ear mites!"

"Sounds as though the pet population is growing at the Thompson estate," Charlie laughed.

"By leaps and bounds... leaps and bounds... and slithers," Rachel agreed with a giggle. "Say, you're awfully dolled up. Going somewhere?"

"If I'm lucky. That's what I wanted to talk to Luke about."

"I can go get him—"

"No, I can wait," Charlie said hastily, wondering why her sandal-clad feet suddenly felt so cold.

"Well, I hope it works out. You look great."

"Thanks. You don't think this dress is too bare, do you?" Charlie twirled around, showing the cutout back of Gina's strappy sundress.

"Gracious, no!" Rachel closed the daybook, reached for her purse and sighed enviously. "Lord, I wish I was able to wear something as sleek as that."

"You do?" Charlie smiled in bemusement as Rachel came around the counter. "I've always wanted to be more voluptuous up top. I barely have anything to hang a dress on at all."

"Well, count your blessings. I've been what my daddy calls 'robust' since I was twelve." Rachel shook her head. "It's not easy. I've been called every vulgar name in the book at one time or another, and I couldn't begin to count all the wolf whistles and adolescent leers—all because I have to wear enough whalebone to keep Captain Ahab in business!''

"This body image business gets out of hand, doesn't it? We'd all be better off if we could simply accept ourselves as we are.''

"I'll say," Rachel grinned. "When they filmed *Steel Magnolias* here in Natchitoches a few years back, I was nearly hired as Dolly Parton's stand-in. Only one thing kept me from getting the job.''

"What was that?''

"For the first time in my life someone told me I was too flat-chested!'' Rachel guffawed behind her hand. "Can you imagine?''

"What an ego deflator," Charlie said, chuckling.

"Are you kidding? It was worth not getting the job just to hear that at least once in my life!''

Charlie's smile softened. "Are you in discomfort? I had a friend in Charleston who had a breast reduction surgery.''

"No, I've never had any problems to speak of. I guess if the Lord put me together the best He knew how, I'd better not tamper with His handiwork. Still, I'd give my eyeteeth to wear a dress like that.''

"Hmm. Let's not be too hasty." With a critical eye Charlie examined her friend's figure under the shapeless lab coat. "I'll bet there's a dress out there with your name on it. What if we go shopping Saturday to see if we can find it?''

"Oh, I'd like that," Rachel said.

"Then it's settled.''

They had their heads together making plans when Luke, Rob and Mikey appeared from the rear of the clinic. Luke's deep voice held a teasing note.

"Better get that rabbit hutch built tonight, cuz. You know how fast rabbits multiply."

Mikey carried a box with three furry inhabitants, and he looked up, exasperated. "Uncle Luke, bunnies don't know 'rithmetic!'"

His comment evoked a chorus of laughter, but Luke's chuckle disappeared abruptly when his eyes met Charlie's.

"Hello, Miss Charlie!" Mikey piped.

"Hi, Mikey, Rob. It's nice to see you," Charlie said, refusing to let Luke's glower undermine her determination. "I see you've acquired a few new members of the family."

"Yeah," Rob said, a rosy flush under his cheekbones. "I guess this makes me the world's biggest chump."

"I think it's very sweet," Rachel said. "A country boy like Mikey needs lots of animals, right, sport?"

"Right!" Mikey beamed proudly at the newest additions to his menagerie.

"Even country boys need to be well rounded," Charlie said. She knew she was chattering like a magpie, but her tongue seemed to have a will of its own. "Have you ever thought about letting Mikey attend the summer arts program at the university, Rob? We're starting a new session next week. It's only two weeks in the mornings, and we have a lot of fun drawing, painting and making things."

"Gee, Dad, could I do that?" Mikey asked hopefully.

"I know you'd have fun, son," Rob said, frowning slightly. "The problem is getting you home after it's over. I have to work, you know."

"Pooh, that's no problem," Rachel scoffed. "I'd be glad to run Mikey to the sitter's."

"We couldn't impose like that, ma'am," Rob insisted uncomfortably.

"Don't be silly," she said. "Luke won't mind if I take a few extra minutes at my lunch hour, just for two weeks, would you, Luke?"

Luke hid a smile. "Well, no, of course not."

"See?" Rachel demanded triumphantly.

"Please, Dad? Please?" Mikey begged.

"Well, if you're certain..." Rob's ears were red, and when he swallowed, his Adam's apple bobbed convulsively. "Michael and I would be much obliged."

"Hooray!" Mikey shouted.

Charlie smiled brightly. "Wonderful. I'll sign him up tomorrow."

"Thanks." Rob nodded. "Come on, son, we've got to get home."

"I'll walk you out," Rachel offered. "You'll lock up, Luke?"

"Sure." Luke stuck his hands into his jeans pockets, his gaze on Charlie's pink face.

"See you tomorrow, then," Rachel called, adroitly ushering the Thompsons out the front door. "I've got the perfect names for those bunnies, Mikey. How about Flopsy, Mopsy and..."

Charlie fidgeted with the clasp of her straw clutch bag and chewed the peachy lip gloss off her bottom lip. "I guess you're wondering why I'm here. Well, it's not what you think and—"

"Forget it. Just let me take a look at you," Luke said mildly. His golden brown gaze made a leisurely inspection from her head to her polished toenails. "You look good enough to eat."

"Well, that's the general idea." She groaned inwardly at the mishmash she was making of this. "I mean—"

Luke leaned forward and dammed the flow of babble with a kiss. "I've missed you."

Charlie melted under the heat of his gaze. "I've missed you, too," she whispered. "I wasn't trying to put you in an awkward position before. Honestly, Luke. Our... friendship has nothing to do with Milady."

"All week I've been kicking myself for being such a jerk." He ran his index finger under the shoulder strap of her dress, smiling slightly at the gooseflesh his touch raised. "I worried I'd pushed you too hard. I worried I was giving you too much space, then not enough. That you'd think I'd taken advantage of you and never want to see me again after such a stupid ultimatum."

Her laugh was wobbly. "Hardly. I've spent most of my time trying to figure out a way to explain without sacrificing my pride," she confessed.

"Me, too. I'd decided crawling to Evening Star on my hands and knees might work."

"Sounds a bit drastic." Charlie's smile was tremulous. "Maybe I could persuade you to have dinner with me instead?"

He trailed his finger across the back of her hand. "Any special reason?"

"As a matter of fact, there is. I need someone to help me celebrate. You're looking at a woman who's just received a major commission for four stained-glass windows from the Charleston Historical Society."

"Charlie, that's wonderful!" Luke's wide smile was full of admiration and pride. He smacked a kiss on each cheek. "Congratulations!"

"I'm really on my way at last," she said, pink and breathless with pleasure. "At least I think so."

"Wait a minute." Luke drew back with a sudden frown. "This doesn't mean you're going back to Charleston, is it?"

She reached out and flicked a button on his shirt. "Would you care?"

"Don't kid me, Charlie," he growled, catching her hand.

"I just wondered." Her smile was satisfied. "No, I can work here. There's a possibility I'd have to deliver the panels and see to their installation, but that's down the road. So, will you have dinner with me? I'm buying."

"Now that's an offer I can't refuse." His thumb made lazy circles in her palm. "Where do you want to go?"

Charlie was having a hard time thinking about anything but the languorous feelings his touch evoked. She stirred herself with an effort. "I've never been to the Mariner on Sibley Lake, but I've heard it's good."

"It is, but I need to get cleaned up. Let's run by my house, and I'll buy you a drink while I change."

"Deal."

A short time later Charlie was sipping a mineral water and lime and watching the splendor of a Louisiana dusk spread over Sibley Lake through the floor-to-ceiling windows at the rear of Luke's house. The air conditioner hummed softly, and she could hear Luke's shower running. She smiled to herself, pleased that their relationship was back on a friendly footing. Where it would lead, she wasn't certain, but being with him was such a simple and complete joy that for now it was enough.

The phone shrilled, and she hesitated, then went to pick it up. "Dr. Duval's residence." A harried farmer on the other end of the line poured a frantic tale of woe into her ear. "Just a moment. I'll get him."

Charlie tapped on Luke's bedroom door, then pushed it open. "Luke? There's a client on the phone...."

He appeared at the door of the connecting master bath, one towel hitched around his lean hips, another rubbing at his tousled mane, and her breath stopped short at the sight. The width of his shoulders and the corrugated muscles of his flat belly, dusted with a thatch of fair hair, made her mouth go dry.

She would have hastily backed from the room, but as Luke picked up the bedside extension phone, he stopped her with a wave. Helpless, she allowed herself the luxury of observing him through her lashes, her heart thumping as she admired the lean and muscular length of his legs, the play of tissue and tendon down his bare arms and back. She didn't even try to follow his one-sided conversation and was startled when he slammed the phone down with a muttered curse.

''What is it?''

Luke's mouth twisted into a rueful line. ''God, I'm sorry, Charlie. We're going to have to postpone your celebration. Bill Dozier's prize bull is down.'' He draped the towel he held over his shoulders and shrugged apologetically. ''That's the life of a vet. It's always fire engine stuff.''

''Fire engine?''

''Emergencies. Like now, damn it.'' He raked his fingers through his damp hair.

His chagrin was so obvious that her disappointment took second place to her desire to reassure him. ''It's all right. I understand. Do you have to go right now?''

''I told him I'd be out within the hour. We could still go on over to the restaurant, but I'd have to leave you there.''

Charlie smiled at his frustrated expression and walked over to stand in front of him. She grabbed the two ends of the towel hanging over his shoulders and tugged his head down, brushing his lips with hers. ''Don't worry about it, I said.''

Luke pulled her close, kissing her gently. "A truly understanding woman," he murmured, then broke off with a sudden indrawn breath.

"Something wrong?"

"Did you realize someone forgot to put a back on this dress?" His voice was hoarse, and his hand splayed out warmly over her bare spine, inching down inside the dress to the upper curve of her hips.

"I was wondering if you'd noticed," she purred. She ran her palms down the hard planes of his chest, then paused tantalizingly at the line of damp terry at his hips. "Luke?"

He groaned in her ear. "Hmm?"

She leaned against him, slowly tugging the towel free. "I say let's forget about dinner."

"I'VE GOT TO GO."

"I know."

Charlie rubbed her hands across Luke's sweat-dampened back, waiting for her heart to recover from the aftershocks of fast, furious and totally satisfying love-making.

"No, I mean, I've *really* got to go." Luke's warm breath caressed the side of her neck as he lay atop her in his wide bed, utterly sated and relaxed.

"Uh-huh."

"When I can move again." He drew a deep breath. "Lord-a-mercy! How did that happen?"

Her voice was demure but faintly amused. "I believe I seduced you."

"You shameless hussy." Lifting his head, Luke smiled down at her, his tawny eyes full of laughter.

"I don't seem to have any willpower where you're concerned," she admitted.

"When I get my strength back, remind me to thank you."

"Mr. Dozier's waiting," she reminded him, nibbling at his shoulder with her teeth.

"Yeah." He rolled onto his side, propping his head in his hand. The other hand cupped her waist possessively and his leg pinned hers. "We've got to stop meeting like this. I want us to take our time."

"Who's complaining?" she asked, blushing. "That was perfect, except for one tiny detail."

"What?"

She giggled and tugged at the bedclothes. "These sheets are cotton."

"At least it's a step up from feed sacks," he said with a chuckle. His expression sobered, and he ran a fingertip along her collarbone. "I don't suppose I could persuade you to stay the night?"

Charlie glanced away. "I can't."

"Okay." He sighed regretfully. "Dozier's bull could take a while, anyway."

"You'd better go."

"You're a nag, you know that?" He lowered his head and feasted on her lips. "A beautiful sexy nag."

"Sweet talk will get you everything, but not right now," she said, laughing breathlessly. "Get going."

Luke rolled to his feet and went to the walk-in closet in search of clothes. Charlie got up, her limbs still undeniably shaky, and slipped on a shirt Luke had thrown carelessly across a chair. It covered her modestly to midthigh, and she buttoned it as she headed for the kitchen. When Luke joined her a few minutes later, tucking his shirttail into his jeans and pulling on his boots, she'd assembled two huge Dagwood sandwiches out of everything she could find in his refrigerator.

"Eat first," she ordered.

"I'll take them with me," he said, scooping up the paper plate one-handed. "Thanks."

"I'll lock the door when I leave," Charlie called after him.

Luke paused at the back door, then deliberately set down his sandwiches and returned to snatch her into his arms and kiss her until she was dizzy and clinging weakly to him.

"You look so absolutely right standing in my kitchen barefoot and naked and rosy with my loving," he murmured.

"I'm not naked."

"You will be if I stay another minute. I'll take a rain check on dinner, okay? Tomorrow?"

"All right." She took a deep breath and fiddled nervously with the buttons on his shirt. "Howard's got a filly running at Louisiana Downs tomorrow afternoon. If you're free, maybe you'd like to go and we could have dinner in Shreveport?"

"With Howard and Gina?"

Lifting her head, she met his gaze squarely. "If you want. I'm not trying to prove anything to my family, but they may as well get used to seeing us together."

Luke's eyes blazed with a golden fire. "I like the sound of that. Charlie..."

Her fingers brushed his lips, halting his words. "Don't say anything else. One step at a time, remember?"

Disappointment clouded his expression, replaced almost immediately by a look of impatient resignation. "All right, Charlie. For now." She smiled softly, and he groaned again, swallowed harshly, then released her with an effort.

"You're temptation incarnate," he said with a strained laugh. "The races it is, then, if I can get someone to cover for me. I'll call you tomorrow."

Long after he'd slammed out the back door and gunned his truck down the driveway, Charlie stood grinning into space. When she finally came back to herself, she took pains cleaning up the kitchen and remaking the tumbled bed. Mischievously she even took her atomizer and sprayed the pillows with her scent. If Dr. Luke Duval returned to his bed tonight, she hoped he'd find it as hard to sleep as she knew she would.

She was still in a euphoric mood when she drove down the dark lane to Evening Star sometime later. The house was empty, with Gina and Howard still out, and Milady had apparently already retired to her own rooms. Even Miss Scarlett had disappeared for the night, but Charlie's attitude was so buoyant that she couldn't make herself go to bed yet. She was in the process of dragging out her portfolio to work on the design for Louise Bewley's new bay window when the phone shrilled, and she hurried to the foyer to answer it before it could disturb Milady.

"Hello?"

Tyler's enraged voice blared in her ear. "Just where the hell have you been?"

CHAPTER TEN

GUILT, FEAR, hopelessness, rage.

Emotions produced by years of conditioning poured through Charlie at the sound of Tyler's voice. So many times his brutal verbal assaults had begun unexpectedly, sundering the foundations of her confidence, shredding her ability to defend herself. With an enormous effort Charlie caught hold of her reeling senses. No longer did she have to answer to this man.

"Go to hell, Tyler!"

She slammed the phone into its cradle, then began to shake violently in reaction. A minute later the phone's peal jarred her again, making her jump. For an instant she contemplated letting it ring, then her jaw firmed. No, she'd come too far to let Tyler intimidate her now. She lifted the receiver to her ear.

"What do you want?"

"Don't hang up, please. Charlotte, I'm sorry." Tyler's mellow tones were calm, abject with remorse. "I didn't mean to upset you, darlin'. I've been trying to get in touch with you all evening and I was worried, that's all."

"I'm not upset," Charlie declared coldly. "I simply will not tolerate rudeness . . . from anyone."

"Now you sound like Milady," Tyler said with a deep laugh. "How is the old lady? Does she ask about her favorite grandson-in-law?"

"She's well, thank you, and no, she doesn't. Is your concern for Milady's health the only reason for this call?"

Tyler's "tsks" of reproach echoed over the lines. "My, you're prickly tonight, darlin'. Actually, I wanted to tell you how proud I am of you. Bunny told me about your coup with the Historical Society. You *are* serious about this art thing, aren't you?"

Charlie didn't bother to hide her annoyance. "I always have been."

"Well, when you come back to Charleston, maybe we can see about building that studio you were always nattering on about—"

"I'm not coming back to Charleston."

"Now, Charlotte, I know we've had a lack of communication in the past, but I'm willing to work on it."

"Well, I'm not," Charlie said flatly.

"Listen here, darlin'," Tyler ordered, "you've had your fling down there with those trashy friends of yours. Don't you think it's about time you quit slumming and came back where you belong?"

"I can't believe you have the nerve to say such a thing!" Charlie gasped. "We're divorced, Tyler."

"A mere technicality, sweetness. My lawyers inform me I can contest the action."

"Why?" Horror-stricken, Charlie clasped the receiver to her ear with both hands, her voice hoarse. "Why would you want to?"

"Darlin', I miss you. I really do. Everyone says we're the perfect couple, you know. We've let our friends down. We've let ourselves down. No matter what our problems, I've always loved you. I still love you."

"No." The word was a whispered denial of that obscene lie.

"I can see we can't settle this over the phone. I'll come and see you—"

"No!" This time Charlie's word was a shout. "Don't come here, Tyler. It would be a waste of time."

"Don't think I won't fight for what I want, Charlotte." Tyler's tone was soft and silky with menace. "We belong together."

"Forget it." Against the lurching of her stomach, Charlie fought to keep her voice steady. "I don't want anything to do with you, Tyler. If you come here, I'll have the sheriff on you with a restraining order so fast your head will swim."

"Threats, Charlotte?" Tyler laughed in her ear. "How unbecoming. And how useless. You know I always get what I want in the end, and I *will* get you back."

"You've lost your mind, obviously. Don't come, and don't call. We're through, and that's final."

"Don't be stubborn," Tyler returned angrily. "You can't afford to cut yourself off from me."

"What? Why?"

His laugh was a taunt. "Ask Howard."

Then he hung up.

Mystified, Charlie listened to the buzz of the dial tone for a shocked moment, then her knees turned to jelly and her gorge rose. She barely made it to the hall bathroom in time.

When the spasms eased, she leaned over the commode weakly, giving mental thanks she hadn't eaten one of Luke's Dagwood sandwiches herself. A damp washcloth appeared in her field of vision.

"Here," Milady said, "wipe your mouth."

Embarrassed, Charlie flushed the toilet and shakily accepted the cloth, rubbing the cool terry over her flushed face. "Thank you."

Milady, looking tiny in a lace-edged dressing gown, eyed her narrowly. "You sure you're through?"

"Positive."

"So is it the flu or are you pregnant?"

Charlie stiffened, and her lips felt numb. "Neither."

"Are you sure? I may be old, but I'm not blind. You're seeing Luke Duval, aren't you?"

Charlie carefully folded the washcloth on the edge of the sink and reached for her toothbrush. "That's none of your business."

"Don't be impertinent to me, miss! I just don't want you to get your tail caught in a crack."

"It's my tail." She rinsed her mouth and slid the brush back into the rack. "Besides, it's clear I'm not able to carry children."

"Is that what the doctors say?"

"It's what *I* say."

Milady sniffed. "Well, you'd best be careful, anyway."

"But wouldn't that suit your plans to marry me off again?" Charlie asked nastily.

"It might, except why would any man buy the cow when he's getting the milk for free?" Milady asked in disgust. "I gave you more credit than that, Charlotte."

"And that's exactly why I won't marry again," Charlie retorted angrily. "Simply to avoid those kinds of destructive, dominating games. Tyler's still trying to use them on me."

Milady's gray eyes flashed behind her golden-rimmed glasses. "He was the one who called?"

"Yes."

"What did he want?"

"Some lunacy about wanting to come here to see me to work things out." Charlie laughed harshly. "You see what the very idea did to me."

Milady frowned. "A reaction like that means something, Charlotte. Maybe you should hear him out—"

"No!"

"But—"

"I said no!" Tears sparkled in Charlie's eyes. "How dare you try to interfere again? Haven't you done enough? I may have to live here, and your age demands a certain respect, but you've lost the right to any affection from me with all your secrets and manipulations."

"Charlotte!"

"Enough is enough, Milady," Charlie said, ignoring the hurt in the old woman's eyes. "You don't own me. From now on, stay out of my life!"

"YOU'RE AWFULLY QUIET."

Charlie set the racing form down on the small table in Howard's private box at Louisiana Downs the next afternoon and smiled at Luke. "You would be, too, if you'd just lost ten dollars on the daily double."

"Rich artist types like you can afford it."

Luke stretched his arm along the back of her chair, idly watching the parade of horses taking the course for the next race. The towering glass wall of the grandstand separated them from the fierce afternoon heat, letting them enjoy the drama of Thoroughbred racing in air-conditioned comfort. On the infield the electronic tote board flashed a constantly changing display of odds and payoffs.

Charlie laughed. "If that were only true! The Historical Society is giving me an advance on the commission, but the materials to do it right will cost a small fortune."

"Is that what's got you so preoccupied?" He leaned toward her, tugging gently at a curl behind her ear, and his voice went low. "Or dare I hope it's something else?"

Charlie flushed and straightened the crease in her white linen trousers. "Have I been ignoring you? I'm sorry."

"Admit it. You've been miles away for the past hour. I guess I'm paranoid, but I keep thinking maybe you've decided last night was a mistake."

Startled, Charlie looked up into Luke's golden brown gaze, and her color deepened further, her cheeks nearly matching the deep rose of her blouse. "N-no, it's not that."

"Then what's bothering you?"

She looked away, following the line of horses and jockeys in their bright silks as they made their way to the starting gate. Although she felt the impulse to blurt out about Tyler's disturbing phone call, his veiled threat to contest their divorce and her uneasy suspicion that somehow Howard was involved with him, she bit her lip and held her peace. After all, there was nothing Luke could do, and she had to learn to deal with her problems herself. Instead, she shrugged.

"I didn't mean to be poor company. Milady and I had another disagreement last night, that's all."

"What about?"

She shook her head. "It wasn't important."

"But—"

"Drop it, Luke. Please."

He sighed and rubbed his knuckle down her cheek. "All right, but I hate to see you at odds with your grandmother. You're both as hardheaded as they come, you know."

"Thanks for that wonderful assessment of my character." She pulled a face at him.

"Oops." He grinned, unrepentant. "Time to change the subject, huh? So, who do you like in the next race?"

Relenting, she bent over the racing form with him. "Howard's filly, of course. Here she is—Diamond Lady, number four. Fifteen to one odds. She's not the favorite, but the jockey's experienced, and Howard's positive she'll come in with the leaders."

"Let's hope she does better than those other 'sure things' Howard's been giving us advice on."

"If it's any consolation, he hasn't done any better than the rest of us," Charlie said with a laugh. "Worse, in fact, if the looks Gina's been giving him mean anything."

"Poor devil. Nothing worse than a nagging woman," Luke teased with a lecherous gleam.

"You men!" Charlie spluttered, then thrust some bills at him. "Here. Go place this on Diamond Lady to win before I throttle you."

"A whole two dollars? Yes, ma'am, anything for the lady who likes to live dangerously." Luke scraped his chair back just as Gina, looking spicy as a chili pepper in hot pink, fuchsia and acid green separates, appeared at the box's open rail.

"Luke, you darling. Bring me a fresh margarita on the way back, will you?" Gina pursed her lips and pouted prettily. "I'm positively dry and Howard's too busy talking business with every horse owner here to look after me."

"It'll be my pleasure, Gina." He cocked an inquiring sandy brow at Charlie. "You want anything?"

She smiled up at him, liking the way his navy knit shirt stretched over his broad shoulders. "As you said, I like to live dangerously. Surprise me."

Luke nodded, then turned to make his way up the stairs to the promenade containing betting windows and concession stands. Gina slipped behind the railing and gratefully sank into another chair.

"Whew!" she said, fanning herself with her program. "Some of these horse folks can talk your ears right off your head!"

"You and Howard certainly seem to know a lot of people," Charlie commented.

"You know racing. Dallas, New Orleans, Hot Springs—they come from all over." She shrugged. "But you never know when connections like this will come in handy. In fact, one of the track officials was asking me if I wanted to help with a charity fund-raiser connected with next fall's Super Derby."

"What's that, honey?" Howard asked, sliding his bulk into a seat beside his wife. A faint sheen of moisture shone on his brow, and the malty odor of beer hung over him. "Kaiser been trying to sweet-talk you again?"

"Just to run a fashion show."

"With your experience it sounds like a good idea." Howard's dark eyes glowed, and his voice was a bit too loud, a tad too jovial as he leaned toward Charlie. "My little lady has a way with those ritzy folks, Charlotte. She could sell an Eskimo a refrigerator if she took a mind to."

Gina tittered and brushed her shoulder against Howard's. "But why should I want to, sugar, when I've got a big, strong man like you to take care of me?"

Howard guffawed and squeezed Gina in a beefy hug. "She sure is sassy, ain't she? But she knows which side her bread's buttered on, that's for certain."

"That's because you do it so well, sugar," Gina purred.

Charlie laughed with the clowning couple, but a sudden doubt niggled at the back of her mind as she took in Gina's designer clothes and sumptuous jewelry. Though less flashy in his dress, Howard sported a Rolex on his wrist, and Charlie knew an owner's box didn't come cheap. For the first time she wondered if the good life Howard and Gina led was really within their means.

She'd assumed all of Howard and Milady's altercations over Evening Star's finances were due to differences in temperament, but what if it was more than that? And what exactly had Tyler meant by that ominous "Ask Howard?" Perhaps she had no right to pry into Evening Star's financial affairs after abdicating her interest for so many years, but if Tyler thought he had some leverage over her, she had to find out what it was. At the first opportunity she was going to have a serious discussion with Howard.

Gina stretched and languidly fanned again. "Speaking of bread and butter, Charlie," she said, "Howard said you turned down an opportunity to dust Frank Murphy's farm. Considering your recent, er . . . financial difficulties, I can't believe you'd give up the chance to make oodles of money flying."

On the step above the box, Luke hesitated with a loaded tray in his hands. Charlie hadn't mentioned the offer to him, and now his stomach twisted at the thought of her going up on a regular basis. Maybe he didn't have the right to feel so protective and possessive, but the operative word to add to that phrase was *yet*.

Charlie accepted Gina's comment with a shrug. "It gets complicated if I do it for other people. I'd have to take a refresher course to get a permanent aerial applicator's certification, and there's all sorts of paperwork. Besides, my time will be limited once I begin on my commission, and that's what I want to concentrate on now."

"And it's tough, hot, dirty work for a woman," Luke said, joining them. "Not to mention dangerous."

"Spoken like a true chauvinist," Charlie returned tartly. Her green eyes sparked with a militant light. "Dodging power lines and handling potentially toxic chemicals isn't a sex-linked talent."

"Better back off, boy," Howard advised sotto voce. "You ain't gonna win this one."

"Ouch. You're right." Luke grinned and passed Howard a beer. "Hunger's taken my brain out of gear, obviously. Mea culpa, Charlie. I only meant that crop dusting can be a risky proposition and I'd be concerned about any friend of mine pursuing it."

"No riskier than anything else, if you know what you're doing," Charlie replied. She lifted her chin and looked him straight in the eye. "And my daddy taught me not to take chances."

Was there a message in her words? Luke wondered. A warning? "But—"

"Better a nacho in your mouth than your foot," Gina interrupted with a laugh, reaching for her lime-green margarita. "And the way you're going, Luke, it's a good thing you brought enough food for a siege."

"By all means, eat," Charlie ordered, dubiously eyeing the mound of jalapeño-topped nachos, sausage po-boys, chips and cold drinks.

"Maybe you're right." Luke nodded and handed the food around, finally passing Charlie a giant cup of frozen strawberry yogurt. "For you."

Her lips curled upward in a reluctant smile. "Trying to sweeten me up?"

"Always, princess." Luke's voice held a husky intimacy that touched her cheeks with color. She tasted the creamy concoction, licking it from the spoon with sensual enjoyment.

"Maybe it'll work," she said softly, and touched the tip of her tongue to her upper lip to lap at a drop of sweetness that lingered there.

Luke swallowed hard. He was really a hopeless case, he thought. She only had to look at him, and all he could think of was making love to her again. He wanted to whisk her off somewhere where it would only be the two of them and pour out all that was in his heart, but instinct told him she was still too vulnerable to push.

It was aggravating and confusing for a man who had always been the one in control of his relationships, the one who called the shots. But this time he was the one who wanted assurances and sweet words of commitment. Even though they'd made love, he still had the feeling that for every step forward he took toward Charlie, she retreated two. It was damn frustrating.

The track announcer's voice boomed over the PA system. "They're at the post."

Instantly Howard was on his feet. "This is it," he said, his words tense. "Come on, Diamond Lady—it's now or never."

Luke and the women turned their attention to the track and the distant starting gate located on the backside stretch. There was a hush, then the clang of the starting bell, and the announcer's explosive: "They're off!"

The horses bolted from the gate, and the crowd noise grew. Gina's excited cries rose as Diamond Lady held her own near the head of the pack. The horses raced down the backside and took the first turn.

"Look, she's in the lead!" Gina shouted, jumping up and catching Howard's arm. The tension and excitement in the grandstand made the air crackle, and the wall of sound became a roar as the battling horses took the home turn.

There was a sudden groan from Howard. Diamond Lady fell back, passed by one, two, three, then four other horses as they raced toward the finish line. The announcer called off the three winning horses, and Howard sat down heavily.

"Oh, too bad, hon," Gina murmured, patting his arm. "I thought for a moment..."

"Yeah, I did, too." There was a curious whiteness about the corners of his mouth, but he made a grimace that was almost a smile. "Well, *c'est la vie*, as they say. The accountants will be glad to have another write-off."

Charlie spoke hesitantly. "If you'd rather go home now, Howard, Luke and I don't mind."

Her cousin sat up straight. "Hell, no! Don't let a little thing like that worry you, Charlotte. All in a day's work for an owner, you know. I expect I'll have more winners once I get my own trainer situated at Evening Star where I can oversee things personally. You came here today for a good time, and that's what you're going to get."

"Don't put yourself out on our account," Luke said. "We're easy to please."

"Nonsense!" Howard reached for his beer cup, took a deep swig and gave a satisfied sigh. His eyes were bright again, his smile jovial, as if his disappointment over Diamond Lady's loss had never been. "We're going to show you both the best damn time you've ever had!" he insisted.

It would have been churlish to refuse, but as Luke nodded his agreement, Charlie's expression flickered, and Luke had the distinct impression that what he saw lurking behind her gray-green eyes was suspicion.

LUKE WAS SO BUSY over the next several days that he hardly found time to see Charlie or talk to her over the phone more than a few minutes at a time, much less concern himself with a fleeting and perhaps erroneous impression. He was contemplating a cool shower after a blistering day administering vaccinations to a herd of ill-tempered cattle and wondering if he could entice Charlie into going out for dinner when he opened his clinic door to pure chaos.

A long-legged man sprawled on his stomach in the middle of the floor, scrambling for something beneath the waiting room chairs. A high-pitched squealing rent the air, and from the rear kennels every dog in the place seemed to be howling his lungs out. A middle-aged woman clutching a shivering Chihuahua and an elderly man with a terrified cat stapled to his chest stood cringing on the seats of the chairs.

"What the hell—!" A small black-and-white streak of lightning zigzagged between Luke's boots, hightailing it on cloven hooves down the hall.

"Get him!" Rachel's blond head popped up from behind her desk. "Luke! Thank goodness! I—Rob, watch out!"

A second bolt of squealing animal lurched from under the chairs, and Rob Thompson grabbed for it, missed, bumped his head on a chair rung and came up cursing.

"Where the devil did these pigs come from?" Luke roared.

Rachel's expression was thoroughly miffed. Pattering down the hall after the retreating piglets, she jerked a thumb at Rob, who was sitting in the middle of the floor, holding his temple. "Ask him."

Luke groaned, extending a hand to his cousin and pulled him to his feet. "Good God, man! Are you raising your own bacon now?"

"It seemed like a good idea at the time," Rob mumbled, still rubbing the tender spot under his black hair. "I don't know how they got loose so quick. I was trying to show Rachel—Lord, she's mad. I'd better see if I can corral those pigs."

He followed the sounds of mayhem erupting from the rear of the clinic. Stifling a chuckle, Luke turned to help his shaken clients and their pets down from their perches on the chair seats. By the time he'd soothed their ruffled feelings, Rob had reappeared, retreating before a small blond termagant who held aloft two subdued piglets by their curly tails.

"And furthermore, if you *ever* create such a ruckus in here again, Rob Thompson," Rachel said sternly, "I'll ban you from the premises permanently, relation to the doctor or not! This is a place of business, not a barnyard. Now take these creatures—no, not like that! Hold them by their tails like I'm doing."

Rob hesitated, looking faintly horrified. "Doesn't it hurt?"

"No, of course not!" Rachel glared at him indignantly. "I wouldn't hurt a baby of any kind. They don't feel it, but they can't escape, either. Now, here."

Gingerly Rob grappled with the pigs' tails. Sure enough, the two miniature porkers hung upside down like a couple of complacent bats, silent except for a mildly interested snort or two. Rob was obviously at a loss what to do next, his homely face sporting a strained and baffled expression. Luke couldn't contain himself any longer. His rich laughter filled the office, and his clients added their own amused chuckles.

"Don't be so hard on the poor guy, Rachel," Luke said between chortles.

"Luke..." Rob grimaced, his expression pleading.

With another guffaw Luke relented. Wiping the tears of laughter from the corner of his eyes, he gave a helpless wave. "Let me get you a travel cage for your friends. Are they bound for the sausage maker, or have you given them names? I can't wait to see Mikey walking his hogs!"

"I was kind of thinking he could raise them as a 4-H Club project," Rob muttered.

"Mikey isn't even old enough to belong to the 4-H Club yet!" Rachel protested.

Her fists were perched on her rounded hips, and her attitude was still belligerent. While Luke retrieved a wire cage from under the front counter and expertly slipped the two contentedly swinging piglets into it, Rachel shook her finger in Rob's face and continued to give him a piece of her mind.

"I think this pet thing with Mikey is getting totally out of hand, Rob Thompson. You've bitten off more than you can chew. Why can't Mikey be satisfied with a dog and a cat like most kids? You've got to start getting this under control or the Humane Society will step in and—"

"Aw, it's not as bad as all that, Rachel," Luke interrupted with a grin. He gave Rob a companionable slap on the back and handed him the cage. "Is it, cuz? Take Porky and Porkette here home, and I'll stop by to check them out later."

"Sure." Rob ducked his head, mumbling. "Sorry about everything, Rachel. Er, thanks." Red-faced, he ambled out the door, holding the cage containing the Hampshire piglets straight out from his body as if he couldn't quite believe his eyes.

Rachel took a deep breath and smiled at the clients. "Mrs. Jamison, Mr. Parker. So sorry about all this. If you'll just step down the hall, the doctor will be with you in a moment."

With the clients ushered into their respective examination rooms, Rachel expertly pulled their pets' files from the cabinet behind her desk and handed them to Luke.

"Never a dull moment around here, is there?" he asked mildly.

"Really, Luke," Rachel said, still exasperated, "I think you need to have a serious talk with your cousin. I understand his wanting to make up for Mikey's not having a mother in any way possible, but really! How many pets does he think a child needs? If you weren't giving him a discount, he'd need a good banker just to afford all the veterinary bills."

Luke gave Rachel an affectionate chuck under her chin. "You know, for someone who's usually as bright as a button, you can be a real dodo sometimes."

"Now what's *that* supposed to mean?"

"Don't tell me you had no idea Rob's been gathering animals like Noah before the flood just so he could come in to see you."

"Me!" Rachel's mouth made a perfect O of amazement.

"Absolutely you." Luke nodded with sagelike solemnity. "I'd say he's been smitten by a pint-size Venus."

"Well, he's got a funny way of showing it!" Rachel gulped. "Why doesn't he just ask me out?"

"I told you he's kind of a shy guy. He'll get around to it." Luke turned toward the examining rooms.

Rachel propped her chin in her palm and stared sourly into space. "Yeah? Before or after he brings in that herd of elephants?"

"YOU DON'T MEAN IT!" Charlie said with an incredulous laugh. "Pigs?"

Rachel giggled and nodded as she and Charlie fol-

lowed a skipping Mikey out of the arts building after the
next morning's session of Charlie's class. "It wasn't funny
at the time, but the more I think about it . . ."

"It must have been something to see," Charlie agreed
with a smirk. "And I guess it explains these." She held out
a sheaf of Mikey's drawings, showing black-and-white
splotches. "I thought they were Holstein cows, not
Hampshire hogs. No wonder he gave me such a funny
look when I asked if they gave milk."

Laughing, they pushed through the double glass doors
into the steamy July heat and paused on the sidewalk.

"Wait up a sec, Mikey," Rachel called, digging into her
straw shoulder bag for her keys.

"Okay, Miss Rachel!" Mikey changed his beeline from
Rachel's car, waiting in the parking lot, to a gnarled and
multibranched old crape myrtle that had become his favorite climbing tree. Scrambling like a monkey, he found
a notch with his tennis shoe, boosted himself onto the first
low branch, then flipped over and hung upside down by s
knees, waving at the ladies.

"Wow, he's full of energy today," Rachel said.

"After a morning cooped up inside, they're all ready to
run and romp," Charlie agreed. "I can hardly believe his
two weeks are almost over already. He's such a sweet kid.
I'm going to miss him."

"Yeah, I know what you mean," Rachel agreed. Her
expression was a bit distracted, but Charlie dismissed the
flicker of loneliness behind Rachel's cornflower-blue eyes
as a product of her own disturbed thoughts.

Try as she might, she hadn't been able to get anything
substantial from Howard regarding Evening Star's financial status. Whether he was being deliberately vague
or merely patronizingly contemptuous of a woman's

ability to comprehend such matters, she was unable to determine.

To compound her frustration, she and Luke had seen little of each other over the past week. All sorts of "fire engine" work had kept him occupied every day and most nights, and doubts flayed Charlie. Having left a disastrous marriage, and being a novice at love affairs, she was too cautious to put a name to her growing need for Luke.

She hungered for him on a basic, physical level, and she longed for his warmth and understanding on an emotional level, but the force of her feelings gave her pause. Was she falling back into a cycle of dependency? The possibility frightened her immeasurably. At all costs she had to keep her hard-won sense of independence. She had learned the hard way how much it hurt when you lost that essential part of yourself.

So even while she longed to tear down the walls, another part of herself kept adding stones, and the conflict within her own heart made her glad in a way that nothing more had been said about continuing their physical relationship. Until she was more certain of herself, her strengths, what she truly wanted—perhaps that was best for both of them.

Charlie blinked away that painful thought and turned the conversation to a more cheerful subject.

"By the way, have you talked to Becky since we went shopping?" she asked Rachel. Charlie, Rachel and Becky Turner had made a ladies' day of mall shopping and lunch in Alexandria the previous Saturday.

Rachel shook her head. "No, why?"

"It seems you're going to have an opportunity to wear those smashing new outfits you bought sooner than you expected," Charlie confided. "Audrey and her boyfriend announced they're getting married. Church wedding, reception, everything—in two weeks!''

"No kidding! Mrs. Gilchrist must be frantic with the preparations."

"For having such an event sprung on them like this, Becky says everything's more or less under control." Charlie walked side by side with Rachel up the blistering sidewalk toward their parked car. "Becky's going to be matron of honor, Regan is the flower girl, and they've even talked Mikey into being ring bearer."

"That little scamp!" Rachel said with a laugh. "He never said a word this morning."

Charlie smiled. "Ring bearing takes second place to pigs, didn't you know?"

Rachel's reply was cut off by a sudden thump and a shrill wail of pain.

"Mikey!"

The little boy sat at the base of the crape myrtle, clutching his arm and shrieking in terror. Rachel got to him first, and her face blanched at the crimson spurting from under his fingers. Whipping off her neck scarf, she wrapped the wound, applying pressure, and lifted the sobbing child into her arms.

"Hush, Mikey, hush," she crooned. "It's going to be all right."

"How bad is it?" Charlie asked, startled at the amount of blood already staining the child's shirt and shorts.

Rachel shook her head and swallowed. "We need a doctor—fast."

CHAPTER ELEVEN

CHARLIE PACED the highly polished tiles in the corridor of the Natchitoches General Hospital Emergency Room, wrinkling her nose at the acrid smell of disinfectant. It was interesting how an odor could evoke a strong emotional memory, she thought. Against her will, images of another hospital flickered across her mind's eye: the green of scrub-suited nurses moving briskly about their mysterious business, the prick of a needle against the soft flesh of her arm, the giant claw of pain ripping her unborn child from her womb.

"Where is he?"

Rob Thompson's abrupt question jerked Charlie from her own private misery. He strode toward her, his homely face etched with fear. Charlie reached out to him instinctively, placing a calming hand on his tanned forearm.

"Mikey's in there with Rachel." She indicated the closed door of an examination room. "It's not too serious, just a bad gash, but the doctor wouldn't do anything until you were here to sign the papers."

Grim-lipped, Rob nodded, gave her hand a grateful squeeze, then entered the room. Before the door swung shut again, Charlie got a brief glimpse of Mikey, white-faced and wide-eyed, lying on a gurney with Rachel standing at his side, animatedly spinning some yarn to keep them both occupied.

"Damn," Charlie muttered, and resumed her pacing. If a hospital environment made a full-grown adult like herself nervous, what must all those shiny instruments and menacing machines be doing to a five-year-old? Thank goodness both Rob and Rachel were here now.

After a few minutes, the door opened again, and Rachel appeared, her expression strained and pale. Charlie stepped forward and placed her hand on the shorter woman's shoulder. "Are you all right? How's Mikey?"

Rachel blinked owlishly. "Oh, Charlie. You're still here."

"Of course." Charlie frowned. "You'd better sit down. You look wobbly."

Rachel drew a shaky breath. "I'm okay, and so is Mikey. They're bandaging his arm now. It took eight stitches to close that wound."

"My goodness! All from hitting a broken stub when he fell?"

"He was lucky it wasn't worse." Rachel swallowed. "I think I will sit down a minute."

Charlie ushered her to one of a series of chairs lining the wall. "How about some coffee? There's a machine—"

"I'm late getting back for work. I need to call Luke—"

"I've already talked to him. He said take as long as we need. Maybe I should go in for you. You'll have to go home to change, anyway."

Rachel looked down in surprise at the reddish-brown splotches of drying blood smeared across her blouse and slacks. "I hadn't realized."

"I'm in awe, Rachel. You really were coolheaded."

Rachel shook her head, laughing weakly. "Not me. But you should have seen how Mikey took everything once we got him settled down. That's one gutsy kid." Suddenly she flushed and laughed again. "And do you know what that little troublemaker did?"

"No, what?"

"While I was blathering on, asking him about his being a ring bearer, he took the notion that he wasn't going to be in Audrey's wedding unless I'd come, too, and sit in the pew with Rob so he wouldn't be lonely! Wouldn't let the doctor stitch him until I'd promised."

"That rascal!" Charlie grinned at Rachel's chagrined expression. "You stay put. I'll get that coffee."

She was up the hall at the vending machines fumbling for change when Rob came out of the room, spotted Rachel and went over to her.

"Rachel." His voice was a deep rumble in his chest. "Thanks for everything. I don't know what I'd have done if you hadn't been there."

Rachel gulped for breath, and her yellow curls quivered. "It was all my fault. You trusted me to take care of him, but I only had my back turned for a minute and—"

Rob hunkered down in front of her chair, frowning. "Whoa, there, honey. You're shaking like a leaf. You've been the Rock of Gibraltar. Don't go to pieces on me now."

"I'm so sorry," she said, almost on a wail. "You must think I'm a terrible, careless person—"

"I do no such thing!" Rob reached out and pulled her against his shoulder. Her head nestled in the crook of his neck, a bright contrast to the pitch-black of his hair. "Shh," he murmured, "I think you're great. Gosh, things like this happen all the time when you're a parent. Mikey's lucky he's got a friend like you."

She pulled back, embarrassed. "Look, you don't have to take me to Audrey's wedding. That son of yours—"

"Did his tongue-tied dad a favor. I wouldn't dream of letting you weasel out on me, okay?"

"But—"

Impulsively Rob leaned forward and kissed her. "I mean it. Okay?" he repeated softly, anxiously.

Rachel's blue eyes were the size of saucers. "O-okay."

Standing at the coffee machine, Charlie began to smile. Her smile widened even further when a nurse peeked out of the examination room.

"Mr. Thompson? You and your wife can come back in now."

Rob rose without correcting the nurse, pulling Rachel up beside him. With his arm looped possessively around her waist, they walked through the door together.

Charlie lifted the tepid cup of coffee to her lips, not even minding the cardboardy taste. Cheerfully she considered the prospect of answering the phone for Luke during the afternoon. Unless she missed her guess, his receptionist had just taken the rest of the day off.

"MORE COFFEE, Miss Scarlett?"

Charlie poured the lukewarm dregs of her Saturday morning coffee into her saucer and placed it on the floor for the old dog. Miss Scarlett's toenails tapped across the wooden floor, then, with the air of a queen performing a boon, she daintily lapped the milky liquid.

"You treat that animal better than you do your own grandma," Sudie said from the sink.

Charlie reached down and gingerly scratched Miss Scarlett's ruff. "She doesn't bite—at least not as often as Milady does."

"Hmph. That isn't a very Christian attitude. And your grandma isn't as hearty as she once was. You can ask Dr. Melford if you don't believe me."

Charlie placed her chin in her palm and sighed. "Sudie, don't lecture me, please. You know better than anyone why Milady and I aren't getting along."

"I also recollect how Miss Margaret's raised you up since your mama died, God rest her soul. That ought to count for something."

"It does, of course, but all my life I've had the feeling Milady's tried to make me over into my mother. I've tried to please her, but I've reached the point where I've got to be *me*, not what Milady thinks I should be."

"Yes, I can see that, honey," Sudie said tiredly, wiping her wet hands on a dishcloth. "You always had too much of your daddy inside you to go down without a fight, no matter how sweet you looked on the outside."

"They sent me a picture of Daddy's marker," Charlie said, looking out the French doors. In the backyard Pigeon and Hector were setting up sprinklers to water the wilting azaleas and beds of striped caladiums and hot-pink impatiens.

"Maybe you can visit his grave someday. That would be a healing." Sudie poured herself a cup of fresh coffee and sat down at the oak table with Charlie. "Your daddy wouldn't expect you to take on so about not knowing about him. After all, the man was a tumbleweed by his own choice! Why, I can just hear him laughing, poking fun like he used to over what a trick he'd played on us all."

"Maybe you're right," Charlie said slowly. "I suppose Milady thought she was doing the best thing."

Sudie patted Charlie's hand. "There you go. You got to forgive her. After all, she loves you best in the world."

Guilt made Charlie's heart buck. "Maybe. After Evening Star, that is."

"Now, Miss Charlie..." Sudie's chocolate-brown eyes were reproachful.

"I'll try, Sudie, I promise. It's just that making peace with Milady is like waltzing through a minefield."

"Well, there's lots of ways to be a loving granddaughter. I'm just wishing you can find your right path before too much longer." Sudie rose and rinsed out her cup, frowning out the window over the sink. "Look at that Hector! Don't he know Pigeon's supposed to be up to the horse barn helping with Mr. Howard's new horses?"

"They're here already?" Charlie asked in surprise.

"Delivered yesterday. Pigeon's flat beside himself over working with a real trainer. Course nobody's seen hide nor hair of *him* yet." Sudie busied herself washing out the coffeepot, muttering under her breath. "Those animals don't look like much to me, leastways not for what Mr. Howard paid for them, but what do *I* know about such-like? Hector asks me."

"I'm not so sure about some of Howard's enterprises myself," Charlie confessed, chewing her lip.

Taking Sudie's words to heart, it occurred to her that part of being a dutiful granddaughter to Milady was making certain Evening Star was safeguarded and its assets weren't being squandered. If she and Milady couldn't see eye to eye on anything else, perhaps they could still find common ground when it came to their home. Perhaps her fears were groundless, Charlie thought, and Howard could easily alleviate them with a few minutes' explanation. It was simply a matter of asking the right questions in a tactful manner. Throwing down her napkin, she went to look for Howard.

She found out shortly that what she considered tactful and what Howard thought were two different things altogether.

"Why, Charlotte, I'm deeply hurt," Howard said. He sat behind his desk in the study, his dark eyes glistening with rebuke. "Are you accusing me of trying to hide something from you and Milady?"

"No, certainly not." Charlie let out a deep, exasperated breath and shoved her hands into the back pockets of her jeans. "All I wanted was to see Evening Star's books. I'd just like to know how we stand financially. That's a reasonable request, don't you think?"

"Really, I haven't got the time to go into all that now, dear. Besides, it's all fairly complicated—mortgages, second mortgages, crop liens and the like." He waved his thick hand vaguely. "I've got to check those new horses this morning and then get out to the western quarter. That milo you planted is coming up nicely, by the way."

"I'm glad to hear it." Stubbornly she refused to be sidetracked. "But back to the books. I don't mind digging it out for myself."

"Now see here, Charlotte," Howard blustered, rising to his feet. "Much as I'd love to humor your whim, I'm not quite certain where all this sudden concern is coming from. It seems a bit mercenary for you to develop a proprietorial interest after years of neglect, don't you think?"

Charlie blushed. "Perhaps it does, but that's not my intention. I'd simply like to be apprised of the situation so Milady and I can discuss it—"

"Well, that really tears it!" Howard slammed a folder down on his desktop, and his swarthy face went dull red with suppressed rage. "First you don't trust me, and now you're trying to undermine the trust I've built up with Milady over nine years!"

"There's no need to get so defensive," Charlie protested.

"I'll bet Luke Duval's put you up to this." Howard ground his teeth. "Grasping son of a—"

"Luke doesn't know a thing about it," Charlie snapped. "Actually, it was something Tyler said."

"Tyler!" Astonishment made Howard's heavy features go slack. "What has he got to do with this?"

"That's what I'd like to know." Her gaze narrowed. "What kind of business are you doing with him?"

"With Tyler?" Howard's voice cracked as he laughed. "You must be joking. Why would I go to a private individual when there are perfectly good banks around?"

"I don't know. You tell me. Tyler said to ask you."

Howard sat back down in his chair and folded his arms belligerently. "Well, that explains it. Tyler's playing mind games with you, Charlotte, and I don't appreciate your putting me in the middle of them!"

Charlie hesitated. Howard could be right. It was just the sort of sly, vindictive trick Tyler would use. "If that's what it is, then I apologize, but I still want to see the books."

"Fine!" Howard's chin jutted at a pugnacious angle, and he gestured around the study. "Help yourself. Everything's here. Let me know if you find anything untoward, and I'll hand in my resignation that minute!"

"Now, Howard..." Charlie bit her lip, but he was already back on his feet, grabbing his Panama hat and stomping toward the door.

"Save it, Charlotte! When you're over this tantrum," he flung, "then you can apologize."

Charlie stared after Howard uncertainly, feeling guilty for upsetting him. Obviously she'd insulted him grievously, but she was at a loss to understand exactly why. Shrugging, she went to the desk and opened the ledger.

THE BEAD OF MOLTEN LEAD splashed onto the crimson glass of a soldier's coat. Cursing under her breath, Charlie set down her solder gun and carefully wiped up her mistake, taking care not to burn herself. This was the last window for the Charleston commission, and she was determined that each would be as perfect as she could make it. When she picked up the solder gun and made exactly the same error again, she knew it was time to stop.

Rotating her stiff shoulders, she attempted to loosen muscles tightened by too many hours futilely pouring over Evening Star's books, compounded by an equal number of hours hunched over the workbench in her sweltering studio. As far as she could discern, there was nothing remotely out of the ordinary about the state of the plantation's finances. Howard was an able manager, and they were no more or less in debt than many other farmers. Why this finding wasn't as reassuring as she'd thought it would be was a question that only made her impatient with herself.

Sliding from her stool, she picked up the wooden-framed three-by-four-window she'd finished earlier, grunting and struggling under its awkward weight as she manhandled it toward a safer storage area along the shed's far wall. She was halfway there when a pair of strong hands gave her some much needed assistance.

"My, you're a stubborn woman," Luke said, his tone somewhere between disgust and admiration. "You're too small to handle this all by yourself. Why didn't you wait for some help?"

"I can do it!" Charlie puffed indignantly. But when they set the window against the wall she gave a deep sigh of relief.

"Yeah, sure." Luke gave her a skeptical glance, then focused his attention on the trio of completed windows, each depicting a famous scene from Charleston's history.

In a saggy T-shirt and denim cutoffs washed almost to whiteness, he looked more like a beach bum than a successful veterinarian, but his blatant virility and sexy good looks were enough to make Charlie's mouth suddenly go dry. Swallowing, she tore her gaze away from him and examined the windows herself.

"These are great, Charlie." Luke studied each piece in turn. "You can almost feel the action in them."

She blushed with pleasure, but she wasn't falsely modest. She knew this was the best work she'd ever done. "I'm pleased with the way they've turned out. Only one more to go and then I can ship them off."

"I doubt if the Historical Society expected you to have them finished so soon."

"No, they gave me as much time as I needed, but . . ."

He turned and smiled at her in understanding. "But you had something to prove?"

Threading her sliced and scabby fingers through the sweat-dampened hair at her nape, she shrugged. "Maybe."

"You've been working too hard." He closed the distance between them, his faint smile a bit accusing. "Do you realize I haven't even seen you since the day Mikey got hurt?"

"I'm not the only one who's been busy," she pointed out tartly. The musky odor of his skin mingled with a piny after-shave, and she balled her hands into fists to keep from reaching for him. Despite everything between them, she was still at a loss where their relationship was concerned. She forced a casual tone. "Have you seen Mikey? How's he doing?"

Luke ran callused fingertips down her arm to encircle her elbow. "Didn't slow him down one iota, as far as I can tell. In fact, Rob and Rachel took him up to Shreveport to spend the day at Hamel's Amusement Park."

"I'm glad they're seeing each other."

"If that's what you call dancing attendance on a five-year-old. I've a mind to tell Rob he's going about this courting business all wrong. They've taken Mikey everywhere they've been so far."

"Maybe Rob feels more comfortable that way," Charlie suggested. "It's as good a way as any to get to know each other. And after all, Rob doesn't have your smooth-talking charm with the ladies."

Luke laughed softly, fitting his hands around her waist and hooking his thumbs into the belt loops of her jeans. "Much good it's done me lately. And there's only one lady I'm interested in these days. That's why I'm kidnapping you."

"But I really should finish—"

"Oh, no, you don't! I've got another vet taking call for me this afternoon, and I'm not going to waste it. Let's take the boat and go find some place to cool off."

Tempted, Charlie bit her lip.

"What?" he demanded, his hands tightening. "Got another offer?"

"It's not that." Her laugh was shaky, a bit embarrassed.

"Then what is it?"

"We were going to take things one step at a time, remember? Lately, when we're alone, I seem to be unable to keep my hands off of you, and—"

His deep, relieved chuckle cut her off. "I'm not complaining."

"But, Luke," she gulped, "I don't think I'm being fair to you."

He touched her cheek, shaking his head in confusion. "Princess, you just lost me."

Pulling away from him, she clasped her hands together in agitation. "I . . . I had hardly had a chance to learn to be on my own, before we . . . we . . ." Blushing, she stumbled on. "And I may have given you the wrong impression about what I can give you at this time in my life. We learned the hard way before. I'd rather die than hurt you, but if you come to count on me or vice versa and either of us realized that we'd rushed into a physical relationship, then . . ."

"You call nine years rushing things?" he asked quietly.

She looked at him with misery shining in her green eyes. "No, but—"

"Are you saying you don't want to see me anymore?"

"No!"

He grasped her twisting hands. "Then what are you saying? I'm crazy about you, and yes, the sex is good—fantastic—but that's not all there is between us and you know it."

"Do I? Maybe I'm only using you, and later I'll change my mind and one of us will get hurt."

"Look, Charlie, have I asked you for anything? Made any kind of demands?"

She shook her head uncertainly.

"And I won't."

Not yet, he amended mentally, *not if it kills me.*

The path of the conversation had taken him from the heights to the pits in just a few words. His heart pounded with fury that she could be so blind to what he felt for her, that she couldn't feel the force of his love and trust in it.

The next moment he nearly exploded with fear that if she
did, she'd bolt like a skittish filly, and he'd never see her
again. So he forced himself to grit his teeth and say the
hardest words of his life.

"We're both adults here. Maybe neither of us wants or
needs a lifelong commitment right now, but as long as we
go into this with our eyes and options open, that doesn't
mean we can't enjoy each other. As far as our relationship goes, my feeling is that 'if it ain't broke, don't fix
it.'"

Charlie swallowed. "It sounds so cold-blooded."

"You can't have it both ways." He drew her closer,
crossing his arms across her back and positioning her next
to him, hip to hip, thigh to thigh. "Besides," he muttered, "what you do to my blood is make it boil."

"And that's enough?"

He moved his hips in an erotic mimicry of lovemaking,
avoiding the answer with a question of his own. "What do
you think?"

Charlie arched against him, her hands moving in tantalizing patterns over his chest to clasp around his neck.
Relief and mischief mingled in her impish expression. "I
think that as long as you're sure, we ought to look for a
place to go skinny-dipping."

"I MUST SAY, I had exquisite taste when I insisted you buy
that dress," Charlie said smugly. "You're a vision,
Rachel. I'll bet Rob's eyes popped when he picked you up
for the wedding this evening."

Rachel's rosebud mouth compressed into an annoyed
moue. She swept a careless hand over the skirt of her linen
sheath, its fabric so deep a purple that her eyes appeared
nearly violet. "He was so busy fussing with Mikey that
I'm not sure he even noticed."

"He'd have to be blind not to!"

"Yeah, well, he must have thought I was an eggplant in disguise," Rachel said flippantly. She cast a look at Charlie's yellow suit. "Maybe I should have come as a daffodil, too."

Charlie laughed and took a sip of champagne from her fluted glass. "Don't worry," she said. "We'll make sure he gets another look at Miss Eggplant before the night's out."

Charlie caught the crook of Rachel's elbow, and the two women strolled arm in arm across the large candle-lit and flower-bedecked backyard of the Gilchrist home, enjoying the postnuptial festivities and the cool night air.

Hurricane lanterns glowed in the arbors of the white-latticed gazebo in the rear of the yard, and a four-piece band played softly on the brick terrace. Charlie could see the top of Luke's tawny head as he talked with Rob and Howard in line at the bar set up in the carport, and she waved briefly to Becky in her gauzy matron of honor gown, standing beside the young bride and groom as they beamed for the photographer. Milady, regal as ever, held court with the dowagers just inside the sliding glass doors leading into the house, while Mikey and Regan Turner surreptitiously took finger scoops of confectioner's icing from the base of the lavish marzipan wedding cake on the bride's table.

"Maybe I'm wasting my time," Rachel said in a morose tone. "Much as I like Rob, I don't want a man to date me just because his son approves!"

Charlie chuckled. "I'm sure it's more than that."

"I'm not. We've seen each other constantly, and the man hasn't given me so much as a good-night handshake! I don't want to sound like a hussy, but a little physical demonstration of affection every now and then wouldn't be amiss. Don't you agree?''

Charlie choked on her wine, and a rosy tide rolled across her cheekbones at the memory of a certain swimming expedition and its inevitable passionate outcome. She and Luke had cavorted in the sun and water of a secluded corner of the lake like a couple of shameless oversexed kids, and it had been wonderful, exhilarating and liberating, like finding a part of her youth she hadn't realized she'd lost.

Luke Duval was really the most surprising, sexy, understanding man in the world, she decided. A no-strings affair was what they both wanted, even if Charlie had been forced to swallow a bit of feminine pique that he'd agreed with her ''no commitments'' agenda with such alacrity. While Charlie could relate to Rachel's frustration, thanks to Luke she wasn't having to endure anything of that nature.

''That just means Rob's a gentleman,'' Charlie hastened to assure Rachel. ''Besides, I saw him kiss you at the hospital.''

''And that's been it. I'd take the lead myself, except he's so shy I'm afraid an aggressive female would scare him off completely.'' She made a face. ''Not the type of woman he'd want raising his boy, you understand.''

''And you'd consider that? Raising Mikey, I mean.''

They paused at the edge of the terrace and set their glasses on a nearby table. Rachel bit her lip and shrugged. ''Maybe. Given the right incentive. I really admire how Rob's raising his son, and Mikey's such a precious little dickens. It would be easy to mother him, but I'm no martyr. There would have to be more than that between us before I'd think of marrying, but how am I ever going to find out?''

"Patience," Charlie advised with a laugh. She saw Luke and Rob crossing the lawn toward them, and mischief lit her eyes. "And a little feminine guile. Come on, there's nothing like a little slow dancing to raise a man's thermostat."

With a minimum of maneuvering on Charlie's part, the two couples joined the group on the terrace swaying to the music. Nearby, Gina, in apparently her latest attempt to keep Howard "on his toes," or at least get his attention, executed a flashy series of pirouettes with Harry Humphries, their efforts producing a smattering of applause. Charlie wondered briefly if Gina's philosophy masked a certain insecurity regarding her marriage, then dismissed the thought as her attention reverted to Rob and Rachel. Rob held his petite partner awkwardly at first, then gradually relaxed, folding his tall form closer to hear Rachel's comments. Their conversation was too low to hear, but Charlie smiled in satisfaction.

"What kind of shenanigans are you up to?" Luke murmured in her ear.

She gave him an innocent smile, then nestled closer to his chest, rubbing her cheek against the dark fabric of his suit coat. "Hard to tell at this point."

"Should I warn Rob?" There was a laugh in the husky tone of his voice.

"Certainly not! He can watch out for himself."

At that moment Mikey appeared on the dance floor, tugged at his father's pant leg and whispered some urgent message. With an apologetic smile Rob allowed the boy to drag him off the terrace toward the house. Rachel caught Charlie's eye, shrugged, then drifted off toward the gazebo to wait.

Charlie stifled a sigh. "So much for shenanigans."

"You women shouldn't be conniving, anyway," Luke admonished.

"I don't know." She swayed even closer, luxuriating in his closeness. "Look what it got me."

"She devil," he said, laughing. "Were you planning this nefarious attempt on my self-control during the entire ceremony?"

"Mmm."

Maybe she had been, Charlie thought, her hand tightening in Luke's. The wedding hadn't been comfortable for either of them. Sitting side by side in the pew of the First Methodist Church, Charlie couldn't help but feel Luke's tension. She'd been party to her share of it, too, for the familiar recitation of vows had reiterated her own shattered ones, tormenting her with memories both poignant and painful. The fact that she sat beside a man who was nothing at all like her former husband, and who had made no impossible demands on her, was the only thing that got her through it. It would be nice to think somehow she could make it up to him now.

"How about we get out of here?" Luke whispered in her ear.

"The bride and groom haven't left yet," Charlie reminded him. "That would be rude. But just as soon as they do..."

With a barely audible groan Luke drew her closer, and for a long interval they danced oblivious to everything but each other.

"Hey, you lovebirds, break it up." Becky, harried but grinning, stood at their side, her carroty hair a mass of curls under a headdresss of satin ribbon and baby's breath. "Hate to interrupt such a pretty scene, but I need to steal Charlie for a minute. Okay, Luke?"

She was dragging Charlie away before Luke could frame a protest.

"What's going on?" Charlie asked with a breathless laugh.

Becky's cheerful expression faltered and a worried pleat creased her brow. "Rachel raced through here a minute ago with an awful look on her face, and now she's locked in Mom's bathroom. Could you see about her, please? There's so much to do...."

Alarmed, Charlie hastily agreed and hurried through the Gilchrist house to the master suite to tap softly on the bathroom door. "Rachel? It's Charlie. Let me in."

The lock rattled briefly, and Charlie entered to find Rachel blotting suspiciously red eyes and peering into the mirror over the washbasin.

"Rachel? What is it?" Charlie asked in a gentle voice.

Rachel sniffed and continued to work at the smears of mascara under her lashes with the sodden tissue. "Don't mind me," she said with a cracked attempt at a smile. "It's nothing new. I can handle it."

"Handle what?" Charlie's expression was thoroughly puzzled.

"This. Me." Rachel indicated her amply endowed figure with a gesture. "God, it's rich, isn't it? Rob won't touch me, but other men think they can at will." Her voice broke with bitterness. "I'm not trash, but when they see these knockers—heigh-ho, it's time to grab the goodies."

Charlie was instantly indignant. "Who did? Did someone offend you? I'll—"

"Never mind. It's nothing." Rachel was suddenly busy poking through her handbag.

"What do you mean, nothing? No one has a right to touch you unless you want it. You can't let whoever did this get away with it scot-free."

"Forget it, please, Charlie."

Charlie's voice was as stern as an old maid school-teacher's. "Rachel."

"Really, it was probably just my imagination. I was feeling low because of Rob, you know." Babbling, Rachel snapped her purse and hurriedly moved toward the door. "I'm sometimes oversensitive. I must have mistaken Howard's intention—"

"Howard!" Charlie's jaw dropped. Aghast, then suddenly furious, her face paled, then flamed. "My God!"

"It's all right," Rachel said, her tone a bit frantic. "I'm sure he didn't mean anything—"

"The very idea! If you don't give him a piece of your mind, I sure as hell will!"

"It'll only make it worse." Rachel's expression was miserable. "I don't want a scene."

"I can't believe you'd protect him," Charlie protested.

"I'm not! It's just that now I'm not sure exactly what happened, and there's Gina—" she swallowed and her voice grew very small "—and me."

Charlie patted Rachel's hand. "All right, I understand. But I'm still going to have a word with my cousin. Don't worry. I can be very discreet. I've had plenty of practice."

Shaking with the effort to suppress her indignant fury, Charlie took Rachel to sit down with Milady and her cronies. Milady took one look at Charlie's expression and instantly turned on the rarely used but legendary Montgomery charm, drawing Rachel into the ladies' conversation.

Crossing the terrace, Charlie scanned the crowd of wedding guests, and was immediately intercepted by Luke.

"Have you seen Howard?" he asked, a distracted air about his lean features.

"You're looking for him, too?"

"Yeah, it's fire engine time—there he is at the bar, still tanking up." Luke strode off, leaving Charlie to tag along or not. Nonplussed, she hastened after him, coming up short just in time to hear what he had to say.

"Howard, you'd better come with me."

"Wha—?" Howard squinted drunkenly at Luke. "Hell, what for, Doc? I was just fixin' to have me another drink."

"Pigeon called. Your new colt's down, and it doesn't sound good."

CHAPTER TWELVE

"THE INSURANCE COMPANY called again."

Gina made the announcement in a low voice, then took her place of vigil beside Charlie, peering over the plank divider into the horse stall. In the gray predawn light Gina's bare face was as pale as her ivory silk dressing gown, and she paid no attention to the muddy mixture of dew and dust that stained her satin mules.

"Tell them there's been no change." Luke knelt beside the prostrate horse, where he and Pigeon had been most of the night, working with tubes and buckets and gallons of mineral oil.

"Maybe that's good?" Howard asked hopefully from the other side of the stall. Like the rest of the group, he'd changed into old clothes on their arrival, and now wrinkled garments and haggard faces testified to the night's toll.

Luke sat back on his heels, rubbing his jaw in frustration. He'd sent Pigeon off to catch a nap earlier, and his own eyes felt grainy with fatigue. "It'll be a miracle if this fellow makes it. Damn it, Howard! Why'd you insure him for a hundred grand? He's not worth half of that."

Bleary-eyed and stubbled, Howard cursed between his teeth. "Hell, I'd just had my best horse struck by lightning! Anyone could see why I'd get as much insurance as possible. And from the looks of things, Doc, it's just as well I did."

Luke grunted. "Guess so. Damn bit of bad luck. I'd better give the insurance company's consulting vet a call, but I'm doing everything I can think of—fever reducers, painkillers, tubing. We can keep trying, but I never saw a case of colic take one down so fast." He stood and stretched. A sandy eyebrow lifted when he saw Gina's and Charlie's tired, intent faces watching him over the stall divider. "You ladies go on back to bed. There's nothing you can do here."

"Maybe some more coffee?" Gina suggested, stifling a wide yawn.

"Sounds good, hon," Howard answered, his dark eyes focused uneasily on the suffering animal.

"I'll go make that call," Luke said, and caught Charlie's eye. "Coming?"

She shook her head. "I'll watch with Howard until you get back."

Nodding, Luke followed Gina out of the barn. Howard glanced at Charlie curiously.

"To what do I owe this show of solidarity?"

"Nothing I can think of." Her tone was short and her eyes smoldered with resentment. "All I wanted was a moment to tell you what a snake I think you are."

Howard's complexion went pasty, and beads of sweat popped out on his swarthy brow. "I…I don't know what you're talking about."

"I'm talking about the pass you made at Rachel Aubert last night," Charlie hissed.

Howard looked blank, then gave a nervous chuckle and rubbed a shaky hand over his forehead. "Your imagination's run away with you. I was only being amiable, and I certainly didn't make a pass."

"Whatever you call it, you upset Rachel, and I think you owe her an apology."

"I was a little drunk last night," Howard muttered sullenly. "All I did was give her a friendly hug. How that can be misconstrued, I don't know."

"Misconstrued or not," Charlie countered icily, "I'm certain Gina wouldn't appreciate it, either."

Howard's expression was suddenly stricken. "It was nothing, I swear. I'll apologize first chance I get."

"Relax," Charlie said in disgust. "I'm not tattling to Gina unless you pull something like that again. Just keep your paws to yourself from now on. You've got enough trouble with the horses and the farm. Only a fool or weakling would jeopardize his marriage, too."

"Coming from you that means a lot," Howard said, attempting to rebuild his battered dignity with a snide dig.

"I'm delighted at your insight," she returned sweetly. "So be warned, Howard. You see, Tyler was both foolish and weak, and just look what he lost."

Turning on her heel, she stalked out of the barn. In the distance the red globe of the rising sun balanced on the treetops, and a thin white haze hovered over the dark green cotton fields. She took a deep, cleansing breath, filling her lungs with the cool scents of earth and dew and life.

She felt better for having confronted Howard for his stupidity. Maybe he wouldn't make the same mistake again. At least Gina had been spared the embarrassment of knowing what an ass Howard had made of himself, and Charlie was glad of that. Whatever Gina saw in her husband, she really seemed to love him.

Which goes to prove there's no accounting for taste, Charlie thought, smiling to herself.

She looked up the lane, spotted Luke walking her way and faltered at the piercing warmth of emotion that swept through her core. His face was lined with fatigue, his shoulders drooped with dejected frustration, the luster in his tawny eyes was dimmed by preoccupation—and still he was so beautiful and dear to her that the breath choked in her throat.

My God, she thought, dazed. *I love him.*

When had caring and passion turned to more? Only love could explain the powerful tenderness that she felt for Luke, the longing to ease his burdens, the urge to share everything, not only the good and happy things that life brought, but the heartaches and disappointments as well. Had she always loved him? Perhaps love had lain dormant until now, reawakening like a flower opening to the sun's warmth. Or perhaps it had been necessary for both of them to endure and experience life in order to come together at this point in time. By whatever means or circuitous path, it had happened, and Charlie's heart swelled with love—and fear.

"Are you all right?" Luke asked, reaching her side. He frowned down into her pale face, then placed his arm over her shoulder and drew her close. "You look exhausted."

Heart racing, Charlie pressed her cheek into his shirtfront, inhaling the masculine musk of man and horse and honest sweat. "I'm fine," she murmured, but clung to him almost desperately.

How ironic to be hoisted by her own petard! she thought. By insisting on a free, no-ties relationship, she was caught in a trap of her own making. Now, when her love bade her cry out her need for Luke and her desire for something permanent between them, she held her peace. How could she demand from him what she hadn't been willing to risk, and perhaps even now was still unable to give herself?

"Something's wrong," Luke said, startling her with his intuitive grasp of her mental state. "What is it, princess? Did you and Howard have words?"

Gratefully Charlie grasped at that excuse. "Yes, that's it. He... he insulted Rachel last night and I called him down for it."

Luke scowled. "He got fresh?"

"He said he'd had too much to drink. Maybe Rachel overreacted. I don't know. But it's settled now, so don't worry. You've got to concentrate on saving that horse."

"If I can." Rubbing his hand up and down her back absently, he stared down the lane toward the horse barn, his expression perplexed. "It looks like colic, but there's something not quite right.... I can't put my finger on it yet."

"Isn't colic in horses caused by bad feed or overfeeding?"

"Sometimes. But Pigeon and I checked all that. The feed wasn't mildewed, and the Coastal hay Howard's been using is good. Not that we could really tell what the animal had eaten. Whoever cleaned the stall last did such a good job there wasn't a grain left in the manger or blade on the floor. Anyway, it could be caused by a dozen other things. The colt's in such apparent pain, it may mean a twisted gut."

"Will you try surgery?"

"Only as a last resort."

Charlie tightened her arms around him. "You're tired. Can't I convince you to rest a while? You could use my bed."

A ghost of a smile tugged at the corner of Luke's mouth. "Only if you're in it, too, and then I don't know how much rest either of us would get. No, much as I'm tempted, the colt's condition is deteriorating too fast. I'd better get back."

"All right. I'll see if I can get Sudie to bake a pan of buttermilk biscuits to go with your coffee."

Luke grinned and dropped a brief kiss on her mouth. "Sounds good. Then take a nap, will you? No use both of us having bags under our eyes."

"Okay." Charlie smiled, soothed and warmed by his teasing and his caring concern. Nothing had really changed except the name she put on her feelings. Why shouldn't they just go on as they had been? There was something of her relief in her eyes, and Luke paused, then grabbed her close again.

"There isn't anything else the matter, is there?"

"No," she said in a soft voice. "Not anymore."

THE HORSE DIED AT MIDDAY. By the time the second veterinarian required by the insurance company arrived, and he and Luke had conducted the autopsy, it was nearly dusk. Milady and Gina sat in the porch rockers while Charlie stood on the tall front steps, watching Howard and Luke in the front yard shake hands with the visiting vet as he prepared to leave.

"Why Howard thought he could raise racehorses in the first place is beyond me," Milady sniffed. "Gina, you've got sense enough to know better. You'd better talk that husband of yours into getting out of the business before it drags him under altogether."

"It's just a run of bad luck," Gina said, shifting restlessly in the wooden rocker. For once she'd foregone her elaborate makeup, and her face was curiously pale, showing a smattering of auburn freckles. Absently she picked at a place on one fingertip, grimaced, then stuck the finger into her mouth and sucked. "And it's important to him to make it big on something that's all his own."

"Poppycock! Evening Star's big enough for anyone," Milady snorted.

"Don't worry." Gina stood up, then leaned against the porch railing with her arms wrapped around herself as if chilled by the cooling evening air. "You heard Dr. Hankins say there wouldn't be any trouble filing on the insurance. He and Luke agreed at the autopsy that it was just an unavoidable case of colic."

"Then why did they take all those tissue samples and specimens?" Milady demanded.

"It's the usual procedure, Milady," Charlie said. "Luke sends them off to the veterinary diagnostic lab at Texas A & M. Just in case the animal died of something that might start an epidemic in the entire herd."

"Which they're certain isn't the case here," Gina added.

"Well, I still think Howard's bitten off more than he can chew."

Out in the yard Dr. Hankins made his final farewell, climbed into his car and drove off. Howard and Luke walked silently toward the porch. Howard said nothing to Charlie as he passed her on the steps. Ignoring Milady as well, he gestured tiredly to Gina. "Hon, I think I need a drink."

Arms still clasped around herself, Gina shivered and nodded. "Me, too."

Without another word they went inside.

Milady stiffly levered herself out of the rocker. "Miss Scarlett! Come along, it's time for supper. Oh, where is that wretched animal?"

The animal in question had been dozing under Milady's rocker. Grumpily she climbed to her feet, stretching and yawning, then slowly followed her mistress into the house.

Luke stood at the base of the steps, and Charlie smiled in sympathy. "Been a bad day, Doc?"

He snorted and ran a hand through his hair. "I've had worse."

"But not recently," she guessed, attuned to his frustration, seeing the fatigue that made his lids heavy and etched new angles into his lean, stubbled cheeks. She rose, placing her hands on his bare forearms. "I'm so sorry."

"You win some, you lose some." He shrugged philosophically.

"And I know you hate it every time you lose one, no matter how blasé you try to appear. You're too good a vet not to care." She slid her hands up his arms, but he caught her waist, holding her away.

"I wouldn't get too close if I were you," he said with a wry laugh. "I'm filthy and need a shower."

"As if that matters," she muttered, reaching up to pull his head down for her kiss. After a little while, she asked, "Do you want something to eat?"

He shook his head. "I'm too tired to be hungry. I think I'll head home and catch some rack time. Walk me to the truck?"

"Sure."

It felt good to Luke not to talk, not to think, just to walk hand in hand with Charlie, feeling her unspoken support. He was professional enough to know he'd done everything he could for Howard's horse, but nonetheless he was drained. They walked past the barn housing Charlie's studio, and Luke felt her hesitate.

"What is it?"

"Is that door open? Hold on a minute. Let me check." She frowned and peered into the gathering dusk, then pulled free of his grasp with an apologetic smile. Crossing to the ramshackle door, she pushed it open. "That's funny. I never forget to lock—"

Her sharp cry of dismay brought Luke on the run. He skidded to a halt in the doorway. Charlie was already inside, but he couldn't see her in the dim interior, only hear her husky, "Oh, no!" Moving blindly, he stepped inside, swinging his hand overhead until it connected with the dangling light cord, then pulled.

The studio was a battle zone.

Charlie stood rooted in the center of the work area, her hands pressed to her mouth in horror, staring at the carnage. At her feet lay the remains of her stained-glass windows, those marvelous moving scenes shattered into rainbow-hued bits and pieces no bigger than postage stamps, their wooden frames splintered into kindling. Even the half-finished one had been thrown from her workbench, the lead beading twisted into an obscene Medusan mass. It was utter, wanton and deliberate destruction on a scale that took Luke's breath away.

Cursing, he reached for Charlie, crushing her into his chest. "Don't look."

Trembling, dazed, her voice seemed to come from a long distance. "How could this happen? I'll have to start from scratch again, but the arts program job is over now and I won't have the money to replace everything! Did they fall? I was so careful—"

"It's no accident. Someone did this on purpose."

She jerked, then leaned back, staring at Luke in disbelief while her mind reeled in bewilderment.

Who? her brain screamed. *Who?*

If this wasn't simple vandalism, who could have acted with such viciousness? Had she angered Howard more than she realized? Even Milady had denigrated her project more than once. Who would strike at her most vulnerable point, undermining the self-esteem she'd begun to achieve with her new career?

Suddenly she knew. "Tyler."

Luke scowled. "Tyler? Why would he—"

"I should have known!" Fury surged like molten lava through Charlie's veins, and she pulled free of Luke's restraining hands. Glass shards crunched beneath her feet, and she smote the air with her fists. "Damn him! He said he'd find a way to make me come back. If he thinks this is going to break me, that he can drive me away from Evening Star so I have to come crawling back to Charleston, he's crazier than I thought! I'll—"

"Wait a minute." Luke's jaw clenched. "When did you talk to Tyler?"

"He called . . ." She waved her hand in distraction, her eyes overbright.

Jealousy scorched Luke, hot and raw. He caught her wrist in a hard grip, and his words were a snarl. "Why didn't you tell me?"

"It didn't concern you!"

"When are you going to realize that everything about you concerns me?" he roared, infuriated.

"Don't yell at me!" She jerked her wrist free, and her eyes glistened with moisture that she fought valiantly to contain. "I don't need this from you now."

Luke controlled himself with an effort, drawing a deep breath. "What makes you so sure Tyler's responsible, anyway? You don't think he came all the way from Charleston just to vandalize your stuff?"

"Probably not, but he wouldn't have to. Tyler could always find someone else to do his dirty work," she replied bitterly.

Luke ran an exasperated hand over the back of his neck, rubbing the tired muscles. "You can't be positive. It may have been kids, burglars, anybody!"

"It's Tyler's handiwork," she said, the soft line of her mouth clenched stubbornly.

"When were you here last?"

"Yesterday morning."

"And you hadn't been back until now?"

"No. We went to the wedding, remember? And then we were up all night, so I slept during the day today...."

"So anytime from yesterday noon until now someone could have sneaked in here. What about the key?"

"Whoever did this broke the lock," she pointed out dully. Suddenly her eyes overflowed. "It doesn't matter who—I'll never be able to pick up the pieces!"

"Princess..." Unable to stand her anguish, Luke pulled her into his arms, burying his nose in the flower-fragrance of her hair while she sobbed brokenly. "Don't cry. God, it kills me to see you cry."

A wave of protectiveness crashed through Luke, a determination not to let anything hurt this woman ever again. "I love you, Charlie," he choked. "Marry me. Let me take care of you."

He knew the instant she stiffened in his arms he'd said the wrong thing.

Furiously she pushed away from him, wiping her wet cheeks. "Is that your idea of a solution? I'm not some helpless little twit who has to depend on a man at any cost—I'm not!"

Dismayed, Luke battled against a sense of hurt rejection. "I'm not suggesting you are. But it's all right to need someone."

"Not for me." In a rage she kicked at a pile of broken shards. "Damn it! I'm going to prove to everyone I can make it on my own. I'll rebuild these windows somehow, and I'll do it by myself.''

"But you don't have to.'' Bewildered, Luke felt himself sinking deeper and deeper into a morass of emotional quicksand. He caught her shoulders. "Didn't you understand what I said? I love you Charlie! I want you to be my wife. I want to be there for you.''

"And don't you understand I can't?'' Charlie's eyes were as green as the sea on a stormy day, and Luke thought he saw a momentary flicker of panic. Her mouth clamped down tightly, and she threw up her chin. "I can't!''

"You're lying to yourself.'' Jerking her close, he caught the delicate angle of her jawbone on either side of her face, holding her still to ravish her mouth with a blistering, demanding kiss. They were both shaking when he lifted his head. "Now tell me you aren't in love with me,'' he taunted softly.

She gasped for air. "Luke—''

"Admit it.''

"Yes!'' She stared at him in defiance. "Yes, I love you, but I can't marry you.''

A giant fist smashed Luke's heart. "Can't or won't?'' he croaked.

She looked away. "It's the same thing.''

"Not to me. Not if you really love me.''

"Don't push me, Luke.'' Her voice was ragged. "You don't own me.''

His mouth twisted, and he slowly opened his hands, releasing her. "That's not the issue. We love each other. We should be together. It's as simple as that. What are you really afraid of?''

"Of making another mistake!'' She closed her eyes and pressed her fingertips to her throbbing temples. Her breath soughed between her parted lips, but her voice was lower as she fought for control. "I just got free of a damaging relationship. No matter how I feel about you, I need time to learn to be *me* first."

"That's a flimsy excuse. Look deeper, princess. Is it independence you really want, or are you afraid of making a commitment?"

"What if I am?" she cried. "Is that some kind of crime? Look at what shaped me, Luke! My parents, then Tyler, even my unborn child—everyone I cared about left me in one way or another. You can't blame me for being cautious."

"Maybe you can be satisfied with some kind of crazy open-ended relationship, but I can't." His voice was flat. "Not anymore. I want you in every way a man can want a woman, now and forever. Damn it, Charlie! Can't you see I'm not Tyler? What will it take for you to trust me?"

"It's not you. It's *me*." She trembled visibly, and her voice was pleading. "Why do you have to pressure me now?"

"Because you need me!" Luke exploded. He gestured sharply at the debris littering the little studio. "Any idiot can see that."

Her lips compressed angrily. "Well, this *idiot* has to prove to herself that she can cope on her own. It would be easy for me to lie down, give up, let you handle everything, but I won't do it because..."

"Why?"

She took a deep breath and met his gaze fearlessly. "Because if I depend on you, without knowing I can depend on myself first, then I'll always be afraid that someday you'll let me down when I need you the most—and I won't survive."

"That's not true! I'd never let you down."

A sudden sadness clouded her face, and her answer was soft. "You did once before."

He was as surprised as if she'd slapped him, and when he could answer, his voice was harsh. "As the saying goes—That was then, This is now."

"Here's another one that's just as apt," she snapped. "Once burned, twice shy."

"That's just another excuse." He held up a hand to forestall her protest. "All right, have it your way. Be Miss Independent. Do what you have to, Charlie. I just hope you know what you're about." He started for the door, but Charlie's cry made him pause.

"Luke, wait!"

"What for, princess? I think we've covered it all." He stood in the doorway, a dark silhouette against the graying sky, and his voice was weary. "Just remember that it can get pretty damn lonely while you're out there standing on your own. If you need me, you know where to look."

Charlie stared after him, confusion and conflicting emotions tossing her mind like a ship caught in a hurricane. Broken glass crunched beneath her feet, and suddenly she couldn't deal with the consequences of the disaster, nor her hasty and heated confrontation with Luke. A sob lodged in her throat, threatening to choke her. Without thinking she sought the only refuge left to her.

The Stearman looked lonely in its hangar-barn, but Charlie knew that was only a reflection of her mental state. Her hands shook when she ran them over its yellow fuselage and peered into the open engine compartment. Hector had evidently been working on the aircraft following the last round of pesticide applications she'd completed for Evening Star. She decided against climbing into the cockpit as had been her intention, fearing she might inadvertently interfere with some fine-tuning Hector was working on. Muttering, she circled the plane, prowling the barn, until finally, with a dejected sigh, she threw herself down on a mound of hay in the last stall to brood.

If she hadn't felt so miserable, she might have laughed at the irony of discovering in the course of a few hours that she loved a man and then had turned his proposal down flat. A witness to the situation would no doubt conclude she was "a brick short of a load," as the old boys down at the co-op would say. She couldn't blame them, either.

Scooting into the corner of the stall, Charlie leaned against a portion of a square bale lumped beneath the piles of loose hay. Elbows on upraised knees, she chewed on a golden straw, sniffing occasionally and irritably wiping at the leakage of moisture from her eyes that she told herself was due strictly to an allergy to hay dust.

The loss of her glass pieces was devastating, but not irreparable. Hard as it was, she could do the windows again, given enough time and replacement materials. And proper protection from Tyler's machinations. She frowned fiercely. She wouldn't underestimate him again.

What was worse was the hurt she'd seen in Luke's eyes. Swallowing, she tossed the chewed sprig aside. If she hadn't been so upset, she would have had a little more care with his masculine pride. How could she make him see it wasn't him she was rejecting, but the feeling of helplessness that could drag her back down into the black depths of despair and self-loathing? If she never achieved the sense of independence she so desperately coveted, she knew deep in her soul she would never be truly worthy of Luke's love.

And that was what she really wanted, she realized, shifting against the uncomfortable prickle of the hay bale. Rising, Charlie brushed the loose hay aside, uncovering the offending lump, a grayish-green mass of compressed leaves and stems, then sat down on it, deep in thought.

Somehow she had to prove herself, to achieve the goal of independence, so that she could meet Luke as an equal. Then they could explore what their love for each other meant, and what, if any, commitments were possible.

Feeling somewhat calmer, Charlie drew a deep breath. Somehow she'd make Luke understand. And somehow she'd find the funds to replace the broken glass and complete her commission on time. The question was how?

Straightening, Charlie focused on the Stearman. Suddenly her eyes widened and a half smile materialized at the corners of her mouth. The answer was staring her right in the face.

LUKE CAME AWAKE SLOWLY, groaning in protest at the sound of someone pounding on his back door. Hershey the Labrador whined and pressed his cold nose into the palm of Luke's dangling hand.

"All right, boy," Luke mumbled, "I hear it."

Rolling to his feet, he fumbled for a pair of ragged Auburn University gym shorts to cover his nudity, pulled them on and stumbled for the door, Hershey bounding ahead of him. His eyes were gritty and his mouth tasted like the bottom of a kennel. The digital clock on the microwave oven in the kitchen said 9:30, meaning he'd been asleep for only about three hours since returning home from Evening Star. Luke muttered a curse for whoever had decided to circumvent his answering service and prayed it wasn't another fire engine call. He'd had enough for one day.

Flinging open the back door, Luke glared blearily at the intruder. The man in shorts and T-shirt held a beer can in one hand. The index finger of his other hand was hooked in the plastic connection loop of the remainder of the six-pack.

Rob Thompson let out a low whistle. "Whoo-ee, man! What the hell happened to you?"

Luke mumbled something incoherent and vaguely obscene and held the door open. Rob ambled in.

"Saw your truck. Thought you might want some company."

"I was asleep."

"Hey, sorry! Why didn't you say so? I'll be on my way—"

Luke cut Rob off with a wave. "Never mind. I'll stay up awhile." He went to the kitchen sink and splashed water onto his groggy face. Facing Rob, he pointed to the six-pack. "One of those for me?"

"That's the idea."

Moments later both men were sprawled in loose-limbed comfort in Luke's oversize den chairs, sharing a beer and a companionable moment of silence. The cool liquid eased Luke's dry throat, and the malty taste was soothing. Luke felt muscles that had been tensed since the quarrel with Charlie finally begin to relax, and his sleepy brain kicked into gear.

"Where's Mikey?"

Rob fiddled with the television remote control, turning on the set and then flipping through the cable channels until he found the sports network. "He's sleeping over at a friend's. How come you hit the hay so early?"

Briefly Luke brought Rob up to date on the demise of Howard's colt. "If only I could be satisfied I knew what killed the animal," he said, gnawing at his frustration like an old bone. He took another swallow and shrugged. "Guess the definitive answer—if there is one—will have to come from A & M lab."

"After a day like that, no wonder Charlie gave you the night off," Rob said with a sly grin.

"Yeah."

Any other time Luke would have responded to the friendly ribbing, but his emotions were still too raw. He could kick himself for being so stupid! He'd known in his gut from the very beginning that pushing Charlie was the worst thing he could do. He'd seen her vulnerable and down, seen how valiantly she'd fought to rescue her own soul from the shipwreck of a failed marriage and a lost child, and then he'd had the utter gall to try to force her down a path for which she was obviously not ready.

It was a wonder she hadn't told him to get out of her life and stay out! One step at a time had been working fine— why had he been such a dunce? Luke only hoped there was some way to salvage what was left.

With an effort he stirred himself to be a cordial host. "Got another one of those?"

Rob pulled loose another can and tossed it to his cousin. "Nothing better than a beer and a ball game, right, cuz?"

"Humph." Luke eyed Rob narrowly. "That's a matter of opinion. Why aren't you and Rachel doing something tonight?"

Rob crossed his hairy ankles on the coffee table and stared at the hole in the tip of his jogging shoe. "Dunno. After the reception last night, she was acting real cool, like she didn't want to see me anymore."

"You dummy! That had nothing to do with you," Luke said in disgust. "Charlie said she got teed of at Howard for getting too chummy."

Rob's feet hit the floor with a thump. "What! Is she all right? Why didn't she say something?"

"Lord, how do I know? Believe me, I can't figure women at all!" Luke said in a wry tone.

Rob surged to his feet. "Cripes! I'd like to teach Howard Montgomery a thing or two. A lady like Rachel..." Bending, he picked up the rest of the six-pack and dropped it into Luke's lap. "Have a party, cuz. I'm going to see about my lady."

"Hey, that might not be such a good idea," Luke warned. "Better let it drop if she didn't say anything...."

But it was already too late. The back door slammed behind Rob, and with a deep exhalation Luke sank back down into his chair. Hershey came and pushed his head into Luke's lap, whining to have his ears scratched, and Luke obliged.

"If he'd just listened, boy," Luke told the dog, "I'd have explained to him that women can be damn sensitive."

Hershey yipped inquiringly, and Luke frowned.

"I don't know, boy. I just hope Rob isn't about to make as big a mistake with his lady as I did with mine."

CHAPTER THIRTEEN

THE GOSSIP AND THE COFFEE ran hot and heavy down at the Natchitoches Parish Co-op Monday morning. Everyone already knew that Howard Montgomery had lost another horse over the weekend.

"What does a dirt farmer know about blooded racing stock, anyway?" Preacher Lamar wanted to know.

"From what I hear this last batch ain't the same quality as what he's had before," Bertell Dickson said, sipping the potent black brew from his disposable cup.

"Still, it's a shame," Bill Dozier said, "even though everyone knows old Howard stands to make a tidy killing off the insurance. The boy isn't a complete fool, that's for sure, but I sure feel sorry for the doc, losing an expensive animal like that."

"Speaking of the vet," Melton Snipers said, "I'll bet he'll have his hands full dealing with his secretary this morning."

"How's that?"

Melton leaned on his bony knees, imparting his news with all the secrecy of General Patton planning an invasion. "Bessie's cousin's boy lives next door to Rachel Aubert, and she and Rob Thompson had a real set-to right there in her driveway Saturday night. Looked like she was kicking him out, giving him the old heave-ho."

Sympathetic murmurs circled the group.

"Yeah," Melton said mournfully, "good old Rob never says a cross word to nobody. Why, he was so mad he peeled off rubber leaving her place. Looks like all the old ladies hoping to get those two youngsters together are in for a big disappointment."

Gray heads nodded, a silent chorus of perennial male mystification: women!

"It's been a bad weekend all the way around for Evening Star," Deputy Arnold Herbert added, pouring himself a free cup of java to take on his morning patrol. "Why, the sheriff went out in person yesterday evening when old Miz Montgomery called to report a case of vandalism."

Ears perked up at this tidbit. "What happened, Arnie?" someone prompted.

In his official police monotone the deputy gave the crime report. "A person or persons unknown got into Ms. Charlotte Kincaid's studio. Someone broke up all the stained-glass windows ordered by that fancy society over Charleston way. I mean tweren't nothing bigger than a splinter left. The family was all upset, and there ain't a clue who did it."

Scowls of disbelief and anger scored the old men's lined faces. It gave them the shivers to think of such a thing happening in their nice little town.

"Makes people jumpy," the deputy continued as he helped himself to a couple of doughnuts. "Makes 'em so they're constantly looking over their shoulders, or forgetting to be as friendly as they ought to be to newcomers."

Several pairs of rheumy eyes flicked to the potbellied stranger in the English driving cap chatting at the cash register with Bob. Bertell Dickson hemmed and hawed

and made a big production about what he had to add to
regain their attention.

"Am I the only one who knows anything around
here?" he demanded in mock disgust. "Miss Charlie's
already been in to the co-op this morning, way before any
of you lazy slug-a-beds were up. And—" Bertell paused
here for emphasis "—she picked up pesticides so she
could get right on to crop dusting the Murphy boy's cotton acreage this very day."

"Imagine that! Pretty lil ol' thing like her, flying that
dirty and dangerous old contraption of her pappy's."

"I heard she did some dusting for Howard," Melton
said, "but that's family and understandable. Why on
earth would she take such a damn fool notion, anyway?"

"Believe it or not," Bertell said, "she said she needs the
money."

A Montgomery in need of money? Impossible! Or was
it?

All the old boys shook their grizzled heads, mumbled
into their coffee cups and wondered what the world was
coming to.

"WHAT IS THE WORLD coming to when I can't offer my
own flesh and blood a loan if I want to?" Milady demanded from the middle of her heavy poster bed, a Mil-
lard creation made in New Orleans over a hundred years
earlier.

Charlie, fresh from the shower after a hot day's worth
of dusting, tucked her damp hair behind her ears, shoved
her hands into the pockets of her new shorts and sighed.
"I appreciate the offer, but—"

"But nothing!" Propped on a mound of lacy pillows,
Milady scribbled in her checkbook, tore the paper out
with a loud rip and held it out to her granddaughter. "It's

not much, but I'd give all I had to keep your feet on the ground.''

"I'm perfectly safe." Charlie made no move to accept the check.

Shrugging, Milady laid it down on the bed within her reach. "I'm not questioning your flying ability, girl! But the fellow who broke those windows did it out of pure cussedness. There's no telling what might happen, so I don't want you taking any chances.''

"I'm not. And I'm not going to take your money. Mr. Murphy gave me an advance, and I've already ordered the materials I need to start on my commission again.''

Miffed, Milady glared through her gold-rimmed spectacles. "Where did you get this stubborn streak? You're not at all like Emmie.''

Charlie sat down on the edge of the bed, and a reluctant smile twitched the corners her mouth. "Aren't I? Luke says I'm just like you.''

"Why, that impertinent—'' Milady broke off with a pursing of lips that only delayed her inevitable chuckle. "That scamp! Did he really?''

"Uh-huh.''

"Well, the boy's got sense. Never said he didn't." Her silver eyebrows arched. "Though I don't recall us ever scrapping as bad as we have recently.''

Charlie carefully wet her lips. "I always tried to please you.''

"Charlotte..." Milady's voice cracked. "Girl, I know I've been hard on you, but you've always pleased me. After I lost your grandfather, and then your mother, you and Evening Star were the only things I could count on. I've always been proud of you.''

Her grandmother looked tiny and frail in the massive bed, and Charlie felt a pang. No matter how angry Milady had made her, Charlie still loved the old lady, and she realized that their estrangement harmed no one but themselves. This was their first civil conversation, and she prayed that the tenuous thread of communication wouldn't snap over yet another battle of wills.

"Then try to understand why I can't accept this." Gently she caught the old lady's hand and folded the check back into it. "Since Tyler and I broke up, I've realized I've got to do some things just for myself. It's important to me."

It was odd how she'd said these same things to Luke, Charlie thought, trying not to dwell on the lonely ache that filled her. But she was determined to see things through on her own before attempting to mend any bridges with the man she loved. Then, if it wasn't too late . . .

Shying away from that painful "if," Charlie watched a gamut of emotions cross her grandmother's lined face. She could only hope Milady understood better than Luke had.

"You've got more backbone than I gave you credit for, standing up to a domineering old biddy like me," Milady said finally.

There were other things Charlie wanted to say, things she hoped to hear from Milady, but then the old woman returned to her usual brisk manner and the moment was lost, or at least postponed. Stifling a sigh of disappointment, Charlie resolved to be patient. At least Milady had accepted Charlie's decision with what was, for her, very good grace indeed.

"Well, if you won't take this," Milady was saying, "then I'll be able to make my donation to the Women's Missionary Society. Lord knows I've been hard-pressed to keep up with my charitable obligations as I like."

This startled Charlie. "Why is that?"

"Last year was tight, you know, and Howard had to spend most of our cash on new equipment."

Charlie felt suddenly cold. "That's not what the books show. Howard's figures show a surplus."

"Surely you read them wrong." Milady's brows drew together in a perplexed frown. "We barely have enough to cover household expenses each month, and Howard hasn't been drawing his regular salary, trying to avoid re-financing at this point...."

"Milady, I don't know what's going on, but there's definitely a discrepancy between what the books say and what Howard's told you. What could be the reason for that?"

"I can't imagine."

Charlie chewed her bottom lip. There it was again, that suspicion that had nagged at her, the sense that Howard wasn't being completely truthful about Evening Star's condition. But Charlie thought better about upsetting her grandmother for such nebulous, unsubstantiated concerns.

"Well, ah, perhaps I misunderstood what I was reading," she hedged. "Maybe I should have another look."

"Better than that. If you're really interested," Milady suggested, "why don't you go down to the bank tomorrow and talk with Edgar Gideon? After all, you're going to inherit Evening Star one day. You might as well know the realities of farming a place this size, and Edgar will be glad to fill you in. Tell him I sent you."

"Thanks. That's a good idea."

But when Charlie spoke with the bank president during a midday break in her dawn-to-dusk dusting schedule two days later, the information he was able to give her was even more confusing and unsettling. The interest payments on Evening Star's note hadn't been paid in over a year, but with harvest in only another two months, Mr. Gideon was willing to wait.

When Charlie questioned him about any other outstanding debts, he suggested she check the parish records. After an hour in the clerk of court's office, Charlie walked to her car with a tight lump of anxiety clogging her throat.

Not only was Evening Star mortgaged to the hilt, but the paper trail of second mortgages she'd uncovered wasn't reflected in Howard's bookkeeping. She knew equipment, fuel and labor costs were exploding, but Evening Star owed an exorbitant amount of money, and bills that should have been paid hadn't been. Something was definitely wrong, and Howard, who possessed Milady's power of attorney, was the obvious culprit.

She climbed into her car, then sat frowning into space. What had Howard done with all the money? She hadn't been privy to Howard's private financial records, only the ones that concerned her inheritance. Had he skimmed Evening Star's profits to finance his own personal Thoroughbred project? Or was it something more sinister?

Milady would be furious if Evening Star had been jeopardized, but Charlie reasoned that demanding explanations from Howard at this point would be useless. Without more concrete information he would only deny any accusations, do some behind-the-scenes juggling and come up smelling like a rose. If there was only someone she could ask, someone who knew something, some detail, that might give her an inkling into the total situation....

She had it!

Glancing at her watch, she smiled to herself, a slow calculating grimace that caught the rotund gentleman in the squash-pie cap climbing into the sedan next to her by surprise. Swiftly Charlie started her car and pulled into the busy Second Street traffic. She was scheduled to meet Hector and resume the dusting on the last of the Murphys' fields shortly, but there was enough time for her to enlist the aid of the one man in the parish who knew everything about everyone.

"WHAT HAPPENED TO YOU?" Rachel demanded.

"Nothing." Luke's tone was sullen as he limped through the clinic toward his office.

"Nothing?" Rachel's Cupid's-bow mouth pursed in a knot of irritation. "I sent you off to the auction barn this morning all in one piece, and you come back this afternoon looking like something the cat dragged up. What happened?"

"I got stepped on, okay?" Luke snapped.

He wasn't in the best of tempers. It seemed every contrary cow in the parish had been on the auction block this morning, and one old bull had definitely gotten the better of him while he'd been thinking about Charlie instead of paying attention. He'd spent almost as much time dodging nosy questions about the goings-on out at Evening Star over the weekend, for once irritated by the idle curiosity of his neighbors and clients and even one old coot in a tweed cap he'd never seen before. Missing Charlie, but held back by pride and a sense of caution that told him they both needed a breathing space, he'd spent a totally miserable day.

Besides, his foot hurt like hell. Dropping into his desk chair, he gingerly tugged off one heavy boot and then peeled down his sock. His instep sported a mottled bruise in the half-moon shape of a hoof.

"Holy Jehoshaphat!" Rachel gasped. "Is it broken?"

"No, it's not broken," Luke returned sourly. He flexed the injured foot, grimacing.

"How do you know? I think it needs to be X-rayed. You'd better let me call the doctor."

"Just get me some ice, will you?"

"Ice won't help if it's broken—"

"I tell you it's not broken!" Luke exploded. "I know when something's broken or not!"

"Well, excuse me!" Rachel drawled sarcastically, then flounced out of the door, her eyes suspiciously bright.

Luke leaned his head back on the edge of his chair, groaning, not only at the pain in his foot, but at his stupidity. Just because his life was in a shambles didn't mean he had the right to take it out on Rachel. She returned in a moment with a plastic bag of ice in one hand and a chocolate bar in the other.

"Here," she said, tossing the candy down on the middle of the desk, "I'll bet you didn't eat lunch, either."

She shoved the ice bag at him, but he caught her other hand instead. "Hey," he said, "I'm sorry. And you're right about lunch. Thanks."

Rachel's militant stance wilted a bit. "It's all right." She took an extra lab coat off a hook on the door and folded it into a bundle.

"Stick your foot up here," she ordered, placing the makeshift pillow on the desk. Luke obediently leaned back in his chair and did as he was told while she settled the ice pack on top of the bruise. "There. Elevation and ice ought to help."

"Thanks. Sorry about being such a crank." He peeled the foil paper away from the chocolate bar, carefully broke it and, with great solemnity, offered her half. *"Pax?"*

Rachel allowed herself to soften, accepting the offering with the proper gravity. Propping her hip on the corner of the desk next to Luke's injured foot, she took a tiny nibble, then examined the candy thoughtfully. "Sometimes love stinks, doesn't it?"

Luke nearly choked on an almond. "You got that right."

"Your cousin is a lunkhead."

Swallowing the last mouthful, Luke said mildly, "Had a spat, did you?"

Rachel glared at him and took another tiny, vicious bite of the candy. "Since we never were officially together, it makes it kind of hard to break up—but that's what we did. Finis. End of story. Love stinks."

"That's just my foot," he joked, but got no answering smile. "Come on, out with it. What happened?"

"Who are you, my father confessor?"

"I'll get the particulars from Rob, anyway."

"You wouldn't!"

"I can guess." He steepled his hands under his chin and examined the ceiling. "Let's see . . . Sir Robert, operating in his white knight mode, rushes to Fair Damsel Rachel's rescue, threatening to beat a certain dastardly party to a pulp for insulting her, whereupon the fair damsel says she's a big girl who can take care of herself, and pitches said knight out on his ear."

Rachel's face was flaming. "How'd you know about . . . ?"

"Charlie mentioned it. You should have blackened Howard's eye." He studied her carefully. "Anyway, have I got the scenario down right?"

She looked away. "You know Rob pretty well."

"I know what he tried to do to me when he thought I was two-timing you with Charlie," Luke replied, his voice dry. "But don't tell me you've given up on Rob over a goof like Howard?"

"No, it was everything else. Things finally came to a head, that's all." She sighed and passed him the rest of her bar. "Why can't it ever be simple?"

Luke stared at the chocolate candy, then crammed the whole thing into his mouth. The taste was sweet, but his words were sour. "Yeah, I know what you mean."

"It was pretty frustrating trying to have a relationship with a man whose main concern is finding a mother for his kid."

"Sure, that's one consideration, but certainly not all that's on Rob's mind, especially these days." Luke laughed. "The man's a basket case, he's so crazy about you."

"Ha! Much you know!" Rachel jumped up and began rearranging the ice pack on Luke's foot, ignoring his gasp at her less-than-tender ministrations. "He's shy, you said. Be patient, you said. Well, let me tell you, there is nothing more humiliating to a woman than practically throwing herself at a man—and then he turns her down flat!"

The last was almost a wail. Luke grabbed the ice bag she was mashing into his bruise and rescued his abused foot.

"Ah, you mean you, er..." He gestured helplessly.

Pressing her hands to her crimson cheeks, Rachel nodded, and silver tears welled over in her eyes. "Uh-huh. I couldn't have made it any clearer that I was ready, willing and able to move forward with the relationship, but he just stood there, looking at me as if I was crazy! That's when I kicked him out."

Luke swallowed and patted her shoulder awkwardly. "Don't take it so hard, honey. I'm sure it wasn't what you thought. You see, Rob's real cautious because his ex-wife burned him. Told him she was taking care of things, and when she got pregnant, he felt obligated to marry her even though they both knew she was using him as a ticket out.''

"What!'' Rachel shrieked. "He's afraid I'm trying to trap him? Why, that sorry—''

Luke got to his feet, shaking his head and waving his hands. "No, no! He's just gun-shy.''

"And now I've scared him off for good.'' Rachel's expression was stricken. "Now he *knows* I'm not the kind of woman he wants for Mikey's mother!''

Alarmed at her tears, Luke hastily seated her in his chair. "I'm sure that's not true....''

"He's bound to be positive I'm some sort of sex fiend,'' she sobbed. "I'll b-bet he thinks I egged Howard on.''

"He knows better than that.'' Luke hovered helplessly.

"Never mind.'' She wiped her wet cheeks and took several deep breaths. "It's too late. Crying won't help. It always gives me a headache, anyway.''

Luke took the ice pack and plopped it down on top of her head. "Try this. And calm down. You really care about him, don't you?''

"Of course I do! Would I be blubbering like an idiot if I didn't?''

"I'm sure if you talk to Rob—''

"Oh, no!'' Rachel jerked the ice bag off. "I've got some pride! One crushing rejection is all I can take. If he changes his mind, next time he'll have to come to me.''

"A very immature attitude,'' Luke chided.

"You're a fine one to lecture me, Luke Duval!'' Rachel's blue eyes flashed. "I'm not the only one who's been as grouchy as a bear with a sore paw, and if you're not in a similar pickle with Charlie, I'll eat my hat.''

Luke propped himself on the edge of the desk and gave an exasperated sigh. "That's what bugs me about you,

Rachel. You're always jumping to conclusions—and damn it, you're usually right."

"Thought so." She rummaged in the pocket of her lab coat for a tattered tissue and mopped her face. "You haven't said a word about her, and when Charlie called me to ask if she could store her glass at my place, she didn't mention your name once."

Luke shook his head. "Pride is cold comfort, I can tell you. Maybe I ought to listen to my own advice. You say Charlie's working on her glass already?"

"Not yet. She's waiting for a shipment of materials."

"I see."

Luke chewed the inside of his cheek. It made sense that Charlie would look for another, safer place to work on her project, but it hurt that she hadn't come to him. Damn her pretty, independent hide! Would it kill her to ask for his help?

"Besides," Rachel continued, "she hardly has time while she's dusting for the Murphy's."

"What?" Luke's heart plummeted with a feeling of sick dread. "She's flying?"

"Sure, every day."

"Good God!" He was on his feet and heading for the door. "Cancel the afternoon appointments, okay?"

"Going out to Evening Star, are you?" Rachel grinned in sudden mischief. "What about your pride?"

"Pride be damned!" Luke returned, his expression harried. "I've got to talk some sense into a hardheaded woman!"

"WOMAN, YOU'LL BE the death of me yet."

Charlie looked up from the clipboard where she was making notations about pesticides, flight times and weather conditions. Disarmed by surprise, her expression was a mixture of pleasure, hope and vulnerability. "Luke?"

Striding into the old barn hangar, he took a deep breath at its coolness, a welcome relief from the blistering temperatures outside. "Hector said I'd find you here. I don't want you flying anymore."

Charlie stiffened at this blunt pronouncement, and her features went still and blank. She carefully hung the clipboard on a nail driven into a beam. "Is Hector ready for me? I told him to give a holler when he had the Stearman refueled."

"Charlie, are you listening to me?" He jammed a hand through his hair in exasperation.

"Unfortunately you haven't said anything I care to hear. Excuse me. I have work to do." She stepped around him, only to be swung to a halt when he grabbed her elbow.

"Are you nuts?" he demanded. "Need I remind you someone recently vandalized your artwork? What's to keep the same thing from happening again with your plane? You shouldn't be taking any kind of risk until something's resolved."

"How long would that take?" Charlie retorted hotly. "We don't have any idea who did it, if Tyler's involved, or if it was an isolated incident. I've got to earn the money to pay for my materials now, otherwise I'm going to miss the deadline on my commission. I refuse to start off with a reputation for unreliability!"

"They'll extend the deadline if you explain—"

"It's not necessary. I'm handling it. You and Milady are alarmists. Hector and I aren't taking any chances, believe me."

"Blast it all, Charlie! You—" With a groan he pulled her into his arms, taking possession of her mouth with desperate intensity.

One touch, and she was defenseless, melting against him, all her worries—about Howard and Evening Star, about her commission, about Tyler—vanishing in the heat of his kiss. She was dizzy and shaken when he lifted his head.

"Lady, you're making me crazy," Luke muttered. "For my sake, for my peace of mind, don't fly—just for a while. I'm begging you."

With a supreme effort of will she pushed away from him. Her voice was husky with pain. "I'm sorry. Please understand I can't."

Something died in Luke, some portion of his unwavering belief that somehow their love would work out this time. His features were wooden. "Do what you have to, then."

With a deep, shuddering breath Charlie turned away, walking out of the shadows into the blinding sunshine, bitterly aware that she might have dealt a death blow to Luke's feelings for her, but unable to do other than she had. Pulling herself together, burying her remorse and sorrow deep to be examined later, she walked toward the plane.

Hector had just filled the pesticide tanks with the requisite amounts of water for spraying. Charlie forced her voice into a normal cadence, fully aware that Luke had followed her from the hangar and stood watching them from a distance.

"Are we all set, Hector? The tanks full?"

The older man moved away from the plane, nodding. "They're right smart, Miss Charlie. Should be enough for you to finish without havin' to come in again."

"Good. This is the last of the Murphy fields. If I can finish them this evening, then maybe Dr. Luke can quit worrying."

Hector's mouth stretched in a slow grin. "Yes'm, I reckon so. Leastways till next time."

Charlie had to laugh, though it was a bit strained. "I expect you're right. See you later."

Charlie climbed into the cockpit, clearing her brain of everything but the preflight rituals. Concentration was everything in crop dusting, and she was determined not to let Luke's nervousness influence her ability to perform her job. When she touched the starter, the Stearman's engine turned over once, coughed and died. Frowning, she tried again. There hadn't been a hint of a problem when she'd flown earlier that morning. When her second, third, then fourth attempt failed, she climbed down from the cockpit, muttering curses under her breath. Both Hector and Luke were heading for the plane.

"What is it?" Luke demanded.

"I don't know." Charlie watched Hector, who was already shoulder-deep in the engine compartment. "Any ideas, Hec?"

"Good God Almighty!" The mechanic rose, a highly indignant expression on his dark face. "Some dirty so-and-so's done put sugar in the gas tank!"

"Sugar? What does that mean?" Luke demanded.

Furious, Charlie glared at him. "It means you get your wish—I'm not going anywhere!"

"At least not till I flush everything clean again," Hector added, shaking his head in disbelief. "It's gonna take a fair piece of time, Miss Charlie."

"I know. How could it have happened? When? Did you see anyone around here while I was gone?"

"I went home a spell during lunch. I should have stayed...." Hector's face hung in tragic lines of remorse.

"It's not your fault," Charlie hastened to reassure him. "It never occurred to me someone would be this determined to stop me. I should have listened to you, Luke."

"Stop you?" Luke's voice was hoarse, his face unnaturally pale under his tan. "My God, Charlie! Someone's trying to kill you!"

CHAPTER FOURTEEN

"I CAN'T BELIEVE THAT!"

"Open your eyes!" Luke ordered angrily. "I had hoped I was being overly cautious. I didn't want to believe it would ever happen, but someone's made an attempt on your life, and you've got to take it seriously."

Charlie shook her head. "No one's trying to kill me, Luke. Sugar in the gas lines means nothing works. I couldn't get off the ground. You saw that yourself. There are other ways, things a mechanic could do to bring a plane down once it's in the air if that was the real intention. Isn't that right, Hector?"

"Yes'm, it's possible—if you know what you're doing." Hector shook his grizzled head sadly. "But everybody's heard about using sugar to foul an engine. Whoever did it meant to stop you cold."

Charlie fumed. "And it worked, damn it."

"Don't play ostrich with your life at stake!" Luke's hand was hard on her bare arm, as if he could scarcely prevent himself from shaking some sense into her. "We're talking about something more vicious than destroying your art. You may not be scared, but, by God, I'm terrified. If this is Tyler's doing again, it's time we went to the police."

"No! That is. . ." She bit her lip, suddenly unsure.

From what she'd learned today it might be Howard who had more to fear from her. On the other hand, this could well be Tyler's method of trying to manipulate circumstances, thinking it would force her back to him. Whichever, she was adamant in her intention not to involve Luke further in Montgomery family matters, but to solve the problem herself. How that might be done, she was uncertain, and confusion made her frown. "I'm not sure about any of this...."

"Well, I am!" Dragging her by the arm, Luke pulled her away from the plane, seeking out a private spot near the fence that bordered the lane. "If you won't marry me, then at least let me try to protect you. Move in with me, Charlie. Evening Star isn't safe for you right now."

She gasped, taken aback by the ferocity in his expression. "You can't be serious."

"I mean every word. Look, you call the shots. No strings, no obligations, you can even have the guest room if that's the way you want it—but something's got to happen to resolve this mess, and until it does I want you where I can keep an eye on you."

Dismayed, she sagged against the board fence. She couldn't dismiss Luke's misgivings if he felt strongly enough to make such an offer. Yet accepting would be tantamount to admitting she'd failed to solve her problems on her own, and her battered self-esteem wouldn't allow it. "But, Luke—"

Just then a nondescript sedan bounced down the lane, coming from the direction of the house. It passed them in a cloud of white silt, and Luke frowned after it.

"Do you know that guy?" he asked sharply.

Confused, Charlie shook her head, squinting after the driver in the rapidly receding vehicle. "No, I don't think so. He had on a funny cap, didn't he? I think I've seen him around."

"Me, too. Just here lately." Luke's eyes narrowed. "Awfully coincidental, don't you think?"

"What do you mean?"

"You said Tyler would have someone else do his dirty work, and that fellow's the only strange face around. I'd say it bears looking into." He glanced back at her bewildered expression, and the taut muscle in his jaw eased a bit. "Look, don't worry about it now. Let's go pack your things."

"Hold it, Doctor!" Charlie straightened, meeting his gaze squarely. "You may think that's the best solution, but I don't. I'm not running away from trouble this time."

Frustration etched harsh lines into Luke's lean face. "Hell, Charlie!"

"Luke." She touched his cheek, allowing her fingertip to trace the tight corner of his mouth. "I appreciate what you're trying to do, but no one's driving me away from my home, not now, not ever again."

"If you'd marry me," he said in a thick voice, "there'd be no reason for Tyler to carry on this terrorist campaign."

Her hand dropped, and she looked away. "We've already been over this."

Luke's low laugh was brittle with tension. "Are you sure this isn't just another excuse?"

"I've no intention of arguing with you again," she said. Her eyes were smoky with impatience and anger and regret. "Excuse me. I must call Mr. Murphy and tell him the bad news."

Luke watched her walk away, his insides quivering with a mixture of fear and need. Everything in him cried out for action, yet her refusal had effectively stymied his effort to safeguard her.

Now what? he asked himself.

A hazy cloud of white silt still hung in the lane, and Luke's expression narrowed. There were still too many questions. Making a decision, he loped for his truck. It was time someone started coming up with some answers.

Within moments Luke was barreling up the main highway toward town. He pushed the accelerator pedal down hard, ignoring the speed limit, searching the stretch ahead. On the edge of town he caught sight of the car he wanted, slowed down to a reasonable rate as it turned onto the bypass, then followed it into the parking lot at the Holiday Inn. His quarry pulled into a slot at the side of the hotel. Parking the truck beside him, Luke met the man as he climbed out of his car.

"Mister, I want a word with you."

The portly driver glanced up at Luke, then finished locking his car and slammed the door. He was in his fifties, wore a plaid sport coat and an open-collared shirt, and his jowly face was amiable but unrevealing. "Dr. Duval, isn't it?"

"That's right. Who are you?"

"Les Creighton, Doctor. How do." He offered his hand.

Luke scowled. "Cut the crap, Creighton. I want to know what you were doing out at Evening Star."

"Well, now," the older man drawled, rubbing his jaw. "I don't rightly see that that's any of your business. At least not yet."

"The hell you say!" Luke growled, taking a menacing step forward. "There's been some mighty peculiar happenings out there, things I don't particularly care for. Who sent you, Creighton? Are you working for Tyler Frazier?"

"Never heard of him," Creighton said mildly.

"Yeah, I'll bet." Luke's expression grew even darker. "Well, have you ever heard of criminal mischief? Vandalism and sabotage don't set well around here. Maybe we'd better go have a little talk with the sheriff."

"Whoa, sonny! You're barking up the wrong tree now," Creighton said. He took off his driving cap and fanned his balding head. "Look, you mind us getting out of this damn heat?"

"Hell, yes, I mind!" Luke exploded. "Don't play games, Creighton. What's your business at Evening Star?"

"Oh, I get it." Creighton nodded and slapped the cap back on. "The best defense is a good offense, ain't it? Well, Doc, it ain't gonna work."

"What's going to work is your mouth when the sheriff asks his questions. Come on."

Creighton heaved a long-suffering sigh. "It'd be a pity to drag the law in on this. More'n likely won't help the situation—kind of delicate, you see. Sure you won't reconsider, Doc?"

"Reconsider keeping scum like you from threatening a defenseless woman? Why, you—"

"Hey!" The look on Creighton's pudgy features was comically astounded. "You got your wires crossed, Doc." Reaching into his jacket pocket, he flipped Luke a leather folder. "Here, maybe this'll clear things up."

Frowning, Luke opened the case, revealing a badge and an identification card on one Lester E. Creighton, licensed private investigator. "A PI? What's the deal?"

Creighton plucked the wallet out of Luke's fingers. "The deal, Dr. Duval, is a small matter of hundreds of thousands of dollars in fraudulent insurance claims."

"What's that supposed to mean?" Luke demanded impatiently.

"It means I'm onto the scam you and Howard Montgomery are working, destroying horses in order to defraud my insurance company."

"Now wait a damn minute!"

"Oh, I will, Doc," Creighton said, nodding. "I'm a very patient man. And when I find the proof I need, then we'll talk to the sheriff about putting the both of you *under* the jail."

"YOU LOOK PLUM PUT OUT," Gina said to Charlie. "What's the matter, sugar?"

"That's my problem—*sugar.*"

"I beg your pardon?"

From the comfort of the cushy den sofa Gina uncrossed her long legs and put aside her fashion magazine, staring at Charlie in puzzlement. Overhead, a ceiling fan stirred the pleasantly cool air while outside shimmers of heat rose over the cotton fields. As usual, Gina looked cool and pampered in a coordinated safari shirt and culottes, while Charlie's dirty, wrinkled jeans would have disgraced a field hand. Thoroughly disgruntled, Charlie plopped down beside Gina.

"Sugar in the gas, in the tank, in all the lines—it's going to take Hector days to undo what some creep did to the Stearman! Thank goodness Frank Murphy understood."

Gina's glossy mouth hung open in shock. "You mean," she wheezed, "somebody did something to your plane?"

Charlie nodded. "I've had it, Gina. If I could prove Tyler is responsible for this latest disaster, I think I'd take Grandpa's shotgun and fill him full of buckshot!"

"My God! This is horrible!"

"Take it easy," Charlie said, alarmed by Gina's suddenly chalky hue. "Nothing happened, thank God, except another nuisance."

"I don't know how you can be so calm." Rising, the redhead went to the wet bar built into the bookcase and reached for the gin. "You want a drink?"

Charlie leaned her head back against the sofa and sighed. "A mineral water would be nice." When she heard the tinkle of ice cubes, she opened her eyes to accept a frosty glass from Gina. "Thanks. Look, don't mention this to Milady, will you? It'll only upset her."

"And we can't have that, can we?" Gina took a long sip of her drink, her copper-colored eyes darting here and there around the comfortable room. "God knows there's enough happening around here to make the old lady cross. She and Howard spent most of the past hour screeching at each other."

Charlie groaned. "What now?"

"The usual, I guess." Gina's lips twisted. "Do they need a reason?"

"Who was the man here earlier?"

Gina shrugged, finished her drink and went back to the bar. "Insurance adjuster, I think."

"Oh."

"I'm sick of this. I really am," Gina murmured.

"Me, too," Charlie sighed. "Wouldn't a little peace be nice for a change?" The phone pealed, and Charlie rose and walked toward the foyer, waving at Gina to keep her place. "I'll get it."

"Miss Charlotte, is that you?" a voice bellowed through the line.

Charlie held the receiver away from her ear slightly, half amused at Bertell Dickson's refusal to admit a bit of a hearing loss, half afraid of what this call meant. "Yes, Mr. Dickson?"

"About that . . . ah, matter you asked me to check into this afternoon."

"Yes, sir?"

"I asked everybody I knew to ask, confidential like, you know. Miss Charlie, it ain't good news."

Charlie's throat tightened. "Tell me."

"That ol' boy in New Orleans, the one I told you about? He says it ain't unusual for Howard to drop thirty, forty thousand dollars at a time. Racing, poker, you name it."

"Oh, no." Charlie's words were barely a whisper. Gambling! The possibility had never occurred to her!

"My buddy said Howard was into a Dallas bookie for big-time money. It was gettin' to the point of being right nasty—if you catch my drift—but somebody bailed him out."

"You're sure about this?" Charlie croaked.

"Well, you know people talk. But I ain't got to tell you that where there's smoke, there's usually a bonfire. Miss Charlie, if'n I was you, honey, I'd make it my business to find out what the hell your cousin's been up to."

"You're absolutely right. Thank you, Mr. Dickson, and not a word of this to anyone, please?"

"I may be an old fool, but I've been a friend to Margaret Montgomery for over fifty years," Bertell said gruffly. "I know how to hold my tongue when I have to. You can count on me, Miss Charlie."

"Thank you. I . . . thank you, goodbye." Charlie was breathing as hard as if she'd run a marathon. Stunned, she replaced the receiver slowly, one thought running through her head:

We're going to lose Evening Star!

She felt sick. How had it happened? What could she do? Nothing would be worse than losing Evening Star.

A shrill cry of pain rent the quiet house, piercing Charlie's numbness with a new terror.

"Miss Charlie! Miss Gina!" Sudie's frantic call came from the rear of the house. "Come quick! Something's bad wrong with Miss Margaret!"

"HE'S BAD SICK, Miss Rachel. You gotta help him!"

Mikey Thompson stood in the front doorway of the animal clinic, tears streaking his face. Rachel jumped to her feet as Rob appeared behind his son, his face grim and his arms full of lethargic black-and-white dog.

"Is Luke here?" Rob asked, his words clipped.

Rachel shook her head. "He should be back in a few minutes. What happened?"

"Mikey found him this way a little while ago," Rob muttered.

"Pardner's sick, real sick!" Mikey wailed and flung himself against Rachel's leg, sobbing as though his heart would break. "And it's all my fault."

Rachel stroked the boy's dark head tenderly. "I'm sure that's not true, sport. We'll get him fixed up. Bring him to the back."

Rob carried the dog into an examination room, and Rachel followed, urging a sobbing Mikey along. Rob laid the dog on the table. His eyes met Rachel's over Mikey's head, and there was a long moment of awkward silence. The sound of the rear door slamming and Luke's voice broke the contact, much to their mutual relief.

"What's going on?" Luke stood in the doorway of the examining room.

"It's Pardner, Uncle Luke!" Mikey gulped.

Luke nodded at his cousin, stepped to the table and began to examine the stricken dog. "Things not going too well today, Mikey?"

"Everything's rotten," Mikey said, his voice squeaky and high with distress. "Miss Rachel doesn't like me and Dad anymore, and now Pardner's liable to die!"

"That's not true!" Rachel protested. Her hands tightened on the little boy's shoulders. "You know you're special to me, sport."

"Then how come you won't come see me anymore?" Mikey demanded. "Did you and Dad have a fight?"

"Michael, that's enough!" Rob's face was brick-red with mortification. "This is between adults, and none of your business."

"But that's not fair!" Mikey gave a mutinous scowl, scrubbing at his damp cheeks with his fists. "She was my friend first. It isn't fair, is it, Uncle Luke?"

Luke tightened his lips to suppress a grin, keeping his back turned while he pulled open Pardner's mouth to examine his gums. "Not fair at all, Mikey."

"See?" Mikey's expression was a mixture of triumph and belligerence. "I find a great new mom for us, and it's not fair for you to stop liking her—"

"Michael!" Rob's roar drowned out the rest of Mikey's words. He shoved his hand into his black hair and looked away from Rachel's pink, embarrassed face. "Besides," he muttered, "I'm not the one who changed her mind."

"Only after you made it clear you weren't interested!" Rachel snapped. Her lip trembled suddenly. Giving the boy a pat, she left the room with a choked, "Sorry, Mikey, it's no use."

Rob blinked, then went after her. Luke grabbed Mikey just in time to keep the boy from following them, but their voices carried clearly from the hall.

"Rachel, wait."

"So you can tell me what a trashy piece of baggage you think I am? Sorry, my self-esteem is low enough as it is! Now let go!"

Rob's voice was ragged. "Not until you hear me out. I can't let you go thinking these things. You're the finest lady in the world, so beautiful and tiny, like a fairy princess. I'm slow and clumsy, afraid if I touched you, I'd make a mistake or hurt you."

"I'm not made of glass," Rachel said in a shaky, uncertain tone. "The only way you could hurt me is not to care."

"Oh, I care—so much that sometimes I think I'm going to explode. I've loved you forever, since before I thought you were Luke's girl, but I don't know how to tell you how I feel."

Rachel's husky, tremulous laugh held a wealth of relief—and love. "I think you just did," she whispered.

There was a long moment of complete silence.

Luke caught Mikey's eye and, with one accord, they peeked around the door. Rob was kissing Rachel, his big hands caressing, pressing her close while she clung to his neck. Their embrace was so passionate and tender that Luke hastily drew Mikey back into the examining room and shut the door.

"Oh, boy," Mikey chortled gleefully. "Now everything's gonna be great!"

"Looks that way," Luke said with a smile, then turned back to his patient. Pardner was sitting up, his tongue hanging out as he smiled his doggy smile, the picture of health. Luke's forehead sported a puzzled crease as he ran his hands over the animal. "You know, Mikey, I can't find a thing wrong with Pardner."

Luke glanced over his shoulder to find the little boy scuffing his foot across the floor and looking remarkably guilty.

"Is there something you're not telling me?" Luke asked.

"Well..." Mikey's blue eyes were guileless. "I had to get Dad to come and see Miss Rachel, you see."

"And?"

Mikey swallowed. "So I fed Pardner raw eggs until he threw up."

"Mikey!"

"He didn't mind, Uncle Luke. Honest!" Mikey threw his arm around Pardner's neck. "At least not until he got sick."

"Young man, I don't want you to pull anything like this ever again," Luke said sternly.

"No, sir." Mikey looked properly abashed. "You gonna tell?"

Luke chuckled and glanced toward the hall where the silence still reigned. "Well, considering the circumstances... just this once it can be our little secret."

"Swell!" Mikey gave Pardner another hug. "I like secrets."

The humor left Luke's face, and he went to the sink to wash his hands. "I wish I did."

Les Creighton's accusations about insurance fraud at Evening Star had put him between the proverbial "rock and a hard place." He had to admit that two equine deaths in a row looked mighty suspicious, but if they'd been intentional, he was damned if he could figure it out. But somehow he had to, one way or the other. If he came under professional scrutiny, he could lose his license, his livelihood and his ability to support Charlie in the manner she'd been accustomed to and deserved. But if in proving his own innocence of any collusion in the matter, he pointed a finger at Howard, Charlie might see that as an attack against her family and Evening Star itself. It was unlikely she'd forgive him for that.

Throwing his paper towel into the wastebasket, Luke listened to Mikey's happy chatter with half an ear. It was a damnable mess. Maybe when those lab reports came back from A & M, he'd have somewhere to start looking for answers. In the meantime he could only hope and pray nothing else happened to Charlie.

"ASHES TO ASHES, dust to dust . . ."

The setting sun cast deep shadows against the raw earth of the open grave, filling it with darkness just as the familiar prayers filled Charlie's mind. Sudie's deep contralto vibrated with the old sweet hymn of comfort.

"In the sweet bye and bye . . . we shall meet on that beautiful shore . . ."

The little congregation of mourners watched the boxy coffin disappear beneath the shovelfuls of dirt. The sound of a strangled sob made Charlie lift her eyes, then slide her arm around her grandmother's quaking shoulders.

"She was a good dog," Milady said in a broken voice.

"The very best. Loyal and faithful." Charlie blinked back a sting of tears behind her own eyelids. "The heart attack was quick. Miss Scarlett didn't suffer."

"You think I'm a foolish old woman," Milady said, dabbling at her eyes with a linen handkerchief. "Carrying on over a mean, ugly, old dog—but we understood each other."

"It's never foolish to grieve over someone you love," Charlie said softly. Behind them Howard shifted impatiently, then quieted as Gina laid a steadying hand on his arm. Hector and Pigeon continued to cover the little grave that lay in the shade of a giant old camellia bush.

"I should have told you about your daddy. I should have brought him home to Evening Star," Milady said abruptly, staring at the grave. "I'm sorry, Charlotte."

"It doesn't matter." To her surprise Charlie found that she could say that without a qualm. Somehow she'd forgiven Milady. It mattered not where Roy Kincaid lay for eternity, for Charlie knew in her heart his soul would always be flying the heavens.

"Promise me you'll bury me here in the good earth of Evening Star," Milady said, fresh tears streaming down her lined face.

"Oh, Milady, you've too many years left to worry—"

"Nothing endures but the earth, Charlotte. I want to know that I'll rest where I spent my life. Promise me!"

With her conscience screaming that it might not be possible, nevertheless, Charlie nodded. "All right, I promise."

"You're a good girl, Charlotte." Milady dabbed her eyes and sighed. "I think I'll go lie down for a while now."

"Here, Milady, let me help you," Gina said, offering her arm. Gina caught Charlie's eye, and Charlie nodded. "I think it might be a good idea to give Dr. Melford a call."

It was indicative of Milady's dejection that she didn't put up a fight on the subject. "Very well, Gina."

They walked slowly toward the house, with Sudie bringing up the rear. Hector and Pigeon put the last shovelful of dirt on Miss Scarlett's grave, then took their tools and went off toward the barn. Howard stuck his hand into the pockets of his khaki pants and turned to go, too, but Charlie was galvanized by the promise she'd made

Milady. She had to know the truth, and now was as good time as any.

"Howard, I want to talk to you."

Howard didn't hide his annoyance. "This touching little ceremony has thrown me all off schedule, and I've got things to do. Can it wait?"

They were partially screened from the house by a bank of large azalea bushes, and the low buzz of summer insects vibrated in the hot, still evening air. In the turmoil of finding Miss Scarlett and calming Milady, Charlie hadn't had an opportunity to change out of her hot denim jeans. Ignoring her discomfort, she shook her head.

"No, it can't. Not when Evening Star's at stake."

Howard took an aggrieved breath and blew it out in a gust. "What is it now, Charlotte? Haven't you done enough around here?"

"Evidently not, since I've only found out today that you're in way over your head."

"Riddles now?" Howard laughed uneasily. "Make sense."

"I know, Howard," Charlie snapped. "About the second mortgages, the delinquent payments, the overdue taxes, and about your gambling."

He tensed, and the lines in his face deepened. "You . . . you're hallucinating, your nerves are obviously shot, and—"

Out of patience, Charlie interrupted him, her words sharp. "No more lies, Howard! Deal with me, tell me exactly what's going on, or I'm taking the whole thing to Milady."

Howard blanched. "She's in no condition to—"

"You'd be surprised how tough Milady can be about the things that matter to her. And Evening Star is number one on her list."

"Why'd you have to come back?" Howard's dark eyes were hostile and accusative. "Everything was okay until you came back."

"Was it? It's obvious you've been using Evening Star's resources for some time to support this habit. Does Gina know?"

"N-not everything," he admitted.

"Oh, Howard." Charlie sighed dejectedly. "How could you do it? How could you risk Evening Star?"

"It's not as bad as that," he said, blustering a bit. A sheen of sweat dampened his brow. "I've just had a run of bad luck, that's all. But that's all about to change. As soon as the insurance settlement comes in, I'll be able to pay off my IOUs. With a good harvest I can get things straight with the bank, too."

"For how long, Howard?" Charlie shook her head. "Gambling on this scale is an addiction. You've got to admit it and get a handle on it, or things will only get worse."

"I've got it under control now." There was a stubborn jut to his chin.

"Look, we're family," Charlie assured him, her tone earnest. "We'll all stand by you, but knowing what I do now, I can't let you continue to jeopardize the property this way. Let's go to Milady, and Gina, too, and get it all out in the open. Then we can form a plan and—"

"No!" A tide of rosy color rushed up Howard's neck. "It's impossible."

Charlie frowned in irritation. "You don't have a choice, Howard. With or without your cooperation I'm putting a stop to it."

"I said no!" He grabbed her wrist, squeezing hard. He spoke between clenched teeth. "I can't afford any waves right now. The situation is rather... delicate. So you're going to keep your mouth shut."

"And how do you propose to make me do that?" she asked, all icy haughtiness.

"By giving you a good reason. Don't make trouble for me, Charlotte, or you and your precious Luke will be sorry."

Charlie flinched at the painful pressure of his hand on her arm and tried vainly to pull away. "Luke? What's he got to do with this?"

"I've got to have the insurance money."

"So? You have a legitimate claim, don't you?" Howard refused to meet her eyes, and her mouth opened in shock. "You mean it's not? Howard, what did you do?"

"You mean what did *we* do." He laughed harshly at her stricken expression.

"You're lying." She jerked her arm free and glared at him. Perspiration trickled at her temples and between her breasts. "Luke wouldn't do such a thing!"

"It doesn't matter what you think, but nothing must stop my insurance claim from going through. Without it, Evening Star goes."

"What? But you said—"

Howard's mouth was a sullen line. "I had to put up the place as collateral against my IOUs."

Charlie gasped, aghast at his audacity. "You had no right!"

He shrugged. "I'm counting on that insurance money to cover the debt, but if anything prevents it, there goes Evening Star... and that would kill the old lady for sure. You wouldn't want that to happen, would you?"

"You low-down, rotten... varmint!"

"And understand one more thing, Charlotte. If I go down because of anything you do, I take Luke Duval with me."

A sudden chill skittered up Charlie's spine. "Wh-what do you mean?"

"Did you know it's illegal for a vet to own a racehorse in the state of Louisiana? If your meddling causes them to throw out my claim, I'll testify that Duval's been a silent partner all along. The State Racing Commission will fine the hell out of him, and he'll lose his license. He'll lose everything."

Charlie's face was ashen with dread. "You can't. You're bluffing. No one would believe it."

"Are you sure? A man with Duval's—shall we say—unsavory background? It's easy to kill a horse and make it look like natural causes—if you have the skill. Who could blame him for trying to grab a slice of the good life?"

It made just enough sense to strike terror into Charlie's heart. As desperate as Howard was, he wouldn't hesitate to make good his threat against Luke. Knowing Luke, she didn't believe for an instant that he'd deliberately kill an animal out of greed, but would others be so certain? How could she be the instrument that led to the destruction of all Luke had painstakingly built—his good reputation, his career, his very identity?

And yet how could she stand by and watch Howard continue to risk Evening Star? The plantation was her legacy, the land of her ancestors, and Milady's heart. Could she remain silent while her cousin defrauded the insurance company, even if it meant saving the land? Howard was confident the plan would work, that he could pay off his IOUs and not forfeit the plantation, but his luck was notoriously bad, and there were no guarantees. Could she chance it?

"Well, Charlotte?" Howard's expression was smug, the look of a man holding all the cards.

"What..." Her voice was hoarse, and when she tried to swallow, her throat was bone-dry. "What do you want me to do?"

CHAPTER FIFTEEN

"WHAT DO YOU MEAN she's gone?"

Sudie's voice swirled through the phone line, her anxious words plowing furrows into Luke's composure. "Miss Charlie's packed up and left, Dr. Luke."

"How?" he snapped, his belly tightening. "When?" *Why?*

Sudie sniffled moistly. "Sometime this evening, I guess, after we buried poor Miss Scarlett."

"Miss Scarlett!"

Sudie briefly recounted the old dog's peaceful demise, then harped back to her main worry. "Something's wrong, Dr. Luke. We're all upset, but Charlie wouldn't go off with no more than a note to her grandma."

Luke weakened against his office desk, supporting himself with the flat of his palm, foreboding looming in his head like a black, angry cloud. "Note? What did it say?"

"Something about visiting friends in Charleston and not to worry." Sudie's tone quivered, betraying her concern. "I can't help but worry, Dr. Luke! Some scoundrel's poured sugar into her plane, Hector says. Somebody's trying to hurt my little girl!"

"Calm down," Luke ordered firmly, though dread clawed at his gut.

Dear God! What had that maniac Tyler done now? Had Charlie fled some new threat? Fear coursed like ice water through Luke's veins. Or worse, had she given in to his tactics and gone back to her ex-husband? Luke shook his head to clear it, fighting to stay rational despite the welter of confusion and roiling emotion threatening to churn his brain into butter. No, Charlie would never do that. If she'd gone to Tyler, stubborn wench that she was, it would be to confront him—but that thought was just as frightening.

"Is she in Mrs. Montgomery's car?" he asked Sudie.

"No, and it's right peculiar, too. Nobody knows how she left."

"She can't have gotten very far then," Luke said grimly. "Don't worry. I'll find her."

But after hours of fruitless effort, Luke had to admit that it was easier said than done. It was long after midnight when he pulled his truck into his carport and killed the engine. Wearily he rested his forehead against the steering wheel. The pain and helplessness he'd been holding off by sheer force of will burned through his tired muscles, scorching tendons and bones with bitterness, piercing his heart.

There was no sign of her.

Neither the airport in Shreveport nor Alexandria showed a Charlotte Kincaid on any manifest. He'd called everyone he could think of, but no one, not Becky, nor Bertell, nor even sleepy-voiced Rob, who'd answered the phone at Rachel's house, had any answers. A check of the bus depot had him racing up Highway One on a wild-goose chase to Shreveport, only to find no sign of her on the other end of the bus route. The moonlight drive back down to Natchitoches had give Luke plenty of time to agonize, to curse the stubborn woman for putting him through this, and to pray.

Pushing away from the steering wheel, Luke climbed from the truck cab, absently greeting Hershey with a pat. He had to believe that Charlie was safe, because otherwise he wouldn't be able to function, and he had to believe that tomorrow he'd find her, even if he had to go all the way to Charleston to bring her home where she belonged.

Hershey entwined himself around Luke's legs, whining softly. Touching the animal brought some comfort, and so Luke paused at the edge of the carport, bending to scratch the dog's ears while the wind whispered through the tall pine trees. Below the house he could see the lake through the parallel pillars of black trunks, scattering the cool and clouded moonlight on its rippled surface. His glance snagged and held on a motionless figure on the long, bleached dock, and suddenly his breath checked and his heart drummed painfully in his chest.

Stumbling down the pine-straw slick hill, Luke halted at the foot of the dock, struck by the sight of Charlie sitting on her suitcase, contemplating the glittering lake. A line from Frost leaped into his head: "The moon, the little silver cloud, and she."

Seeing her safe left him weak.

Seeing her safe left him furious.

He hesitated, unsure which emotion would be expressed if he opened his mouth, and so he clamped it shut, his jaw throbbing with tension. His boot heel hit the wooden planks, and she swiveled on her perch.

"You're home," she said, though she didn't smile. "I've been waiting."

Luke's throat was dry. He gestured at the suitcase. "Come to say goodbye, princess?"

"Not exactly." Slowly she rose, a slender woman in yellow slacks and jacket whose lower lip trembled briefly, then stilled as she lifted her chin. "I . . . I got on the bus."

Luke stiffened, jabbed by her admission. "And?"

Her eyes were luminous, her cheekbones gilded by moonglow. "A bus is a good place to think. . . ."

"You were leaving," he accused.

"I got off at Armistead and caught the next one back."

His voice was hoarse. "Why?"

"Because . . ." She swallowed. "Because I need you."

He closed the space between them, catching her around the waist with one arm and burying his other hand in her hair to tilt her head up to him. His voice was rusty with emotion. "Say it again."

Her words were the merest whisper, an echo of the wind. "I need you, Luke."

He found her lips with his own, plundering her mouth with a heated kiss that spoke of need and desire and love. Her lips were soft and pliant and tasted of surrender. When he pulled back, both of them were breathing erratically. Luke's tone was husky.

"It was worth the wait to hear that."

She clung to him, raw honesty in the tremor of her words. "I've been afraid to admit how much I do need you, Luke. I thought it would be admitting I'd failed again. I've been fighting so hard, against you, against myself—" Her voice cracked. "I guess everything had to hit rock bottom again before I could see I can't do it all by myself. And that maybe I don't have to."

"Is it that bad?" he asked gently.

"Everything's a mess."

"Is that why you were running away?"

"I couldn't think of any other way to protect you!"

"Me?" he repeated, astounded.

"It's Howard's doing. He's up to his ears in gambling debts, Evening Star's mortgaged to the hilt, and he even pledged it against his IOUs. But worst of all, he's threatening you!" Her fingers curled urgently into Luke's firm biceps. "Oh, Luke, he did something to that horse."

"I know." His mouth thinned. "The insurance investigator thinks I'm in on it."

"Oh, no!" She gasped in dismay, then pressed against him, her cheek against his wide chest, shuddering. "Oh, Luke! I'm sorry. It's my fault. If you hadn't been involved with me..."

"Hush, honey." He stroked her curls tenderly. "It doesn't matter."

"But it does! He's desperate for the insurance money. When I realized what he'd done, he said if I didn't leave, he'd swear you'd been his partner all along and make all sorts of trouble."

Luke frowned. "So he's been the one harassing you, trying to drive you away from Evening Star before you could discover all this?"

"Maybe. I guess so." She shrugged impatiently. "I suppose that makes more sense than thinking it was Tyler who broke my glass and then the plane...but I could handle that. It's when he threatened to destroy your name and your practice that I fell to pieces. That's why I let him put me on that bus. I couldn't let him do that to you!"

"So you were going to help me by leaving?" Luke's voice was rough with wry amusement. "Some help! Don't you know nothing in my life is as important as you are?"

She thumped his chest with her fist. "You're in trouble, even if you don't know it. I have to help."

"Is that so? You've continually refused all my attempts to help *you*."

"Well, I was wrong!" She pulled back slightly to glare up at him. "So sue me!"

Luke laughed softly. "Princess, that's not at all what I'd like to do with you right now." Even in the pale moonlight he could see her blush.

"Don't change the subject," she said shakily. "That's why I came back, you know."

"What? You realized two heads were better than one?"

Though his tone was light, her answer was serious. "Yes. And that having the courage to admit you need someone isn't a weakness but a strength. Whatever the risk from Howard's threat, whatever the blow to my ego, I knew I didn't have the right to make a decision like that, even believing my sacrifice was best for you."

"Giving up on self-righteousness, are you?"

She gave a little sigh. "Maybe I can now that the arrogance has been knocked out of me by life. At least I realized you and I deserve a chance to work this out together. I was a martyr with Tyler. In fighting back against what my life had become, I turned into a militant, a...a warrior. I know some of the things I had to do have hurt you, and I'm sorry. Both are extremes that I don't want to repeat."

"So what are you going to be now?"

She half smiled, shrugging. "Maybe a...a magician? Someone who can find joy without hurting anyone, including myself. I thought about those walls you spoke of."

"What about them?"

"They've tumbled down just like Jericho. Every time I tried to build it up, you knocked it down again." She touched his face. "I thank God you're a stubborn, hard-headed man, Lucas Duval, because I don't ever want to wall you out of my life again. Whatever happens, all I know, all I care about, is that I love you.''

''Charlie!'' Luke's throat felt full with emotion. His hand covered hers, shifting it so that he could kiss her sensitive palm.

Shivering at his touch, she smiled tremulously. ''Another thing about walls, Luke. When your back's against one, I've learned it's okay to lean on the man you love.''

''As long as we're together, we can solve anything.''

''I hope so,'' she said, reaching for him, ''but even if we can't, I can bear it with you.''

They came together with exquisite tenderness, as two lonely travelers finding home at last. Tongues met and tarried, swirling in a delicious feast of the senses, and the tenor of their embrace changed as passion flared.

''Let's go to the house,'' Luke said at length, pushing aside the edge of her jacket to stroke the indentation of her waist, then cup the heaviness of her breast.

Shaking, she pressed against him, reveling in the way they fitted together. ''Yes . . .''

Luke grabbed her suitcase and, with a hand pressed possessively into the small of her back, walked her off the dock and up the little hill. The house was dark, but Luke led Charlie unerringly through it.

''What about Howard?'' she murmured. ''We should decide—''

''Tomorrow.''

Luke set the suitcase down inside his bedroom door, then pushed her jacket off her shoulders, letting it fall to the floor unheeded. His mouth traced a path from the fragrant hollow behind her ear down her throat. Charlie moaned softly while his fingers worked nimbly at the tiny pearl buttons of her blouse.

''But, Luke—''

"Shh. Tonight is just for us."

And Charlie knew he was right. No matter what became of the tangled situation in which they found themselves, they could enjoy each other for the first time with no shadows hanging over them, no doubts, no anger—only the perfection and assurance of their mutual love. Gladly she tugged at his shirt, determined to bring Luke as much pleasure as he brought her.

Garments were discarded in haste, and moments later they lay in Luke's big bed, tasting, caressing, exploring all the secret places known only to lovers until neither could stand the distance between them any longer. Rolling onto his back, Luke lifted Charlie, urging her to lead the dance. With a gasp of pleasure she settled onto him, and he shuddered uncontrollably as she sheathed him within her silky depths, greedy for all of him. Palming her hips, he let her set the tempo of their joining.

Her hair shimmered like a dark curtain as she moved over him, slowly at first to prolong the delight, then faster as their bodies' demands overcame all restraint. With a sharp cry she arched her back, her eyes squeezed shut in the throes of rapture, and Luke knew he had never seen anything so beautiful. Her rippling inner shudders milked him, and with a groan he erupted, emptying himself into his woman.

Drenched with sweat, they lay gasping in each other's arms, still joined. Luke's lips moved beside her ear.

"I love this, Charlie. I love what we do for each other. I love you."

"Luke." The one word reflected her wonder. "How can it keep getting better?"

His lazy chuckle rumbled in his chest. "That, sweetheart, is a question that needs a lot more research."

Her eyes widened. "Now?"

"Now."

And in the ensuing hours Luke did his best to explore every aspect of the question. Charlie roused from a slumber of satiated exhaustion only once, vaguely aware she'd been awakened when Luke sat up abruptly.

"What is it?" she mumbled. She lay on her stomach, the sheets twisted around her, squinting against the silvery finger of predawn light seeping through the bedroom drapes.

"Nothing. I thought of something, that's all." His large, warm hand traced the valley of her spine, soothing her back into drowsiness. He placed a brief kiss in the shallow dimple at the top of her hip, then pulled the sheet over her nude form. "Go back to sleep."

Charlie needed no other encouragement. When next she woke, she was alone. Rolling over, she stretched like a cat, realizing that she felt totally rested and marveling at the sense of well-being produced by a night of loving. Except that it wasn't night any longer. She frowned at the slash of brilliant sunlight pouring through the window. A glance at the clock on the bedside table told her it was almost noon!

A call through the house produced no response. Evidently Luke had gone to his office, leaving her to sleep in. Charlie took advantage of the shower, put on a pair of mint-green slacks and a casual knit top from her case, then went in search of a cup of coffee.

In the kitchen waiting for water to boil, she glanced idly through a section of yesterday's newspaper, then picked up an open magazine lying on the counter beside it. The publication was a slick veterinary journal, and she'd almost set it aside as being of no interest when her eye caught on a bold ring of black ink encircling a section of an article. Curious at what had caught Luke's attention, she opened out the pages, scanning the report on deadly insects.

What she read made her frown, then gasp. Included in the article was a section on blister beetles, a tiny flying insect of such great toxicity that it only took a few of them, ingested in alfalfa hay, to kill livestock. And in the case of a horse, the animal died with all the symptoms of colic!

Ignoring the shrill whistle of the screaming teakettle, Charlie chewed her lip. Did Luke think this was the method Howard had used to destroy the second horse? But how—

She stopped, something nebulous tickling at her memory. Hay. Alfalfa hay was imported into Louisiana and rarely used in the summer due to the prevalence of high-quality Coastal Bermuda hay. A sudden vision of herself shifting uncomfortably on a bale of hay filled her head. A strange kind of hay, *hidden* in the old barn hangar!

"That's it!" Heart thumping, Charlie tossed down the magazine, swiftly removed the kettle from the heat and reached for the phone.

"I'm sorry, Charlie," Rachel said a moment later. "Luke's been out all morning. I'm not sure where he is, but I imagine he'll check in soon."

"I've got to talk to him," Charlie said urgently.

If her guess was correct, there was proof of Howard's deliberate attempt to defraud the insurance company at Evening Star. Maybe having hard evidence like that would protect Luke, or at least give them some leverage over Howard. And as for Evening Star itself—well, she couldn't think of that now, but maybe there was still a chance. . . .

If the hay was what she thought it was. *If* it was still there. She knew she had to find out, and she couldn't wait for Luke.

"Tell him I'll be at Evening Star," she said to Rachel.

"Sure will," Rachel responded cheerfully. "Have you heard my good news? Rob and I are engaged."

Charlie gasped in surprise. "Rachel, that's wonderful!"

"Yeah, I'm merely ecstatic. Rob may be quiet, but when he finally gets started that man is a whiz at nonverbal communication! And Mikey is just icing on the old wedding cake."

Charlie laughed. "I'm so happy for you."

"Thanks. Whoops, here comes Mrs. Pierce with her scatterbrained poodle to be groomed. I'll talk to you later, and I'll be sure to give Luke your message as soon as he comes in, okay?"

Charlie agreed and said goodbye, smiling slightly to herself at Rachel's happy news. Her smile faded. She hoped her own future was as bright, as she'd been sharply reminded that no word of marriage had been spoken between her and Luke last night. Of course, she thought wryly, they'd had other things on their minds. Resolving to trust the man she loved, she pushed those worries aside. There was a more pressing matter at hand. Taking the keys to the Mercedes off the rack by the back door, Charlie headed for Evening Star.

The cotton was chest-high now, thriving under the heat of the summer sun. As Charlie drove into Evening Star, there were places where the dusty stalks were so tall and lush that she couldn't see over them from the car. Choosing one of these spots, she parked the vehicle, then set off on foot, passing through the tall rows and circling around to the rear of the old barn hangar. She didn't want to attract any notice until she completed her task.

The barn door creaked alarmingly when she opened it, making her heart race with misapprehension. Thankfully the interior was deserted, the partially dismantled Stearman mute evidence that Hector had been busy. Charlie hastened past the plane, moving like a wraith through the shafts of mote-filled sunlight falling through the overhead beams. Biting her lip, she approached the last stall. Expecting the worst, she let out a relieved breath. Nothing had changed.

Pulling away the concealing, innocuous Coastal hay, she uncovered the remainder of the incriminating bale. Now that she examined it, the leafy composition of the hay clearly marked it as alfalfa. Taking a hunk of it, she shook it loose, sifting through the straw until she found several tiny dried insects husks. She had no doubt now that the hay was contaminated with blister beetles. With Howard's racing and gambling contacts, he'd probably had no trouble acquiring this poison. Why he hadn't disposed of it was beyond her—unless he intended to use it again.

Charlie's stomach lurched as she remembered the suffering horse. No matter that she'd never been overly fond of her cousin, she hadn't thought him capable of such cruelty. It was a measure of his desperation that shouldn't be underestimated.

"So you're back. I knew you couldn't be trusted."

Startled, Charlie gasped and turned, her hands guiltily clutching fistfuls of hay. Howard stood glaring at her, his swarthy face suffused with fury.

"Didn't I tell you what would happen if you came back?" he demanded harshly.

Charlie willed her pounding heart to steadiness and met Howard's glance with a challenging one of her own. "It's not going to work, Howard. You can't drag Luke into this now, because here's the proof of what you did."

"Figured it out, have you?"

"You fed this stuff to that animal the day of Audrey Gilchrist's wedding, didn't you? No wonder you were acting so peculiar at the reception—drinking too much, insulting Rachel—you must have been half crazy waiting for the ax to fall."

"Shut up."

"And no one could connect you with it, either, since you were miles away when the horse fell ill. Except you left behind this evidence."

He laughed softly. "Well, that's easily enough remedied."

Before she could guess his intent he kicked the offensive lump of hay into the center of the dirt floor, pulled a lighter from his pocket and set the straw afire.

"No!" Charlie cried, lunging at the pile, but Howard's meaty hand clamped down hard on her upper arm. He held her back as the dry hay crackled and caught, then with a whoosh flared into an engulfing, incinerating flame that died in seconds, leaving only ash.

"Damn you!" she spit, struggling against his grip. "I still know what I know. This isn't over."

"Yes, it is, only you haven't realized it yet." Grimly, his face damp and clammy, Howard hauled her out of the barn and force-marched her across the backyard. "It's dinnertime. You might as well join us. I think you'll enjoy it."

"Don't bet on it!" Her words were a feline snarl of rage. "When Milady hears..."

"Oh, I don't think you'll have much to say. Not if you care about the old lady at all."

That ominous sentence effectively aborted the rush of heated protests ready to be launched from Charlie's lips. Still hitched together by an iron grip on her arm, Howard dragged Charlie into the house, her foreboding growing with every step. The tantalizing aromas of Sudie's home cooking teased her nostrils, and from the dining room came the muted clank of silver cutlery on bone china. Howard jerked her after him, and she staggered, off balance, in the wide, open doorway of the airy, paneled dining room.

"Look who I found, everybody," Howard announced.

Charlie straightened self-consciously. Milady sat, imperious as always, in her usual place at the head of the century-old mahogany table, and her gray eyes glinted behind her spectacles as their gazes meshed.

"Welcome home, Charlotte," Milady said evenly. "I'm glad you're back so soon. Such a pity if you'd missed our visitor."

In that instant Charlie became aware of the back of a golden head now turning in her direction, the model-handsome features coming into full view, the well-toned physique rising gracefully from the chair at her side.

"Darlin'."

Charlie caught her breath on a wave of icy shock. "Tyler. What are you doing here?"

Tyler flashed the boyish grin that was only a tiny percent of his superficial charm and reached for her hand. "Is that any way to greet your hubby?"

With an abrupt, circular motion she pulled free of his touch, shivering. "I told you not to come here."

"I stayed away as long as I could, darlin'." With an exaggerated show of consideration he pulled out the chair nearest his own. "Come, sit down. Sudie Mae's good cooking will get cold. Look here—pork chops, sliced tomatoes, field peas and cornbread. My, my, I can't get cooking in Charleston like this, and that's a fact."

Standing near the sideboard with a serving dish in her hand, Sudie snorted her disdain, and with one part of her brain, Charlie registered this fact. With the rest of her mind she fought desperately for equilibrium. Hands curling around the back of the chair, she cast an accusing look at Milady, feeling a terrible sense of betrayal.

"Did *you* invite him here?" she croaked.

"No, *I* did."

All heads swiveled at Gina's quiet announcement. She was immaculately groomed as always in a violet silk jumpsuit, but her hand shook as she laid her napkin on the table. Howard's face was a picture of astonishment.

"Sit down, Howard, before you fall down," Gina said.

Blankly he complied. "What . . . why . . . ?"

"Because it's gotten out of hand," she said, the skin stretched taut over her high cheekbones. Her voice was resolute. "I don't want anyone to get hurt."

"And it's grateful I am, Regina, darlin'," Tyler drawled. "It was way past time for me to come take my Charlie-girl home."

"You're joking!" Charlie snapped, rousing from her shock-induced stupor. "I'm not going anywhere with you."

Tyler's pretty-boy features tightened, and he jammed his hands into the pockets of his tailor-made slacks. "As it happens, I'm deadly serious. You can't believe the damage our separation has done my reputation. After all I've done for you, you owe it to me to come home."

"That house we lived in was never a home," Charlie denied, her tone scathing. "I owe you nothing!"

"Well, maybe not you, exactly, but that's not the case with Howard. Is it, Howie? Had to come to your old friend Ty to keep from having your legs broken by a couple of thugs."

Shamefacedly Howard stared at the empty plate before him, seemingly intent on counting the petals of the roses on the delicate old china. A giant hand squeezed Charlie's lungs.

"No. Not *him*, Howard!" she cried in horror. "You owe Tyler? Everything? Even Evening Star?"

"Well," Tyler said reasonably, "just about. Since you were being so stubborn, despite all my...ah, inducements to return—"

"Such as destroying my stained glass?" Charlie demanded stridently.

Gina's voice was small. "I did that."

"What?" The hurt and disbelief made Charlie's throat constrict. A sudden mental vision of Gina's nervousness that eventful day, of the way she'd nursed a wound on her finger—a glass cut?—made Charlie realize it was true. "Why, Gina?" she whispered.

"It was the only way Tyler would agree to help Howard." Gina flicked a tear from the corner of one eye with a lacquered nail. "I'm sorry, Charlie, but he's my husband...."

"Gina, don't," Howard ground out.

"Well, what else was I supposed to do?" Gina flared. Her fury died a quick death with the slump of her shoulders. "But, Howard, tampering with the plane! How could you?"

"It was just another ploy," Howard said sullenly. "It wouldn't have hurt anyone."

"I couldn't take that chance. It has to stop." Gina's copper-colored eyes flicked to Tyler. "That's why I called him."

Milady spoke for the first time, her eyes narrowed behind her glasses. "Perhaps you'd care to explain yourself, Tyler?"

"I suppose it's time to lay all my cards on the table," Tyler said with a bland smile. He reached into his designer jacket and, removing a sheaf of papers, placed them beside his plate. "Or in this case, all Howard's IOUs. Since he's been unable to pay me back, I've come up with an alternative to foreclosing on the plantation. It would be a pity if I had to turn everyone off the place, especially an old lady."

"I told you, the money's coming!" Howard protested.

"And I'm tired of waiting for it." Tyler's smile was sly. "But I'm a forgiving kind of guy. All it would take to make me tear these up is for Charlie to come home with me."

Charlie pressed her hand over her mouth to stifle a gasp of angry dismay.

"Let me see if I have this right, young man," Milady said, her voice starchy. "You want my granddaughter back, and if she doesn't agree, you'll demand the money Howard so very foolishly borrowed, or in its place, Evening Star?"

"Yes, ma'am, I'd say that's about it. Of course, I'd assume all the bank mortgages, too, so it's not all bad news." Tyler looked apologetic. "I really hate to put y'all in such an awkward position, but a man has to look after himself and, of course, Charlie will really be better off with me, anyway. Charleston is where she belongs."

He looked at the stunned group expectantly. "Well, what do you say?"

Gray eyes met gray-green ones over the table, and there was an instant flash of unspoken communication between grandmother and granddaughter.

"I say," Milady said icily, "that you and Evening Star may go to hell in a handbasket for all I care!"

"Wh-what?" Tyler's expression was comically stupefied.

"Would you truly consider going back to this *insect*, Charlotte?" Milady asked. "Even for me?"

Charlie squared her shoulders and shook her head. "I'm sorry, Milady. Not in a million years, not even for you. Somewhere along the line I found that believing in your own worth is more important."

"You are a strong woman," Milady said with supreme satisfaction. "Just like me."

Feeling proud and treasured and connected to something more tangible than any mere plot of earth, Charlie stepped around the table and took her grandmother's hand. "I love you, Milady," she said.

"Just so, my dear child." Milady cleared her throat and peered through her glasses at her former son-in-law.

"So, Tyler, take Evening Star and welcome to it. Nothing, not even this place, is more important to me than my granddaughter's happiness. Wouldn't you agree, Dr. Duval?"

"Yes, ma'am, I do."

Luke stood in the open doorway, the roly-poly figure of Les Creighton at his elbow. The conversation around the dinner table had been so intense that no one had noticed their unannounced entrance, but he'd heard enough. Now, as everyone turned toward him, Luke's smile was slow and dangerous.

"Mrs. Montgomery," he asked, "did you know there's vermin at your dinner table?"

"It's becoming increasingly apparent," Milady sniffed. "Come in, please, you and your friend. If you can stomach it."

"Now wait a damn minute," Tyler growled, his features twisting into an ugly scowl. "We've got family business to finish here—"

"Oh, don't mind me," Luke said, sauntering to Charlie's side. Tenderness made his tawny eyes golden. "I'm a very old friend of the family."

"Luke." With a glad sigh Charlie slipped into his arms, then her expression darkened. "It was the hay, like you thought, and I had it, but Howard burned it, and—"

"It's okay," he murmured, then gestured at his companion. "I believe everyone knows Mr. Creighton. Les, perhaps you'd like to give Howard what you brought?"

Howard's head jerked up, and his face was a pathetic mixture of relief and shame. "I told you the money was coming," he said to Tyler, breaking into the other man's angry concentration on Charlie and Luke. Tyler glared at Howard, mouthing an obscenity.

"Yes, er, ahem." The insurance investigator patted his pockets and pulled out a single sheet of paper with a check paper-clipped to its top. With a flourish he set it down in front of Howard and offered him a ballpoint pen.

Howard's face went slack with dismay and horror. "What is this?" he croaked.

"Well, now, son," Creighton drawled, "we like to settle these things like gentlemen. After talking with the doc and examining the lab reports, I'm afraid this check is all we're prepared to offer to cover the loss of your animal."

Howard's breath wheezed, so agonizingly painful that Gina bolted from her chair and came to his side. Leaning over her husband, she read the check out loud. "One dollar?'

Tyler's vindictive laughter filled the room. "Look's like Evening Star is mine."

"I'm not signing this!" Howard blustered, his swarthy face pasty.

"Well, of course, son," Creighton said, somewhat sorrowfully, "that's up to you. Course, if you pursue this matter, we'll have to file criminal charges against you and—" he nodded at Tyler "—your business partner over there, as well."

"What! What the hell are you talking about?" Tyler demanded.

"Insurance fraud," Luke explained easily. "Killing horses is pretty damn vicious. Making money off it is downright illegal."

"Kingdom's death was purely accidental, I assure you!" Howard said.

"I can substantiate that," Luke agreed. "But I'm fairly sure you and Tyler cooked up that other business between you. I have to give you credit, Howard, poisoning the horse with blister beetles showed real ingenuity. The perfect plan to take the insurance money and pay off your partner."

Tyler looked aghast at Luke and Les Creighton. "But...but I had nothing to do with that! This is the first time I've heard of anything like this. I swear it!"

Creighton shrugged. "You'll have your day in court to prove it."

"This is ridiculous!" Tyler's golden-boy face was beet-red. "What about my reputation? I can't afford to be dragged through court for something like this!"

"Oh, I'm sure everyone will understand," Charlie said sweetly. "Bunny will just love telling everyone all the juicy details."

"Shut up!" Tyler bellowed. He took a step toward Howard, his hand balled into threatening fists. "Sign the damn thing!"

"Don't do it, Howard," Charlie said quickly. She caught Gina's eye, then glanced at the pile of papers beside Tyler's plate. Gina placed her hand on her husband's shoulder.

"Don't do it, baby," she said. "Not until Tyler tears up those notes."

"Are you out of your minds?" Tyler roared. "Do you know how much money this two-bit con artist owes me?"

Suddenly Howard was enjoying having the position of power reversed. A jocular chuckle shook him, and he tossed the pen down defiantly. "You know, Ty, it'll be worth going to jail if we get to share a cell."

Tyler stood there, breathing hard, his face so red with fury and frustration that Charlie thought he'd explode. For the first time ever she saw him as he was—troubled, self-centered, immature, seeking power over others to validate his manhood. In short, a man to be pitied. With that realization she released all her unresolved anger, forgave him and put him firmly where he belonged—in her past.

"Tyler," she said softly, touching his arm. "Tear them up. Consider it my community property settlement if you want."

His face worked with a welter of conflicting emotions. Finally, with a growled swearword, he grabbed the IOUs and ripped them into tiny squares that floated like snowflakes onto the polished wooden floor. Grinning widely with relief, Howard picked up the pen and signed the insurance release.

Creighton accepted the document with a curt nod. "A wise decision, gentlemen. Although an attempt to defraud is difficult to prove in a court of law, Dr. Duval's testimony on the matter most assuredly would have convinced a jury. I'm glad we could avoid such... unpleasantness.''

"I think that settles the question of your claim on Evening Star, Tyler," Milady said acidly. "As much as I value my name as a gracious hostess, I think you'd better leave now."

"With pleasure!"

"One other thing." Luke stepped in front of Tyler, a half smile on his lips, one long finger flicking imaginary lint from Tyler's immaculate lapel. "You've made Charlie very unhappy in the past."

Tyler's blue gaze ranged in scathing contempt from Luke's work-scuffed boots to his shaggy haircut. "It's no business of yours—"

"Wrong. As soon as I can get a license, I'm marrying the woman." Luke's fingers curled into the lapel, and his smile became even silkier. "So, I can forget about your being such a jerk, in that you're somewhat responsible for her finding her way back home to me. But, Tyler, don't try anything like this ever again, because I'll see that you regret it dearly. She's out of your life, and she's into mine, understand?"

Tyler's Adam's apple bobbed, and he gave a jerky nod. Satisfied, Luke released him abruptly. Catching himself, Tyler self-consciously brushed at his wrinkled jacket. Focusing on Charlie, his lip curled in a sneer. "I knew you weren't worth this kind of trouble."

Out of nowhere laughter bubbled from Charlie's throat. Tyler's viciousness had no power over her, nor would it ever again. Luke's deep chuckle joined hers, and he pulled her into his arms. Milady and Gina giggled, Sudie snickered behind her hand, and Howard let loose an outright guffaw. Spitting a final obscene epithet, Tyler turned on his heel and stalked out of the house, escorted on his way by peals of merriment.

"Did you see his face?" Howard chortled. He gazed up at Gina in admiration. "My God, hon, that was inspired."

"Don't be a child, Howard," Gina replied coldly. "It wasn't for you. It was for Milady." She went to the old woman at the head of the table. "I'm so sorry, Milady. I kept believing everything would be all right."

Milady's expression softened, and she patted the younger woman's hand. "Love is blind, Gina. At any rate, Evening Star is safe—for the moment."

Howard scraped back his chair, a new confusion diffusing his relief. "Now, hon..."

Gina pivoted and pierced him with a level stare. "Don't think you're off the hook, *hon*. Somehow, someway, you're going to make good on everything you've taken out of Evening Star. And you can start with those damn horses!"

"But... but Gina..."

"I mean it, Howard." Gina's copper eyes were molten with determination. "Either you start acting like the man I married, or you and I are finished." She lifted her chin. "Excuse me, everyone. I'm not very hungry anymore."

With great dignity and poise Gina marched from the room. Howard gave a panicky glance around the group, then scuttled after her, his voice pleading. "Wait, Gina! Honey...?"

"Oh, dear," Charlie said. She took involuntary step after them, only to be forestalled by Luke's hands on her shoulders. "Do you suppose she really means it?"

"Hmph. I'd say she does," Milady replied, her eyes narrowing shrewdly. "And it just might be the making of that boy. Now, Mr. Creighton, is it? Would you care to join us for a bite to eat?''

''Well, I don't mind if I do, ma'am. Summer's bounty here looks mighty good,'' the investigator said, pulling up a chair.

Milady nodded. ''Sudie, if you'd be so kind as to fetch some clean plates?''

''Yes, ma'am, Miss Margaret!'' Sudie beamed and began to rearrange dishes.

''And, Dr. Duval,'' Milady said, her voice suddenly stern, ''did my ears deceive me, or did you indeed say your intentions toward my granddaughter were honorable?''

''Milady!'' Charlie gasped and laughed, for it was clear her grandmother was back to her old irascible self.

Luke grinned and winked at Charlie. ''The most honorable, ma'am.''

''Then you know that it is customary for a suitor to present himself for the approval of the family on such occasions. I'd say it's high time you sat down to dinner with the Montgomerys.'' Milady waved at the chair to her right. ''Come sit by me, young man, and we'll get to know each other.''

Luke pulled out a chair for Charlie, then seated himself. Beneath the linen tablecloth Charlie's hand reached for his, and their fingers entwined. When he looked at her, he saw love and pride in her eyes. His heart swelled with a sense of homecoming and belonging.

''Now, young man,'' Milady said firmly ''as a prospective member of this family, I have one very important question to ask you.''

Luke stiffened, and he felt Charlie squeeze his hand in silent encouragement. ''Yes, ma'am?''

Milady's sudden smile was coquettish, reminiscent of the Southern belle she'd once been. "Would you please pass the peas?"

EPILOGUE

THE BOARD UNDER the porch rocker creaked rhythmically. This was the time Charlie liked best, when the heat of the summer's day eased and dusk descended on Evening Star. Looking up from the letter she was reading, she smiled at the sight of Luke's brown truck barreling up the lane toward the house.

She could hardly believe they'd been married a year already. It had been a good year. The wide gold band gracing her left hand was only one sign of the love that deepened between them day by day. Even now the sight of Luke climbing from the truck, all long legs and rugged handsomeness, could take her breath away. She smiled her welcome, then stifled a laugh as Hershey dashed around the corner of the house to greet his master joyfully, followed by the half-grown mongrel whom Milady had dubbed Cap'n Butler for the arrogant way the mutt had claimed her bedroom as his own.

"You're early," she said as Luke climbed the steps.

"Yeah, I decided to leave it to James," he said, referring to the associate he'd taken on during the spring to meet the demands of his growing practice. Bending, he pressed a soft kiss to Charlie's upraised mouth. "How are you doing, princess?"

Charlie smiled. "Fine." She waved the letter. "I got a letter from Gina."

"What does she have to say?"

"They're busy, as usual. Howard got a big bonus at the used car lot, so they sent an extra payment."

Luke looked impressed. "You've got to hand it to that girl. Between her modeling and her real estate sales, and Howard's income, she and Howard haven't only managed to avoid bankruptcy, but they've never missed a payment to me."

"They couldn't have done it without you."

He shrugged. "So I've always wanted to be part owner of a plantation. Evening Star was a good business investment, that's all."

Luke's financial bailout last year had meant all the difference to putting Evening Star back into the black, no matter that one more good harvest would repay him twofold. But Charlie knew he loved the old place as much as she did, for all his pragmatic talk. She hid a smile.

"Of course. At any rate, I think they're going to make it, Luke. Howard's attending Gamblers Anonymous regularly, and Gina say they've never been happier. And she got me a lead on another commission. A large piece for a bank foyer."

"What? Hey, that's great!" He rubbed his lean jaw. "Can they wait on it?"

"They'll have to if they want the 'premier stained-glass artist of the New South,'" Charlie said with a laugh.

"Feeling pretty smug about that write-up, aren't you?"

"I never imagined those Charleston windows would create such a sensation. Being featured in *Architectural Digest* and *Smithsonian* means now I can afford to pick and choose commissions."

Luke tenderly brushed a curl of dark hair back from her face. "Have you been missing your work?"

"Yes, a little." Her smile was serene. "But I think it'll be worth it, don't you?"

Her hands settled possessively on the rounded expanse of her stomach. Even now she could hardly believe the miracle they'd made together. Her pregnancy had surprised and thrilled them, even thought at first their hopes had been tempered with caution. But if the stress of her first marriage had made childbearing a near impossibility, this baby was the product of her glorious happiness and contentment. Her doctor assured her everything was perfectly normal, and in slightly over three months she and Luke would become proud parents. Now Luke came down on one knee and spread his broad brown hand over hers, proudly measuring the place where their child grew.

"I think I'm the luckiest man alive," he said huskily.

Charlie stroked his cheek, loving the way his beard stubble rasped against her fingertips. "Giving up my work for the duration so our baby won't be exposed to the lead from the solder isn't much of a sacrifice, considering the reward—a healthy child. Just like crop dusting. I can easily live without that to help ensure that this child doesn't grow up without a mother as I did."

Luke grinned, leaning toward her. "Smart gal. And to ensure you won't miss the flying, I'll do my best to keep you fully occupied here on the ground."

His mouth covered hers in a lingering, probing kiss that left them breathless. Charlie's laugh was shaky.

"Watch it, Doc. That's the kind of thing that got me into this condition in the first place!"

"And I was blaming it all on those satin sheets," Luke murmured with a smile. Their chuckles were interrupted by the sound of Milady's voice, calling from inside the house.

"Charlotte, it's time to come inside. You've kept that great-granddaughter of mine out in the night air too long already."

"She never quits, does she?" Luke said with a smile.

"I think she'll just go on forever, especially now that she'll have someone new to dote on," Charlie replied.

Milady's imperative call rang out again. "Charlotte!"

"Coming, Milady," Charlie called back, then grinned at Luke. "If my husband will help me up out of this chair."

With Luke's help she heaved her bulk out of the rocker.

"Won't be long now," he commented, supporting her with an arm across her back. "Pretty soon we'll really be a family."

Charlie's features softened, and her eyes grew dewy. "That's all I've ever wanted, Luke. You, a family, a home."

Luke's gaze roamed over the old house. "Yeah, I love living here with you, too."

"Silly. We could be just as happy at your dad's place on Black Lake."

"Especially now that you've fixed it up for him."

"He deserves some comfort, as well as our acceptance. But what I meant was that even though our moving in with Milady meant so much to her, my home is wherever you are." She snuggled into his embrace, her cheek resting against his chest. "That's the kind of home I want us to make for this child. A place that's always there, waiting for you, even when you don't deserve it."

"We'll do it together, Charlie," he murmured, his voice tender.

"Oh, look!" She pointed at the single bright point of light shining in the darkening sky. "The evening star."

"Going to make a wish, sweetheart?"

"Don't be silly," Charlie said with a soft smile. "You've already made all my wishes come true."

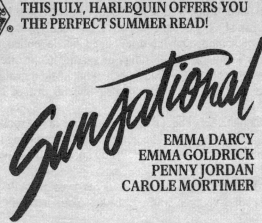

This August, don't miss an exclusive
two-in-one collection of earlier love stories

MAN
WITH A PAST

TRUE COLORS

by one of today's hottest
romance authors,

Jayne Ann Krentz

Now, two of Jayne Ann Krentz's most loved books are
available together in this special edition that new and
longtime fans will want to add to their bookshelves.

Let Jayne Ann Krentz capture your hearts with the love
stories, MAN WITH A PAST and TRUE COLORS.

And in October, watch for the second two-in-one
collection by Barbara Delinsky!

Available wherever Harlequin books are sold.

HARLEQUIN
Romance

**This June, travel to Turkey
with Harlequin Romance's**

**THE JEWELS OF HELEN
by Jane Donnelly**

She was a spoiled brat who liked her own way.

Eight years ago Max Torba thought Anni was self-centered—
and that she didn't care if her demands made life impossible
for those who loved her.

Now, meeting again at Max's home in Turkey, it was clear he
still held the same opinion, no matter how hard she tried to
make a good impression. "You haven't changed much, have
you?" he said. "You still don't give a damn for the trouble you
cause."

But did Max's opinion really matter? After all, Anni had no
intention of adding herself to his admiring band of female
followers....

Back by Popular Demand

Janet Dailey
Americana

A romantic tour of America through fifty favorite Harlequin Presents, each set in a different state researched by Janet and her husband, Bill. A journey of a lifetime in one cherished collection.

In July, don't miss the exciting states featured in:

Title #11 — HAWAII
Kona Winds

#12 — IDAHO
The Travelling Kind

Available wherever Harlequin books are sold.